Scarlet Claimed & Scarlet Cursed

A Raven Vampire Assassin Prequel & Novel

Visit my website at

www.DoraBlume.net

CHAPTER ONE

"Damn, Hope, you're one hell of a shot," Carson shook his head as he dismantled his weapon. His sandy blonde hair fell into his eyes as he carefully placed his gun in the box.

"Whatever, Carson, you just need to work on your reflexes." I jabbed his arm as I walked past him. I pulled the clip from my own gun and placed it in its case.

"So, do you have big plans tonight?" Carson glanced over at me as he holstered his gun.

"Nah, I'm looking forward to some uneventful time at home." I slipped my leather jacket onto my shoulders and turned toward the door of the training room. "What about you?"

"Marissa is making dinner tonight. She'll kill me if I miss another family dinner." He leaned back against the table. "I can't believe your man doesn't have anything big planned."

"Why would he?" I asked.

"I don't know, cause it's your birthday. You don't have a single thing planned?" His eyes bore into me, and I could feel his judgment.

"I don't make a big deal of it."

"It's your birthday, you should make a big deal of it." He shook his head. "Do you want to come have dinner with us? I can call Marissa right now."

"No, I'm fine. I don't really want to spend my birthday with you and Marissa, no offense."

"Oh, none taken," he laughed.

"I just don't see what the big deal is about birthdays. I've never been one to celebrate them. Now can we drop it?" The cold, stale air of the room hit me, and I shivered. I knew it wasn't as cold as it suddenly felt in the room.

"Message received, so, what are you thinking about the case?"

"I think we need to go back and talk to the coroner. Something about their bodies doesn't add up." I had been thinking about the case since we got the call this morning. There was something niggling at the back of my mind. I just hadn't figured out what to do about it.

"What are you thinking?" Carson asked.

"Well, there wasn't that much blood at the scene. But based on their wounds, they would have bled out." I tapped my finger against my lips. "Where did the blood go?" I turned to look at Carson.

"Are you sure there wasn't a drain nearby or something? Blood doesn't just disappear." Carson held the door open for me.

"No, there weren't any drains close enough to the body. It was in an alley." I gave him a duh stare before continuing. "There was nowhere else for the blood to go. Maybe I'll pay a visit to the station before I head home for the night." I pulled out the keys to my Dodge.

"Call me if you come up with anything." Carson's phone buzzed. He pulled it out of his pocket and looked at the screen.

"Marissa?" I asked.

"Yeah, on second thought, I'll talk to you tomorrow. Will you at least do something fun tonight? It is your birthday, after all. And don't stay at the station. I know how you like to think you can pull all-nighters, but then I have to deal with your crabby ass the next day." Carson narrowed his eyes at me. He was dead wrong; I could go at least two nights of no sleep before I was crabby.

"Okay, Dad, I'll try." I smirked, knowing I had no intention of listening. If the case led me down the rabbit hole, I had no problem following it.

Carson hit the button on his phone and turned away from me. "Hey, honey, I'm just finishing up at the range with Hope."

I shook my head and walked to my car. I wasn't sure how Marissa put up with him sometimes. My latest failure of a relationship proved no one was really willing to put up with me that was for sure. Long hours and my inability to leave my job at home certainly affected every relationship I'd ever been in. I wished there was one person out there who was willing to understand my passion for what I do. Michael certainly hadn't understood. We got in regular fights about me staying in the office. He would get mad at me anytime I talked about work. He used to tell me it was just a job, and I shouldn't be so wrapped up in my job. He didn't understand. He never understood. It was too bad. He certainly knew how to please a woman in bed. Damn, I was going to miss that part of our relationship.

I pulled up to the parking lot near the coroner's office. I had to get answers for the victims. There had been two similar murders in the last few weeks. I wanted to know if these murders were committed by the same perpetrator. There was something about the wounds and the blood that was niggling at the back of my mind. Something told me this was an important detail. I had a feeling the connection was in the blood.

I walked through the door to the coroner's office. Laura had her feet up on the desk, a sandwich in one hand and her mouse in the other. A game of solitaire was on the screen. "Hard at work, I see." Laura started and dropped her sandwich onto the desk.

"I'll have you know I'm on my lunch break," she shot back and turned to look at me, her cobalt eyes sharp.

"Oh well, sorry to interrupt your precious lunchtime." I crossed my arms over my chest.

"Careful, Hope, I could make you wait for whatever it is you came here for, considering your shift was up, what three maybe four hours ago." She flipped her blonde braid back over her shoulder. She lounged back in the chair, taking another bite of her sandwich. I knew she was bluffing.

"Okay, Laura, I am deeply sorry for disturbing you. I only have a few quick questions about the man who was brought in this morning. I know you're not the one who completed the autopsy, but you're the best, so I was hoping you'd have a second look." I fluttered my lashes and gave her my award-winning smile.

"You're insufferable, you know that." She rolled her eyes at me. "Fine, let's go take a look." She stood up from the chair and headed into the lab. She signed into the computer and pulled the notes up on the screen. "Did you change your hair? It looks nice," she commented as she read over the notes.

"Thanks, I got some layers and highlights the other day. So, I have a few questions about the wounds." I tucked a piece of auburn hair behind my ears.

"Yeah, it looks like there were jagged knife wounds across his neck. He noted it was rather messy. Let's take a look at the body." She glanced at me and walked over to one of the doors. She pulled the handle and grabbed the table to glide the body out of its compartment. She carefully pulled down the sheet to examine the wounds. With a gloved hand, she touched the jagged lines on the neck. "It's weird how these cuts indicate the killer wanted to really slice up the neck. It looks like they cut several times over the same spot." She stretched out the skin and moved her head closer. "It almost looks like they used the tip of the knife to make sure they punctured the artery."

"Okay, so the victim should have bled out at the scene?" I looked at Laura as she stood up straight. Her hand was still against the man's neck. He couldn't have been much older than eighteen.

"Yes, the artery is punctured. They would have bled out within minutes." She dropped her hand. "Where are you going with this?" Her eyes narrowed as she walked back over to the notes. She pitched her bloodied glove on the way.

"There wasn't much blood at the scene. Certainly not enough to indicate the victim bled out from a punctured artery. Are you absolutely sure they would've bled out from the neck wound?" I asked.

"Positive, there are over two liters of blood missing from the body. The cause of death was exsanguination based on a cut to the carotid artery. There should have been a lot of blood at the scene." Laura shifted her weight from one foot to the other.

"So, the question of the hour, what happened to all that blood?" I blinked up at Laura.

"Maybe a vampire drank it," Laura's eyes sparkled.

"A vampire, really?" I rolled my eyes. "You've been watching too many of those vampire shows. Who's the flavor of the week?" I asked, knowing she was watching one of the many shows about vampires.

"Damon," she answered automatically.

I shook my head. "I think it's more likely we have some weird sicko out there with a blood fetish. I'm going back to examine the evidence. Any other weird things noted about the body?"

Laura glanced back at the notes. "She had a good dinner about an hour before her death. Looks like she had lobster. How often do you eat lobster?" Laura dipped her head.

"Not very often, it must have been a special occasion. I'll look into it. Thanks, Laura."

"You are very welcome, so why aren't you out with Michael tonight?"

"He's busy," I headed toward the door.

"Oh no, you don't. He's too busy to spend time with you on your birthday. That's not like him, spill." She grabbed my arm and turned me to face her. She's lucky she's a friend, or I would have knocked her on her ass for grabbing me like that.

"Michael decided he didn't want to be with a workaholic." I looked into Laura's eyes. I watched as her face softened into a look of pity. "It's fine. I didn't want to be with anyone who didn't understand my passion for the job anyway." I pulled my arm away from her, and she let me.

"I'm sorry, Hope. That's shitty. What kind of guy dumps his girlfriend right before her birthday?" She shook her head.

"What's the big deal with birthdays? Everyone acts like I should be out getting drunk or something. What if I like investigating? This is absolutely how I would choose to spend my day." I pulled on the sleeve of my jacket.

"Examining dead bodies in the morgue is your ideal birthday. Oh honey," she patted my arm before shaking her head and turning away.

"I need to follow up on this lead. I'll talk to you later."

"Sure, call me tomorrow. I have the day off. We can have a girls' night out or something." She gave me a sympathetic smile. Seriously, the pity thing was getting a little annoying.

"Yeah, I'll call you." I turned and walked back out the door. Laura and I were friends, but we weren't that close. Most of the people I hung out with were the people I worked with on a regular basis. My shoulders slumped a little as I thought about that. Maybe I needed to find some friends outside of work. I drove back to the station and opened the file on my desk.

Looking over the photos, I knew it. There wasn't enough blood at the scene to support the victim bled out there. There also wasn't anything to suggest the body was dumped. So, what happened to the blood? I went into one of the layout rooms. I pinned up all the photos from the case on the corkboard. I took a step back and stared at the photos. There had to be something here I was missing.

The door opened behind me. "Aren't you supposed to be at home, celebrating or something?" Reed stood in the doorway.

"No, I am exactly where I should be." I looked at Reed over my shoulder.

"Well, since you're here, you need a fresh set of eyes?" I couldn't help but notice how nice his muscles looked against his blue button-up. His dark hair fell slightly over his eyes, and he brushed it back as he walked up to the photos. He tapped the photo with the body sprawled out on the pavement. "It looks like a straight robbery. Did you search the area for her ditched wallet?"

"What makes you think it was a robbery?" I asked. I wasn't ready to move from my seat yet. I tilted my head as he turned back to stare at the photos. Damn, his ass looked nice in those tight black jeans. I had a rule not to get involved with anyone I worked with, but I might make an exception for Reed.

"Well, he was found in a back alley without his wallet. What else would it be?" he blinked, looking back at me.

"I'm not sure yet." I stood. "Notice the lack of blood in the photo. The coroner ruled it was exsanguination from the knife wounds. If that's the case, where's the blood?" I tapped the photo. "There's not enough blood at the scene to support him bleeding out."

"Maybe it washed down the street or something." Reed turned, facing me. He was close, close enough I could smell his mint and eucalyptus aftershave.

"It didn't rain that night. If the blood flowed somewhere else, there would be evidence of that. There isn't any. I'm starting to think the killer drained the victim somehow before slicing open his neck. The coroner also noted a weird puncture mark in the neck that looked like they stabbed the tip of the knife straight into the artery. I can't imagine why someone would do that." I shook my head as I glanced again at the photo with the man's body.

"Okay, are you sure the blood didn't soak into his clothes?" His eyes shifted to me.

"No, it's not at the scene, and it's not in the body. Someone must have drained him."

'Okay, but why? I've never heard of a case where the killer drained their victim before killing them. What would be the point of that?" Reed scratched the stubble on his chin.

"I don't know why. I just know the blood that should be here, isn't. I can only assume it went with the killer. Until the evidence shows me something else, I'm going with it." I went back to the table where I had all the notes from the scene. "You want to go over these with me? See if we can find something to either support or disprove my theory." I began pulling out the different sheets.

"You don't think I have my own cases to work?" he moved to stand behind me.

"I'm sure you do. But you also came to ask about my case, which means you find this one much more interesting than yours." I smirked up at him. I watched as his head tilted slightly. I knew I was right. He found something about this much more interesting than his own work.

"Alright, you got me there. I'll take some time and go through this with you." He pulled out the chair and rolled himself closer to me. I passed over one of the pages from the file. He smiled and dipped his head. He began reading, and I grabbed up the next.

After an hour, I handed over the last of the sheets from the file. "There's nothing to indicate where the blood could have gone." I pushed the file to the side. "I think I have to go back to the scene," I huffed.

"Yeah, I'm not sure I can join you at the crime scene." He paused, glancing out the window. "I don't think you should go alone, either. Where's your partner?"

"His wife made him dinner. There's no way I'm pissing off Marissa for a hunch that probably won't lead anywhere. I'm just going to stop by and check it out. I shouldn't be long." I stood, slipping on my coat.

Reed stood, "I'd feel better if you had a black and white with you on this excursion. You know the killers often visit the crime scene after the murder is committed. I don't think you should go alone. I'll go see who's available." Reed opened the door and looked around the station. I stepped behind him. The few officers that were in at this hour were either typing at computers or booking someone into custody.

"Reed, I don't need anyone to take care of me. I'll be fine." I squeezed past him and headed for the back door.

"Hope," Reed called. He closed the distance between us. My breath hitched as his arm rested on my shoulder. "Will you promise me that if you notice anything out of line or get a bad feeling, you'll get out of Dodge? No chasing after a killer on your own."

"Come on, Reed. I'm not that stupid. I'd never go after a dangerous suspect on my own."

"Okay," he let out a deep breath. "Are you coming back here after your errand?"

"No, I'm told I should be spending some time out or relaxing or something." I shrugged. His hand moved from my shoulder to squeeze my upper arm.

"That sounds like a good idea. You should do something that doesn't involve work. You hitting up the regular spot?" he asked. All the police at the station had a regular watering hole. It was a rustic bar and grill a few blocks from the precinct. I liked to stop for a whiskey every now and then. My apartment wasn't too far, so I could walk home if I decided to have more than a few. Not that any of the guys in the place wouldn't offer me a ride if I lived further. It always amazed me how many offered to get me home safe. Of course, they may have wanted to make sure I made it all the way into my apartment. The disappointed look on their face when they learned I was a short walk from the bar was always amusing.

"Yeah, maybe."

"I hope to see you there." The corner of his mouth turned up.

The crime scene was a little over a mile away. There shouldn't be too much traffic, so I should be at the scene in a few minutes. I kept racking my brain, trying to figure out where all the blood could have gone. I pulled up and parked near the alley where we found the last body.

The tape had been long removed, but the alley was still devoid of any people. The homeless who had frequented the alley had moved on to somewhere new since they had lost access during the initial investigation. I bent to examine exactly where the body would have been lying. The grit and rocks from the street gave me no clues as to where the blood would have flowed. The drains were at the end of the street. A dumpster was a few short steps from where the body was found. I bent to glance at the bottom. Not even a speck of red remained. Either the cleaning crew had been thorough, or the blood hadn't even made it this far.

"Ugh," I lifted the lid to the dumpster. The crime scene crew had already checked the dumpster. If they had found any blood, it would have been collected. There was nothing in the file about the blood. I studied the inside of the dumpster. Besides the foul smell of rotting food, there was no indication anyone died here. I stepped back, glancing around one last time at the scene. There was nothing. My hunch was leading me somewhere. I just didn't know where yet.

Why would someone drain a person of blood, then cut their throat?

The cuts were jagged across the throat, leaving a mangled pattern. The coroner said it was done with a serrated knife that had been used several times. It was messy. Some would think that it was because it was someone who may not have known what they were doing. I disagreed. I think the unsub knew exactly what he was doing.

I just needed to figure out who they were before they did it again.

There wasn't anything else I was going to learn here. I had no idea why someone would drain another's blood. There were a few diseases that required regular transfusions. Someone without insurance might get desperate enough to drain someone. Maybe some creep needed blood for a ritualistic sacrifice. Those were the only two things I could think of off the top of my head. Either way, I didn't understand what they would need the blood for. I got distracted as I thought about it. The type of person to do something like that would be a real sicko. I sighed. I might as well head to the bar to have a drink. There was obviously nothing else I could do here for the night.

The sound of pebbles skidding across the pavement drew my attention. I thought I was alone here. My hand instantly went for the gun in my holster. It was a habit. I turned to see Reed standing at the entrance to the alley.

"Reed? What are you doing here? I thought you said you couldn't come with me tonight." I furrowed my brow as I dropped my hand from my gun.

"I know, but I didn't feel right with you being here by yourself."

"Oh, well, I already finished up. I was just leaving."

"Excellent, are you ready for that drink?" he asked.

"Yeah, I could really use one." I gave him a weak smile.

"Come on, I'll walk you to your car, and we can head over to Bernie's."

"Sounds like a plan." I began walking in the direction of my car, and Reed was a step behind me. I turned my head to look back at Reed. His hand was in the air seconds from hitting me with the butt of the gun. I blinked in surprise before I felt the sharp pain from the hit and wobbled. My head felt heavy, and the world spun.

"You just had to dig into the blood, didn't you?" I heard him mumble before I lost consciousness.

Chapter Two

The pain in the back of my head was the first thing I was aware of when I gained consciousness. I wasn't ready to open my eyes, so I listened to the room around me. The events from the night were coming back to me. Reed had knocked me out at the crime scene. Why the hell would he do that? Unless he was involved with the murders somehow. I tensed as I thought about the possibility. How could he be involved? What was it he said before I blacked out? Something about the blood? Shit, what the hell had I gotten myself into?

"I know you're awake. You might as well open your eyes." Reed's voice was sharp, and I blinked open my eyes. I tried to raise my hand to my head, but both my hands were bound in front of me with zip ties.

"What the hell is going on, Reed?" I asked. I pulled my wrists against the restraints.

"Isn't it obvious? I kidnapped you." He was sitting in a leather recliner across from me. I was lying on my side on the brown leather sofa. At least a pillow was tucked under my head. My shoulder ached from the angle of my hands.

"Did you bring me to your house?" I asked. I stared at myself on the black screen of the television. I didn't look any worse for wear. Too bad he'd hit the back of my head, not the front. I wouldn't be able to see any bumps from this angle. I could certainly feel one, though.

"Yeah, I didn't want to chance bringing you anywhere else. My house is sound and light proofed. No one will hear you if you scream." There was an edge to his voice. "While it's daylight, no sun will seep through the windows either." His eyes met mine across the room before he focused back on the book that lay open in his lap. A wine glass filled with a red liquid sat next to him on the twisted metal end table. It was a weird piece with jagged lines like the designer couldn't decide which way they wanted the metal to go, so he chose all of them. Reed took a sip from the glass. The liquid stained his lips red. Even now, a heat rushed through me as I watched his tongue glide over his bottom lip. I shook my head to clear it of the absurdity.

"No sound or light? Why would you do that to your home?" I asked. I couldn't fathom the need for a sound and light proofed house.

"How unfortunate? I always thought you were the smart one on day shift. You haven't figured it out yet, my dear, Hope." His eyes never left the book. I watched as he used one finger to turn the page. I was beginning to think I was an annoyance to his reading.

I thought back to what he'd said, my investigation, and the previous murders. "Was the blood missing from the previous victim?" I asked. I didn't like this train of thought. But Laura would be damn proud. It was because of her and those damn shows that my mind even traveled there. Okay, I may have watched an episode or ten of True Blood, but that was it. Those were my kind of vampires. Oh god, what the hell was I thinking? Vampires, was I really going there? The investigator in me was screaming at the ridiculous train of my thoughts.

"Ah, now you're piecing it together. Yes, both victims were drained of blood. I took precautions to make sure no one would think anything of it and only assume they bled out. How is it you were not convinced?" His eyebrow arched as he lowered his book to study me.

"I noticed there wasn't enough blood at the scene. I told you this while you acted like you were helping me with the case." I rolled my eyes. "I should have known. Murderers often insert themselves into the investigation. I thought you were being my friend." I sighed and tried to sit up without the use of my hands. It was difficult, but I managed. I didn't like being lower than he was. I tried to shift to see what was behind me. I needed to figure a way out of this place. Away from Reed. "So, now that you have me here, what are you planning to do with me?" I asked.

"Oh darling, you will be my progeny. You're smart and more than capable of living in this world than most. I knew that the day we met." His eyes sparkled. "I have to get the approval of the council first, of course. As I was not prepared to turn you quite so soon, I thought I would have time to groom you first." His finger traced around the rim of the glass before he lifted it to take another drink. By the look of the stain on his lips, he was drinking blood. My stomach lurched. It was probably the blood from the crime scene. His eyes met mine, and his lips curled into a wicked grin. I pressed my lips together to hold back my nausea. He gave me one last cursory glance before he resumed reading.

"Progeny? What does that even mean?" I asked. I thought it was weird how his speech had changed. In the office, he seemed like a regular cop. Now he spoke as though he were older, more refined. It was giving me whiplash. I needed to get the hell out of here.

"It means, my dear, that as soon as the sun sets, I will go to the council. I will ask their permission to turn you into a vampire. I believe I've made a fine choice in a new progeny. I wasn't planning to turn you quite so soon, but your voracious appetite for investigation has necessitated immediate action from me. I couldn't exactly let you go and tell others what you've discovered, now could I?" He tapped his finger on his lips. "Did you tell anyone besides me what you were investigating?" He closed the distance between us and took a seat on the couch next to me. His eyes locked on mine, and he spoke again. "Hope, dear, who else knew about the missing blood?"

I felt mesmerized by his intense gaze. "The coroner," my mouth moved automatically to answer. I knew I shouldn't be saying anything to him, but I couldn't control my mouth.

"Does your partner know?" he asked.

Again, I felt my control over my answer disappear. "No, I hadn't gotten a chance to tell him at the range earlier. I wanted him to enjoy his dinner with his wife." I blinked.

He smiled. "Good girl, I don't believe the coroner will dig too deeply into it. You were the only one who seemed to be engrossed in discovering where the blood could have gone." His fingers trailed a line down my cheekbone and stopped under my chin, lifting it to meet his eyes again. "Why couldn't you let it go?" he asked.

"It was the only thing that I didn't understand about the case. I am an investigator; it was a lead. I followed it," I answered simply. I was trying to find the killer. Apparently, I was on the right track.

"Hmm, well, that's good. I would hate to have to hurt anyone you care about." His finger felt like acid against my skin as his threat rang through my head. I would find a way to kill this man if he ever went after anyone I loved.

"I'll kill you if you hurt any one of them," I spat back at him.

"Ah, there's the spirit and fire I so adore. I intend to mold that fire in you for my own purposes. Before long, you will have the ultimate gift from me. Immortality. I can only hope you treasure it, as I have treasured my own."

"You know that they're going to ask questions when I don't show up to work today." I probably shouldn't have mentioned that, but I hoped people noticed. Carson, at the very least, would notice. I said I'd give him an update today.

"Oh?" His eyebrow rose. "The guys at Bernie's last night watched you have a few too many drinks for your birthday. The captain said it was the least he could do since he hadn't actually seen you celebrate in years." His mouth curved into that wicked grin that I was beginning to hate. "Sorry, princess, but they think you'll be in bed all day nursing a wicked hangover." He stood; a self-satisfied smile plastered on his pretty face.

I wanted to punch him. "No one's going to believe that. I wasn't even at Bernie's last night." I narrowed my eyes at him.

"Oh? But they believe that you were." He tapped his temple. "A few well-placed memories into an already inebriated mind are child's play." I scowled. He could manipulate people's minds. Shit, what else could he do? I let out a breath. I didn't know what else to say. He'd obviously covered all his bases. I couldn't exactly say he'd been a bad cop in the time I'd known him. He nodded once and strode down the hall.

I whipped my head around, trying to find a way to get out of here. He talked about immortality as a treasure. I assumed he was planning on killing me. He was obviously delusional about having immortality. He was just another sicko murderer who thought himself above everyone else. I saw the door on the far side of the room behind me.

"You'll never be able to open that door. You might as well get some rest before tonight. You're going to need it for what I have planned for you." His voice rang clear down the hall. How did he know I was looking at the door? He must just assume that since I'm trapped here, I would be trying to escape. I pulled on my wrists, trying to loosen the zip ties. I felt the blood as I pulled harder, and the hard plastic bit into my skin. I loosened them slightly but not enough. I yanked harder and tried to slip my hands through the plastic. The blood flowing from the cuts was helping to lubricate my wrists. Maybe I would be able to slip my hands through the small space I was making. I kept trying to yank my hands apart.

I felt his presence before I heard him. "Are you trying to tempt me, young one?" Reed made his way around the couch and knelt before me. He lifted my wrists to his nose and inhaled. I yanked my hands back against my chest, and his mouth broke into a vicious smile. He pulled my hands back toward him. I jerked my legs up and kicked him. The impact of my feet on his calves hadn't even phased him. He licked where the blood was oozing out from under the restraints. His eyes lit as he tasted my blood. My stomach lurched at the hungry look in his eyes. He slid the zip ties down my arm and licked around the wounds. I watched as they sealed before my eyes.

"What the hell?" I asked as I stared wide-eyed at where my wrists had just been bleeding. There was nothing but a small pucker of a line where the plastic had cut my skin. I watched as even that disappeared.

"I told you. I'm immortal. With the blood of immortality, comes certain gifts. I can heal your wounds with my saliva. Do not do that again. Though, I do enjoy the exquisite taste of your blood. It's like a fine wine. I find you to be quite delectable. I can't wait until you trust me enough to share my bed." He licked his lips again, and his eyes darkened with a hungry desire.

"Never gonna happen." I spat in his face. He lifted his hand to wipe away the saliva and blinked down at me.

"That's not what you were thinking at the station. You liked staring at my broad chest while we were working together. You wanted me for more than just the assistance I was offering." His eyes continued to bore into mine.

"That was before you kidnapped me against my will. I thought you were being a nice guy. I didn't think you were a murdering sicko." I sat back, trying to get further away from him. I didn't want to be this close to him. My heart ratcheted in my chest, and I knew I was in danger. More danger than I may have realized. He was a predator, and I was prey. I needed him to turn his focus on anything else.

"I only kidnapped you out of necessity. Please, you need to rest." His eyes locked on mine. He spoke one word, and my eyes drifted shut. I was going to figure out how he was able to do that to me.

Chapter Three

"**W**ake up, Princess. It's time to meet your destiny." I felt a hand on my shoulder and jerked away from it instinctually. "Come now, the council awaits." His smooth voice soothed over me. I felt instantly relaxed before a jolt of shock hit me.

"What? What council?" I blinked my eyes open in the dim room. "Where am I?" I didn't recognize the living room. I blinked a few times before it all came rushing back to me. I yanked on my arms. The plastic bit into my wrists, and I sighed. I was hoping it was all a dream. Reed stopped before me.

A lock of his dark hair fell into his eye. He was wearing a tailored black suit with a thin burgundy tie. I had to admit, he looked dapper in the suit. "My dear, I must present you to the council before they will approve your transformation. I laid out a dress for you in the bedroom. I expect you to be impeccable." He took my wrists and broke the bindings.

"You expect me to put on some gown and accompany you to my death. Uh, no, I don't think so." I sat back against the couch. There was no way I was going to volunteer for whatever he had in store. "I think you forget that you kidnapped me." I crossed my arms over my chest and stared back at him. I didn't intend on letting him bind my wrists again. I was going to exploit a weakness the next chance I get.

He bent so his eyes were level with mine. I looked away. "You will put on the dress."

I narrowed my eyes and glared at him. "No, I won't." I tried to look away from him, but I couldn't manage it. It was like he had trapped me in his gaze.

"You will go put on the dress and join me for the council meeting."

I stood without thought and walked down the hall and into the bedroom. There was a rich burgundy gown on the bed. It matched the tie Reed had on. I didn't want to put on the dress, but my hands moved without my permission. In a few minutes, I was standing in front of a full-length mirror wearing the long dress. It had a slit that went all the way to my upper thigh. It was elegant and sexy. The thin spaghetti straps ran to the two triangles holding in my breasts. It was good I was well-endowed to fill out the dress. I glanced around the bedroom. The charcoal gray bedspread matched the manly feel of the room. The headboard was a rich black leather with a footboard that reminded me of a sleigh. I hated that I was standing in the bedroom of the man who somehow could take complete control of me. I clenched my hands into fists.

The door opened behind me. "Ah, I knew you would be lovely in that dress." He closed the distance and stopped behind me. His arm skated around my waist, and my whole body stiffened at his proximity. My skin crawled where his fingers grazed along my stomach. He looked at me through the mirror. "I can't wait until you welcome me with that fire. You are such a beautiful woman."

"Don't touch me," I stepped to the side and out of his grasp. I turned on him. "I will never welcome you. I don't know why you think I ever would. You are holding me against my will." I stormed out of the room and back into the living room. With my hands free, I went for the door. He was in front of it before I had made it a few steps. He moved so fast he was a blur. "What? How? Uh, how were you able to do that?" I sputtered.

"It's all part of the gift of a vampire. By this time tomorrow, you will know everything," he said. He whispered something into my ear before I could move away. My knees weakened beneath me. I fell into his arms, and everything went black.

I blinked my eyes open in the middle of a dim-lit room. I was stretched out on an altar. There were six people looking down at me from their dais. Reed was standing next to me. I shifted, so my feet were away from the people and stood, brushing my hand down my dress. I couldn't believe I woke up on an altar. It was like I was about to be the sacrifice, and the group was waiting to watch my suffering. By the looks on their faces, maybe they were. I noticed that each person wore a mask of boredom, but something behind that spoke of intrigue. One woman with long hair that flowed over her breasts licked her lips when our eyes met. What the hell was she so excited about? A shiver ran down my spine at the possible answer for her excitement. Reed hadn't exactly filled me in on what was about to happen here. I was surely the sacrifice.

"Progeny, what is your name?" A stern woman looked down at me. She had the strong jawline of Mediterranean women. She wore the mask of boredom like she'd seen this many times before. "Speak, girl," her voice boomed in the open room.

I took a step back, startled. "Hope," I responded. Reed's hand slipped to my lower back, and he guided me forward. I scowled at him. He touched me as though we were intimate. Did these people know he kidnapped me? Was this the standard for vampires?

"Hmm, interesting, is this the detective we spoke of, Reed?" The woman tapped her finger against her thin lips. I wasn't sure what she thought was so interesting about my name. Her focus turned to Reed.

"Yes, ma'am, she is the detective. She has shown promise in the field and will be a welcome asset to our council and the collective." He squared his shoulders after he was finished. I narrowed my eyes. So, I was here because I was a good cop? I thought it was because I discovered his secret. Was he keeping that from them?

"And you Reed swear to teach your progeny the way of our world. You will take responsibility for her actions, all her actions? She will live with you for no more than five years in which you will train her and educate her to be an asset to our collective."

"Excuse me, don't I have a say in this? You actually want me to live with this repulsive man." I turned my head and spat on him.

"No progeny understands the choice and gift we offer. Therefore, no, Hope, you do not have a choice. You would not understand the choice you were making regardless." She waved her hand flippantly. "Reed Longfellow, do you agree to the terms?"

"I do, mistress. I will take responsibility and educate my progeny for a period of up to five years. As soon as she is educated and ready, I will bring her back to the council." He bowed his head. "Thank you for your kindness in allowing me to bestow my gift upon another worthy progeny." He lifted his head, and I noticed him make eye contact with one particular woman on the council. I saw her nod imperceptibly toward him. What was that about? I promised myself I would remember and investigate that later. I wondered about the formality of whatever was happening. They were talking about my death, yet they were so formal about my being educated. What happened after I left Reed? Not that I planned to stick around him for that long. There was no way I was staying with my kidnapper for five years. I'd heard plenty about Stockholm syndrome, no thank you. I was not that girl. I planned on getting the hell away from Reed as soon as I possibly could.

"So, it is decreed, Hope Matthews will now be, Hope Longfellow, under the guidance and protection of Reed Longfellow." She bowed her head, and her hair fell forward, obscuring her face. I felt my heart race in my chest. What had just happened? Did they really think they could make me stay with Reed for five years? No way, I would escape this madness the first chance I got.

The rest of the council spoke in unison. "So, it's decreed."

Something fundamental just happened. I looked between the members. Reed took a step toward me. His arms came up to wrap around me. I held my arms out and backed away from him. I really didn't want him touching me. I didn't know how he kept knocking me out, but maybe I'd be able to leave. I needed to get the hell away from him, from this, whatever it was. I didn't like the way Reed was looking at me. It had my stomach tied in knots. I glanced at the dais. There were six other people here. They wouldn't help Reed keep me against my will, would they? "You can't do this. You're holding me against my will. You have to let me go. I'm a cop."

A perilous laugh came from the dais. "Oh, how I do love this part." The woman who'd looked so stern earlier now had a delighted smile on her face. What was about to happen that she looked so happy about? I wasn't sure I wanted to find out.

My eyes widened as a realization hit me. They weren't going to help me. I was on my own here. I held my hands in front of me, ready to fight. I spent years in the gym combat training. There was no way I was going down without a fight. Reed advanced on me. His arms went for mine, and I jumped back swiftly out of his reach. I kicked my foot up before he realized what was happening and made contact with his chest. It was like kicking stone. He didn't even budge. He grabbed my ankle swiftly, knocking me back on the floor. I hit with a loud thump as my shoulder crushed into the red carpet. He dropped my ankle, and I spun onto my back. I reached my hands to flip myself up. Before I could get my hands in place, Reed was on top of me. His knees moved to straddle me; his weight pinning me to the floor. I lifted my leg to kick him from behind, but his hand reached back and caught it before I hit his back.

"Mmm, I like it when you're feisty." He dropped his head, and his nose moved up my body, taking a deep breath. I was so startled by the motion I didn't move. "You smell good enough to eat."

When I recovered, I tried to punch the side of his head. My knuckles connected with his jaw, and I cried out as I felt the bones in my hand break against his skin. I had thrown a correct punch, so why the hell did my hand break? "What the—" He grabbed my hands and held them firmly above my head. He shifted his weight back to my thighs so I couldn't move my legs. I was trapped. The realization had me panting, my heart already racing in my chest. I tried to pull and struggle against him, but it was no use. He was much stronger than me.

His mouth descended on my neck, and I felt the sharp puncture of my skin. I screamed. It sounded like there was water rushing through my ears. My head began to throb as I felt him pulling against my neck. I tried to jerk my body, but Reed was an immovable force. Something changed after he punctured my neck. My limbs felt heavy like I couldn't move them. I was screaming in my head to fight, but physically I couldn't do anything. His knee moved between my legs, sliding against the apex of my thighs. He rubbed himself against me, and I could feel his hardness against my stomach. My skin crawled, but I felt his arousal as if it were my own.

His mouth left my neck, and he looked down at me with such admiration. It was hard to look away from him. His arms slipped below my back and legs. I was lifted onto the altar when I had awoken. My stomach flipped at the idea of being on full display for the council. I couldn't even move my neck to look at them. Reed moved back over me, his erection resting against my core. I was relieved I was still fully clothed, or he'd be dangerously close to my entrance. For some strange reason, a wave of desire washed through me at the thought. What was happening to me?

His eyes locked on mine as he took something that was handed to him from the right. I saw the glint of the knife as he used it to cut through the skin on his wrist. He pressed the cut to my mouth. I felt my heart flutter in my chest. I could hear the darkness welcoming me like a warm blanket on a cold night. My eyelids drooped. He pressed his skin harder against my mouth. Copper filled my mouth, but I was too tired to drink. I wanted to follow the darkness. Everything felt so light, like I could drift away. Flashes of Carter at the range, talking to his wife. The guys at the bar, roasting me for my last failed boyfriend. Image after image of my failed life filled my head. What was I really holding onto?

"Swallow, Hope, you need to drink," he commanded. My eyes stayed closed. I knew he couldn't compel me with my eyes closed, or at least I hoped that was the case. I would rather die than become like him. His lips pressed against my ear. "Taste the sweetness of my elixir. Drink, Hope, it's delicious." Suddenly, the copper changed to the sweetest thing I'd ever tasted. I couldn't not drink it. I sucked hard against the sweetness filling my mouth. I needed more. My strength began to return, and Reed wasn't holding me down. I gripped his wrist and pulled it tight against my mouth. I swallowed each mouthful of the delicious liquid. When it was taken, I gripped at the air, grabbing whatever I could get my hands on.

"You liked that, didn't you?" a deep voice rasped against my ear. I couldn't think of anything beyond the sweetness. I wanted it back so badly. I was so aroused, my heartbeat pulsed between my legs. I wanted to find the pleasure my release would bring. I ground my hips against the hardness between my legs. My head swam, and I continued to rock my hips. Searching desperately for anything that would provide me relief. It was useless. I wasn't going to find my release that way. I was driven by carnal desire.

A soft chuckle sounded next to my ear. "This is my favorite part."

Lips pressed against mine. I flicked my tongue out and tasted the sweetness. I wrapped my hands around Reed's neck and pulled him closer, gripping his hair between my fingers. When he growled, it reverberated through my body. I wanted more. I rubbed against his hardness, creating a delicious friction. I tasted him with a hunger I couldn't seem to satiate. My tongue explored as my hips ground against the harness between my legs. Hungry, I was incredibly hungry for him. It felt like every nerve ending in my body sparked to life at the same time. Every touch ignited the fire within me. I needed more, so much more.

"Do you want me to soothe that ache inside you?" I felt a hand move down my body. Fire licked every place his fingers grazed the thin fabric of the dress. I moaned, reaching my mouth toward those delicious lips again. I didn't feel like myself. I could think of nothing beyond the desire pulsing through my entire body. I'd never been so filled with need. There was a desperation that I needed filled.

"Yes, oh God, yes," I cried out. My fingers curled around his shoulder, pulling him closer. I needed his body closer to mine. My other hand drifted down yanking open the buttons on his pants. I kept grinding my hips against his leg. I felt like a wild animal, ready to have her way with her prey. Yet, I didn't feel like the predator here. I yanked at his belt, but his hand stopped me from going further. I stared wide-eyed at those dark soulful eyes. A small smile curved his lips.

"Patience, you will be rewarded." I felt myself being lifted from the altar. "If you'll excuse us," he said. My head still swam, and a wave of dizziness hit me. The dim-lit room disappeared, and I was being carried down a dark hall. The door opened, and Reed lowered me onto a soft mattress. His lips lowered to my neck; his heavy body pressed against mine. I relished in the weight of him pressing me into the mattress. It had been too long since I felt the weight of a man on top of me. Oh, God, I was desperate. My head swam with desire. My core ached for a release. I'd never been so desperate. "Hope, I knew you would be delectable. I can't wait to be inside you." A hand slipped the strap from my shoulder, and the soft press of lips moved down my arm. My nipple puckered as soon as it was exposed to the cold air. The cold was quickly replaced by the warmth of Reed's tongue. He lapped at my nipples, sucking them each into his mouth. I moaned at the sensations pulsing through me. I felt ripples of energy running from my nipples to my core. I wasn't sure I could get any more aroused, but as he sucked on my nipple, I knew that was untrue. How was he doing this to me? I felt every lick, every suck as though he were attached to some wire that sent pleasure through me with every touch.

"Oh God," I arched up into his mouth. I wasn't sure how much more I could take.

"Hope, I've wanted you since the moment you walked into the precinct." His mouth made its way down as he slid the dress off my body. There was something about what he said that had me trying to focus around the blur of desire. Precinct, what about the precinct? There was something I was supposed to be remembering. Lips moved down my body, and my back arched again. "Say you want me." His voice sounded pleading. "My blood and passion run through your veins." His head rested between my legs. He licked between my folds, and I moaned, throwing my head back. Finally, I would get what I needed so desperately.

"Oh, God." I cried out, all the sensations hitting me at once. His tongue was amazing. It moved so fast in all the right places. In moments, I was crying out as my climax hit me like a freight train. He kept going, prolonging my orgasm. My hands gripped his hair as he continued to pleasure me. When a second orgasm hit, I pulled his hair and clutched him against me.

"Tell me you want me. I'm not doing anything more unless you tell me, Hope." His mouth left me, and I felt the absence immediately.

"Oh, God, I want you. I want to feel you inside me." I ran my fingers through his lush hair.

"I need you to say my name, Hope," he growled.

"Fuck me, please," I begged.

"Damn, you make it so hard. Just say my name. I want to know that it's me you want. We're going to spend five years together. This is your first lesson. This is what the transformation does to you. I transferred my emotions to you through the blood. I need you to consent before I go any further. Tell me you want me, Hope. Just say my name." His lips found my ear, and he nipped the lobe.

My eyes snapped to his. My head was clearing since I'd gotten the orgasm I so desperately craved. I felt my body relaxing as he kissed down my neck. My mind was returning to thoughts beyond desperately needing release. My hands roamed down his chest. The buttons were open on his shirt. I wasn't sure when that happened. My fingers wandered lower. The button was pulled free from his pants. This was Reed, the man who kidnapped me. The man who just agreed to kill me. He probably did just kill me. My body no longer felt like my own. Something was changing. I could feel it. But did I want this with him?

He stopped and looked down at me. I watched as he bit his lip. "Do you want more blood? I could tell you enjoyed it." His eyebrow rose.

I cringed. "No, I don't want blood, Reed." My voice was surprisingly steady. I looked down to his bare chest. I had to admit I liked the feel of his taut muscles beneath my fingers. He'd already made me come. I could let him finish what we started. It didn't seem like that big of a deal. But something inside me told me it was. I could feel his erection through the fabric of his pants. I lay bare to him. My dress was discarded somewhere on the floor. I felt vulnerable under his penetrating gaze.

"What is it you want, my dear, Hope?" His voice was rough. I could hear the strain of holding back. He wanted me. The desperation in his voice was telling. He wanted to be inside me. I wasn't sure what had stopped him. He could have easily been inside me while I was so lost to the pleasure of my last orgasm. Yet, he stopped. I flipped back to what he'd said. He needed me to say his name, to consent to him. I shook my head to clear it. I didn't want this. I didn't want him. My stomach clenched at the realization of what just happened. Why was I so willing? What was it that made me so desperate? He mentioned transferring his desire. How? How was he able to transfer his desire so that I wanted him beyond all reason? There was so much about what just happened that I didn't understand. "Come on, Hope. I can make it so good for you. I will always make it good for you." His voice came out rough. He was struggling to hold back. A ran my hands over the muscles of his chest, licking my lips.

It was tempting. "I want to go home, Reed. I don't want this."

He froze. Disappointment flashed in his eyes. "Are you sure? You don't know what you're missing. I can give you what you want, Hope. I can give you everything."

"I'm sure I want to go home. You kidnapped me. You think I'm going to want you after you took me against my will. What was it about your blood that made me ravenous for you, anyway? That was not my desire." He cursed and got off me. I shivered at both being exposed and at what just happened between us. My body, my desire, didn't feel like my own. I didn't mind the satiated feeling I had afterward. My body was humming post-orgasm. Reed wasn't wrong about giving me what I needed. He was magnificent, but it was hard to look past the fact that he kidnapped me.

"It's the blood. It makes you aroused. I was aroused by you, so I transferred that feeling to you. Apparently, it didn't last." He smoothed his hand down his trousers.

I smirked. "Wasn't what you were expecting? Did you think your little arousal trick was going to last longer? Were you hoping I'd beg for you?" I smirked, watching the annoyance play across his features. "Too bad, I'll never want you, Reed. Now, are you going to bring me home or what?" I swung my legs over the side of the large bed. I remembered starting in the council room with six people at the dais, watching. I was glad not everything happened with an audience.

He turned on me, pulling his coat taut over his shoulders. "Yes, my dear, I'll bring you home." His lips curved into a coy grin. "We have five years to get to know each other, intimately. I'm sure you'll love it." There was an edge to his voice that had my stomach flipping. *Five years, he thought I was sticking around for five years. Was he delusional, or did he hit his head?*

"No, I'm going home, to my home. Back to my life." I grabbed my dress off the bed and slipped it back over my head. I hated wearing dresses of any kind, and this was the worst. Who went out in gowns beyond those on the red carpet?

"You can't go back to your life, my dear. You are a vampire. As soon as the blood works its way through your body, you will be turned. The life you had before today no longer exists." His voice held a bit of amusement. I wanted to wipe that smirk off his face.

"So, how does it work exactly?" I asked. I wasn't sure what to expect. Would I get that craving for sex again, like when he'd given me his blood? I shuddered. I didn't like feeling like I wasn't in control of my own desires. I wanted to be in control. I needed some of my dignity back. Not that I regretted what just happened. I was a girl. I had needs. He provided for my needs. It wasn't much different than any other one night stand I'd had. Hell, I probably would have taken Reed to my bed at some point if it wasn't for the whole kidnapping thing. I certainly enjoyed admiring him at work. I wasn't going to be a victim here. I wasn't going to regret the fabulous orgasm he had given me. I was in control. He stopped when I asked. That was the end of it. Now, I just needed to understand what was going to happen next? Not that I believed I was turning into a vampire. Maybe Reed was more delusional than I first thought.

"There is one small thing that needs to happen for the full transformation. I wanted to have some fun with you first." He pulled down the collar of his shirt. "Fulfilling your desire and sex is part of the ritual, but you have to ask for me, willingly. Most do. Most actually beg the way you did at first." He licked his lips. My eyes narrowed. I hated that I'd begged him. It was part of it. I couldn't help myself. My core clenched at the reminder of how badly I'd needed him and how well he delivered. Dammit, I needed to get that out of my head. I would not beg for him like that again, ever. A sly smile curled his lips, and I hated that he probably knew what I was thinking.

"What's the small thing?" I asked.

"Your death." His smile turned devious, and he stepped closer to me.

Chapter Four

My eyes widened as the realization hit. I needed to get the hell away from him. I flew off the bed and to the opposite side of the room. I didn't realize this was going to be dinner and a show. I held my hands out in front of me, ready to move into action if I needed to. I had fought him earlier and knew I was outmatched, but damned if I was going to give up. He just said he needed to kill me. I needed to stall him, so I could get the hell out of here. I didn't actually want to die. "Um, so when you say my death, do you mean you're going to actually kill me?" I backed into the wall behind me and flinched. I tried to side-step, but Reed was there in an instant. His finger trailed down my jaw, my neck, my chest. My breath caught in my throat.

"You, my dear, will be a magnificent vampire." He breathed against my neck. "You'll beg for me soon enough. You won't be able to help yourself." he chuckled darkly. "Although, I do love a good chase." He inhaled deeply against my neck, and I stiffened. "I love how you smell with my blood coursing through you. It's intoxicating." My stomach turned, and bile rose in my throat. I couldn't die. Not like this. I had to fight to get away from him.

I jerked my knee up into his groin. He groaned, but it didn't have the effect I was hoping for. Most men were crippled by a knee to the family jewels. Not Reed. I tried it again, jerking my knee up with all the strength I had in me. "I'm not going to be a vampire. Not if you don't kill me."

"Oh, my dear, I'm going to kill you. I've already started the process. You're weak from blood loss. The only reason you feel strong right now is because my blood runs through your veins. I have to say, I love the effect I'm having on you. It doesn't make me want you any less." His finger ran over my neck as the other hand gripped both my hands above my head. I felt his sharp nail scrape down my neck and the trickle of blood in its wake. His tongue slid up my neck. "Mmm, you taste so good, Hope." My name came out like a prayer on his lips.

"You're repulsive," I cursed, trying to yank my hands from his grasp.

"Mmm, I like you in this position." His hands tightened on my wrists.

I jammed my knee up as hard as I could. I watched him wince at the contact for a millisecond before his satisfied mask returned. I was starting to think he liked it when I hurt him. Like he was getting off on it. "I like watching you wince in pain. I know it hurts a little. Otherwise, you wouldn't grunt every time I made contact." I looked back at him, defiantly. "Maybe I'll keep doing it until you let me go. It's not like you can have kids or anything." I jammed my knee up again. A smirk lit my face as he winced. He couldn't hold both my hands and my legs. Could I hurt him badly enough to be able to get away?

"You're enjoying my pain." He licked up my neck again. "I like this side of you. I knew you were devoted to your work but seeing you in action is inspiring." He licked the crook of my neck, and I shivered. "It feels good to cause pain, doesn't it, Hope? You want to hurt me. Come on, Hope, admit you enjoy causing me pain." He pressed himself against me. I could feel his erection against my stomach. He was getting off on this. I was arousing him by hurting him. My stomach rolled.

He was right. I enjoyed hurting him. I wanted him to suffer at my hands. He kidnapped me. Anything I did was a result of being taken against my will. I was trying to survive. The fact that I was enjoying his pain didn't change that. I wanted to see him suffer. I fantasized about hurting him even more. I hated having my hands bound. I hated how he pressed up against me. I hated how much I didn't hate feeling his body pressed against mine. There was something seriously wrong with me. "I can't do anything with you binding my wrists."

"We both know that's not true. You were doing just fine with your legs. I enjoyed having my head between them, giving you pleasure." His mouth moved to nip my earlobe. "You can't hide how you feel from me, Hope. I felt your heart rate increase. I can hear it flutter now with every touch. I know you're not as repulsed by me as you're letting on."

"You're mistaking adrenaline for attraction. You just got me off, and now you want to kill me. I think you're the one who's confused." My voice rose. "Do you normally kill the women you've been with, or is it my sparkling personality?" I rubbed my knee up the inside of his thigh. Maybe I could play on his desire for me. Get him to let me go long enough for me to run. He was talking about killing me. I didn't really want to stick around for that part.

"You haven't seen anything yet." He dropped his hands to my neck, squeezing. I tried to push him away with both my hands, but he was an immovable force. I clawed at his hair, yanking out the strands as I tried to get free. "Although, I do love to feel your fiery passion as you try to fight me off, I'm getting rather bored. I need to be done with this already. I have a job to get to in a few hours." He pressed his lips together. "Sorry, I couldn't enjoy this any further. You're a wildcat I look forward to taming. You are mine." He cupped my face in his hands, and I was mesmerized by the sparkle in his dark eyes. I hadn't noticed before how dark they were. He smiled, and in a flash, his hands moved cupping my head. A sharp crack sounded, and darkness descended on me. In the few seconds before I died, I vowed revenge on Reed. I would make him suffer if it was the last thing I did.

I woke up cocooned in satin. My arm stretched out and felt the smooth fabric of the sheets beneath me. I moaned, my head spinning with the flashes of memories. Reed's hair between my bare thighs, me crying out as an orgasm rocketed through me. Reed's tongue licked up my neck as he held me bound against the wall. The devilish smile that curved Reed's lips before everything went black. I shook my head. What the hell happened?

My body felt strange. I stretched my arms above my head, feeling each of my muscles uncoil as I pulled them. The room around me was strange. The sheets were ruby-red and matched the thick curtains on the windows. A mahogany armoire was directly across the room. It matched the vanity dresser. I focused back on the window. There wasn't even a shimmer of light coming through the drapes. Everything here was so dark. It seemed unlikely that not a single stream of light would penetrate through the dark room. I rolled onto my back. A deep red canopy was above me. What was the deal with the different shades of red?

I threw my legs over the side of the bed. I was dressed in the gown from last night. How did I get here? I couldn't remember anything after Reed's hands were on my throat. I furrowed my brow, thinking. He said he'd gotten bored with me fighting. Did he kill me? I vaguely remembered the snapping before everything went dark. My stomach turned. I couldn't believe how caught up I'd gotten in the pleasure that I forgot about him kidnapping me. I told myself I wasn't going to regret it. Being with Reed was like a one-night stand. He hadn't even really penetrated me, so it was fine. I was chalking it up to it being too long since I'd last gotten laid. It had nothing to do with how sexy Reed looked without a shirt or the fact that his blood made the desire within me insane. What was that? A little attention and arousal, and apparently, I'd forgive anything. I didn't mind the orgasm. It was earth-shattering. I would never regret that part. I licked my lips thinking about it and my core clenched. Damn, I would need to get that under control.

There was a dull ache in my stomach. I got up, glancing back at the room. All the red was bothering me. I would never decorate a room in different shades of red. It was weird. I headed for the kitchen. Something smelled delicious. Reed was sitting at the kitchen counter, a paper in front of him. "I called the chief for you. He hopes you're feeling better soon. He also took your request for the night shift." He didn't look up from the paper. "He agreed that you could switch immediately. Looks like we'll be partners in more ways than one, Matthews. I can't tell you how much I'm looking forward to it." His eyes flashed up to me, and a devious smile split his mouth. I hated him. I hated him so much. How dare he go behind my back to speak to the chief?

I narrowed my eyes on him. "What the hell did you do, Reed?"

"Well, I couldn't exactly have you working on day shift when you can't go out during the day, now could I? You have to earn daylight privileges." He bent the newspaper to look at me when he spoke.

"What the hell, Reed? Why can't I go out during the day?" I asked.

"Oh, my dear, you can't be that incompetent. You understood every facet of what happened last night. Even while you were screaming for more, you knew." His eyes narrowed on me. I didn't like the flutter I felt at his intense gaze. "What we did, there's no coming back from. We're connected. You will be my progeny for the next five years, or until I decide you're fit to go out on your own." He paused, watching me. What did he mean there was no going back? How could one night change so much? My throat felt tight. He nodded as though he understood what I was experiencing. "I explained to the chief that you had the flu, so you won't be expected back for a few days. You'll need to control your bloodlust before you can return." Reed pushed a glass filled with a red liquid toward me. The smell hit me, and I wanted it, desperately.

"What's that?" I glanced down at the glass. The pang in my stomach grew. I needed whatever was in that glass. A small voice in my head already knew what he was going to say. I just wasn't ready to accept it.

"Blood, it will fill the ache you're feeling." His eyes flicked up toward me. His eyebrow quirked up. I could almost see his intrigue. He pushed the glass closer. "Come now, love. You need to control your thirst. You won't be able to be around humans until you're satiated." I licked my lips involuntarily and flinched back. I couldn't drink blood. What the hell was I thinking? Why did I want it so much?

"I prefer coffee in the morning. Maybe some eggs and bacon." The reality of everything that happened hit me all at once. Reed had fed me his blood and snapped my neck. That was the sound I'd heard before everything went dark. This bastard actually killed me. Now I had to drink blood, and I couldn't go out during the day. I hated him. My blood boiled beneath my skin with my hatred. It enraged me that he was right. I could smell the blood in the glass, and my mouth watered. I wanted to drink it. My body craved it. I licked my lips slowly as I stared at the dark red.

"Come on, Hope, you need to drink it. You'll feel better once you do." He stood up and walked around the table, stopping in front of me. He picked up the glass and held it in front of my mouth. He'd reduced me to a whimpering fiend, desperate for the satisfaction only he could bring last night. Now, he was trying to reduce me to a damn toddler by feeding me. No, I was not going to let him debase me like this. I was still Hope Matthews, the badass bitch of a detective. I was good at what I did because I was strong. I could handle his bullshit. I grabbed the glass out of his hand. His eyes widened in surprise.

I watched the liquid slosh against the sides when I took it. I wanted the blood in this glass as much as I wanted air. I couldn't stop myself. My eyes focused on Reed as I gulped hungrily. I licked my lips and set the empty glass back on the table. My glare never leaving Reed. "I hate you for what you've done to me. I will always hate you." I clenched my hands into fists. I wanted to pummel him until I couldn't feel anything anymore. He killed me. He took everything away from me. I knew without a doubt that everything he had told me was the truth. I just didn't know what that meant for me now. How would I continue to live my life as a vampire? Reed took a step toward me. His proximity both made my skin crawl and my core clench. I needed to stop remembering how hard he'd made me come. My eyes narrowed. "What?"

He ran the back of his hand down my cheek, and I stiffened. "I knew you'd make a magnificent vampire. This, my darling, is only the beginning." He paused, his hand still resting on my cheek. Then in a second, he turned away. "We'll begin your training right away. You need to get acclimated to life as a vampire. The sooner, the better. Today is the first day of your immortal life. I can't wait to see how you honor me." He turned back to look at me. His eyes shined with pride. I wanted to wipe that smug look off his face. He was such an arrogant bastard.

"I will never honor you. I hate you." I spat.

"Oh, darling, you will grow to love me, or your life will be increasingly difficult. As I said, this is only the beginning." He walked around me, stopping behind me. I could feel him against my back. He whispered next to my ear. "I promise you, little one, you will honor me. I will break that fiery spirit of yours one way or another." A chill ran up my spine. I wasn't sure I wanted to know how he planned to do that. He'd shown me the night before just how much he enjoyed my pain. Would his training be about breaking me with induced pain? I closed my eyes. I could still feel his breath on my skin. I needed to pull it together. I couldn't think of him as an enemy while my traitorous body heated every time he came near me. My body reacted to every memory from last night. Was that on purpose? Did he want me to react to his presence with desire? Everything felt like a manipulation with him. I needed to be careful. I would not give anything of myself to this man. He would never break me.

"You will never get what you want. I will find a way to kill you." I said between clenched teeth. He let out a laugh.

"Oh, darling, you will never kill me. Not if you value your own life." He stood before me again, his teeth scraping across his bottom lip. "Like I said before, this is only the beginning. It's going to be a long five years if you spend it trying to kill me. We could be spending our time in much better ways." His fingers skated over my arm. "Besides, the vampire council will end your life as surely as you would end mine. It is our most vital law. You cannot kill your maker." A devilish smile broke out over his face. At that moment, I knew my life had changed forever. I vowed to find a way to hurt this man. I would be the one who killed him, so help me God. I wanted to feel his immortal life slip away beneath my fingers. Somehow, I would make that happen, even if it meant giving up my own life.

Epilogue

R eed threw another punch at my face. I ducked it just in time. "You know I already spend hours in the gym working out. Why do you insist on doing even more training after work?" I ducked another of his punches before dropping and swiping my leg in a circle and watching as he fell to the mat. I climbed on top of him, holding his wrists down on both sides of his head. "You forget that being newly made, I'm stronger than you." I gave him a wicked smile.

He catapulted into the air, flipping me over in the process. He landed on top of me, moving his legs fast enough to straddle me on the floor. "Never let your guard down."

"Whatever, Reed, I'm sick of this. What am I even training for? I'm already stronger than anyone on the force." I slid out from between his legs in seconds and stood behind him. I couldn't help but show off with Reed. Our relationship had always been a volatile one.

"You are training to fight vampires. At some point, you may need to fight your own kind or other breeds. You must be able to fight the way we do. The council wouldn't be pleased if you weren't able to fight one of your own." Reed flipped himself into a standing position. "You've had enough for today. We'll pick up again after our shift tomorrow."

"Seriously?" I rested my hand on my hip and glared at him. "I would rather be spending less time with you, not more. You're already my partner on the force. You changed my shift because you don't want me to go out in the daylight. Now, you want me to spend all my free time with you, training? Are you fucking kidding me? I don't want to spend a second more than I have to with you." I began unwrapping the bindings on my hands. I didn't really need to do it anymore, but it was a ritual I had from sparring in the gym. Reed kept telling me that my human habits would fade with time. I wasn't sure I believed him.

"Oh, my darling Hope, those changes were necessary. How many times must we go through this? You are a vampire, not a human. Changes must be made to protect our secret, our legacy. You wouldn't want the council to end your life before it's even begun, would you?" He leaned against the wall next to the door. He didn't need to prepare to spar with me. He would fight in his damn suit without a second thought. I suspected he changed after work for my benefit.

"I would like to point out that you kidnapped me and changed my life against my will. I will never forgive you. If I have to live with you for five years, I'm starting to think death may be the preferable option." I tucked my wraps and shoes into my bag. I didn't need the gym bag because Reed had a gym in our house. Yet, I still carried one with me for my sparring lessons. I did it more because it bothered Reed more than anything else. He seemed to take issue with all my "human" habits. He didn't like that I refused to give up the little rituals he deemed unnecessary. I enjoyed anything that bothered him.

"Oh, my dearest Hope, you'll change your mind eventually." He stalked toward me. I hated that my heart raced when he looked at me like that. One thing that hadn't changed after I'd become a vampire. Stopping in front of me, he took a piece of my hair, wrapping it around his finger. His tongue slid over his bottom lip. "I still influence you. I can hear your heart quicken every time I'm near. Stop denying your desire. We could both be more than satisfied if you'd just give in to me, Hope. Let me give you what you need." His last sentence came out husky, and my core clenched. Damn, I hated how he still had that effect on me after only one encounter.

I rolled my eyes. "You haven't gotten any better at convincing me, Reed. I told you. I'm never going to be with you. Currently, I'm your prisoner because of the laws of the vampire council. As soon as I'm free, I'll be long gone. Feel free to lift my sentence anytime now." I flicked his hand away from my hair.

"You are not a prisoner. You may come and go as you please. The council only specifies that you live with me for the first five years to acclimate to your new life. It's really for your protection, darling. I'd hate to have you run into another vampire without my protection." His voice dropped low, dangerous. "As long as you are my progeny, you are safe with me." He stepped back, his eyes darkening.

"I have yet to see another vampire who might be dangerous. The only dangerous vampire I know is you." I flipped my hair over my shoulder and sauntered out of the room. Our relationship wasn't getting any better. I couldn't believe I had another five years and six months stuck in this place with Reed. He wasn't entirely wrong. I felt a strong attraction to him anytime he was near me. It didn't matter. There was no way I was giving into him. He took my human life from me. For that, I would forever hate him. At least I got to keep some of my life intact. My friends, my family, my job were all still a big part of my life. I wasn't sure what it was going to be like to live forever, but at least for now, I was going to enjoy what I had.

Scarlet Cursed

Cursed fangs. Fiery chemistry. A twisted case that could win her freedom... or leave her lifeless.

Death lies scattered at Hope Matthews' feet. Already solving murders by day, the audacious detective resents the overbearing but well-built vampire whose bite flipped her evenings upside down. But when she's offered a blood-oath to escape from her confines, she seizes the chance and starts searching for answers to a string of bodies drained of life.

Taking her investigation to the seedy club where the victims met their demise, Hope revels in the jealousy her attraction to a playful crime scene tech creates with her dark, controlling master. But with supernatural attacks rising and life-changing secrets hanging in the night air, the trail of clues could lead her straight into a shallow grave.

Can the bold sleuth reclaim her freedom before she meets her own gory end?

Scarlet Cursed is the pulse-pounding first book in the Raven Vampire Assassin urban fantasy series. If you like strong-willed heroines, dashes of romance, and worlds dripping with intrigue, then you'll love Dora Blume's red letter.

Buy *Scarlet Cursed* to lift the crimson stain today!

CHAPTER 1

I traded one set of shackles for another. As I stared at the stack of files on my desk, I wondered why I was still here. I had no idea where to begin with my overflowing stack of unsolved cases. I blamed Reed. He had me hunting for vampires more often than we were hunting murderers. It seemed like one hell of a balancing act to play, being both homicide detective and vampire. Yet, for the last six months I'd managed.

A throat cleared behind me. I turned in my chair to see Carson leaning against the door frame. One piece of his gelled hair fell out of place on his forehead. "That's quite the stack. I don't remember you having so many when we were partners. Do I need to get on Reed for leaving you high and dry again?" Carson was my partner on day shift up until six months ago, when my entire life changed.

"Shouldn't you be on your way to have dinner with Melissa? You know how much she hates when you stay late and don't make it home for dinner." I crossed my arms over my chest. I didn't want to talk about the past. I hadn't given Carson much of an excuse for leaving him and switching to the night shift. I owed him an explanation. Too bad, I couldn't give him more. Another reason I hated Reed.

He chuckled. "Yeah, now that we have a little one on the way, she's worse. I used to be able to get away with staying a few extra hours, you know, get in some time at the range." He paused, giving me a meaningful look. "Now, shit, I won't hear the end of it if I show up even thirty minutes late." He rolled his eyes.

I gave him a weak smile. I hated how much our relationship had changed since I switched partners. "You should probably get to it then."

He nodded. "You know you should join us for dinner soon. One of your nights off maybe?" I saw a spark of hope in his eyes.

"Yeah, maybe." I glanced over to the stack of files. "If I ever get a day off, I need to get through a few of these first." I pressed my lips together before I looked back at him.

"Yeah, well, I better leave you to it then. I'll see you soon, Hope." There was so much of our old friendship in the way he'd said my name. My heart clenched. Oh, how I wish things could go back to the way they were. Carson and I had been partners for five years. You didn't spend everyday with someone and not feel like they were an unbreakable part of your life. I missed him so much. I remembered graduation day from the academy. How he'd been so excited for us both. I thought we'd retire together. Unfortunately, going back wasn't an option. I needed to keep pushing forward, no matter how shitty things got. I was starting to understand Reed's insistence at cutting all ties. I'd been apprehensive, but every one of these conversations hurt.

"Yeah, see you later," I tried to give him a wider smile, but I knew he'd see right through me. I probably wouldn't see him soon. This was the earliest I'd come into the station. I had been avoiding everyone I'd worked with before. At first, it was because I feared they would recognize I was different. Now, it was because I didn't want to keep having these awkward conversations, reminding me of a life I could no longer have. The thought of Melissa being pregnant filled me with joy and regret. I would never have that. It's strange how the things you never thought you wanted, become the things that haunt you when you can't have them anymore. A family, children, a life outside of work, all used to be things I thought I could worry about later. I wanted to get ahead in my job before I got serious about my life. Now, all I had was my job. I understood the error in my ways. And there was no going back for me.

"You're thinking awfully hard considering you haven't touched a single one of those files." Reed, his sudden presence in my doorway sent a chill down my spine.

"I thought you weren't coming in tonight?" I asked. He told me he had a lead on a coven of vampires who were suspected of breaking the council's laws. I helped him with some investigation on them, but since I wasn't an official member of the Raven society I couldn't join him on the case. Which left me here, with my stack of unsolved cases. Usually, I loved my caseload. Lately, I found it lacking. The things Reed was doing sounded so much more interesting. Yet, I wasn't sure I wanted the tradeoff. For now, I was fine doing my own thing.

"I thought I'd stop in, show my face to the lieutenant." He strode over to my desk, sitting on the one clear space above my drawer. His eyes darkened. "Why? Did you miss me?" There was a level of salaciousness to his tone. He licked his lips as I stared back at him. I wasn't sure what it was, but when he used that tone a fire ignited inside me. Damn, vampire ritual. I hated that I'd been so vulnerable with him when he'd turned me into a vampire. I knew that somewhere deep inside, I wanted him. I wanted him long before he took me, long before he offered to help me on my last case as a human. I hated how much I still felt that desire.

"Yeah, he was asking about you." I rolled my eyes and shifted my chair away from him. "I covered for you, of course."

"Of course, I would expect nothing less." He slid an inch closer to me.

"I'm not entirely sure why I'm still working here." My eyes shifted to the stack of files. "I mean, have you ever heard of a vampire who works?"

"Would you rather redo high school over and over?" He smirked. "I think you've read too many fanatical stories about vampires. We don't, in fact, live in dark castles in Transylvania. Nor do we traipse around the world, thinking only of our thirst for blood." He licked his lips slowly, enticingly. "We do in fact, have mortgages we have to pay, and need jobs to pay our bills. Just like everybody else."

"Well, I would like to be the first to inform you, that's the lamest vampire story I've ever heard. You should probably think about a full rewrite of that one. Maybe try the rich man living in a nice castle. Maybe try Scotland instead of Transylvania. I hear it's not so dark there. Wait," I paused, tapping my finger against my lips, "Maybe Alaska would be more fitting. We could always try Alaska. Do you think they make igloos shaped like castles? Maybe we could get a huge cabin." I pressed my lips together to stop from bursting out laughing at the look on Reed's face.

The Lieutenant knocked on the door behind me. "It's good you're here. You two caught a case. A body was found in an alley off of Broadway. I've got a few black and whites on scene and Laura will be headed there soon." He tapped the doorjamb before nodding and heading down the hall.

"You got this covered? I still have my other case to work on." He glanced at the door.

"Oh, so you are going to let me go to the crime scene alone, again? You don't think Miller and Elliot won't notice you're not there?" I took a deep breath. I looked at the very white brick wall across from me. I hadn't done much to my office since I'd gotten it after switching shifts. It's not like I needed much. A desk, a couple of chairs, access to the coffeemaker. You know, the simple things. I was the highest ranking detective on night shift. Everyone who'd moved up the ladder like I had, switched to day shift long ago. It was always the rookies on night shift.

"I think you can handle it. Don't you?" His eyebrow rose in challenge.

I hated that he knew me so well already. "Yes, I think I can handle it. It's not like there will be a sadistic vampire waiting for me this time." I fluttered my lashes.

"I'll see you for training in the morning." He dropped his head next to my ear. "You'll pay for that one." His breath skittered across my skin causing the hair on my neck to stand up.

"Looking forward to it." I pressed my lips together in a forced smile. He pushed himself up from my desk and left. I wondered if other detectives would notice how often we left separately. I'm sure that if anyone noticed, they wouldn't say anything. I had a feeling everyone here had a healthy respect for how dangerous Reed actually was. I wish I had any inkling of it when he'd offered to help with the case that ended my life. I had just thought he was being a nice guy.

One squad car blocked off the entrance to the alley. I saw Laura's van backed into the other. I guess she made it there faster than the Lieutenant thought. I parked in a spot on the other side of the cop car. Miller and Elliot had already made it to the scene. Elliot's dark sedan was parked across the street from mine. I hadn't seen them at the station. Damn Reed for having Raven business. I wondered how no one ever noticed his absence before. Did any of the other vampires work on the force? Reed hadn't shared much in the six months since I'd become his fledgling. I couldn't leave my sire for the first five years after being turned. The only exception to that was if you were to become a Raven and work for the council. I wanted that so bad I could taste it. I'd heard nothing but an endless stream of excuses for why I wasn't ready from Reed. I would do whatever it took to be ready.

I tucked my hands in my leather jacket and strode over to the scene. "Hey Davis, busy night?" I nodded at the alley as I stopped next to the officer who'd secured the scene.

"It's our second body tonight. Not sure what's going on in the city, but I wasn't expecting it to be a double homicide kind of night." He rested his hand loosely at his side.

"Huh? You think it's something in the water?" I smirked.

"It's always something in the water." He rolled his eyes and gave me a playful smile.

I glanced down the alley. Laura was glaring at me, her fist rested on her cocked hip. "Matthews, you planning to work tonight?" Her tone was sharp. It sounded like Laura wasn't handling the stress of a busy night all that well.

"Yeah, you wanna check me in." I rolled my eyes at officer Davis.

"I got you down. Conway was the first on the scene." He nodded, pointing his pen to the other side of the alley.

"Thanks, Davis. You getting a drink tonight?" Kyle Davis was a regular at the bar after work. He was an easy guy to talk to after a long shift.

"Ah, I can't. My sister's got a big wedding tomorrow. I need to catch a few hours before I have to get my tux." He stared down at the ground.

"You haven't even picked up your tux yet? Your sister is going to be mad at you." I shook my head.

"Matthews!" Laura called from down the alley.

"Good luck tomorrow." I waved at Kyle before hustling down to meet Laura.

Laura had her blonde hair pulled back into a messy bun with a pencil sticking out the top. Her gloved fingers were holding up the wrist of the man who lay face up on the asphalt. His body looked like it had been flung out of a car. One leg was haphazardly laying over the other and his torso was contorted at the hips. The man was shirtless and his alabaster skin shone stark against the halide street lamps. I appreciated that some of the newer lamps had been switched over to the blue lights of the halides instead of the yellow from the high pressure sodium lights. Elliot and Miller were half-way down the alley. Miller was pointing to the ground, then down the opposite side of the alley. I would check-in with them after I spoke to Laura.

"There are ligature marks on both wrists. Based on the coloring of the wound, he was bound ante mortem." Laura looked up at me. She rolled the body carefully to peer under his back. "He hasn't been here long."

"Body dump?" I glanced around the alley. It was secluded. Most of the restaurants around here would have been closed. No one in this neighborhood would have noticed someone driving down the alley.

"The stiffened arm and placement of the body suggests he was dumped, yes. I'll know more when I get him back to the lab." Laura stood, her royal blue stilettos a stark contrast to the grit of the alley.

"You wore your new shoes to a crime scene?" I rested my fist on my hip.

She held her foot out. "Yeah, aren't they amazing? They match the pinstripe of my suit." She pointed to the thin lines running down the designer suit.

"They are amazing. I just can't believe you wore them to examine the body in an alley. Do you know what happens here? The entire alley reeks of piss and rotting food." Part of being a vampire was the enhanced senses. She'd probably want to wash every inch of her body if she could see the filth that I saw in this alley.

"Oh, like you wearing those is any better." She pointed to my Louis Vuitton's.

"What? It's not like I have anything else to spend my money on. I might as well buy fabulous shoes." I shrugged. What was the point of being a vampire if I wasn't going to exploit the benefits? Not like I could explain that to Laura.

"Alright Matthews, keep telling yourself that. Maybe if you wore those shoes out on the town, or God forbid, on a date, you might find another reason to spend your money." Her eyebrows rose in challenge.

"Yeah? When was your last date?" I crossed my arms over my chest. I knew I had her. I tried not to read her thoughts. I was getting better at blocking out those around me. I already knew the answer. She hadn't had sex in almost a year. I wasn't the only one who needed to get out.

"You know what, you're right. We both need to get out. I have the perfect place. We can go this Saturday. There's this fancy club I've been wanting to check out, and I happened to have met the owner." Her chin lifted, and I caught a whiff of her cockiness. I wondered what kind of club this was going to be. Laura had a thing for the outlandish and a little kinky.

I took a deep breath. "I don't know. The last club you took me to was a little too leather clad for me. I'm not really into the same, um, things as you are."

"Oh, it's not one of those clubs. I promise. It's very classy. You'll love it." Her smile widened. It was like she knew I would agree before I did.

"Ugh, fine, Saturday." I shook my head. I hated how Laura was the one person who could get to me. I loved her. We'd worked together for years, although, we'd been on opposite shifts for a long time. It was nice finally being on the same shift. She'd always been a little odd and loved working at night. She always explained that days were for normal people. She preferred to spend her time with the weirdos since she'd thoroughly considered herself one.

"Okay, any idea on cause or time of death?" I asked.

"Yeah, based on his liver temp, I'd say he died within the last two to four hours. I'll determine the cause at the autopsy. I don't see any other ligature marks or wounds on the body."

I glanced around the alley. It wasn't late, so the body would have been dumped recently. "What time did we get the official call?" I asked.

"You'd have to ask the first on scene. I was already at another scene when I got the call." She pulled down the neckline of the man's t-shirt. "He's got some weird markings around his neck." She pressed her finger down on the skin. "He's got an odd coloring, too. I'll run a full tox screen." She was speaking more to herself than to me at this point.

I moved around the body, looking for tire treads or anything that would have been left behind since this seemed like a hasty dump. The ground was still wet from an earlier rain. "I'm going to ask Kyle when the call came in." I turned to see Reed striding up behind me.

"The call came in at eight-forty-two. Matthews, you're losing your touch." He shook his head, a cocky smile was plastered across his face.

"I thought you had something to take care of?" I rested my fist on my hip. His showing up whenever he felt like it was getting old.

"I was in the area. Besides, it looks like you need me to keep you on your toes." He strode past me and bent next to Laura. His body was practically pressed up to her shoulder. "Did you find any fibers on the body? If they were in a car, there might be some transfer from the trunk."

"No, I will do a thorough work-up in the lab." She stood motioning to the two younger men waiting by her van. They hurried over with a body-bag and a stretcher. "Let's get him loaded and back to the lab." She pressed her mouth together in a hard line then she glared back at Reed. "I do know how to do my job, Carter." I smiled, Laura was the one person whom Reed's charms didn't work on. I loved her for that. Everyone in the office seemed to be either smitten or terrified of Reed. Not Laura, she often looked like she couldn't stand him.

Reed stood, walking over to a dumpster that looked like it had been pushed back slightly. There was a white line along the side. I moved to stand next to Reed. I held out a glove to him. "Don't you think you should be wearing gloves if you are going to examine the evidence?" I smirked. It served him right for questioning mine and Laura's competence.

"Actually, I have my own." He pulled a pair of leather gloves from his back pocket and slipped them on.

"Of course you do." I shook my head. "So, partner, what are you thinking?" I shifted my weight and looked down at him as he examined the side of the dumpster.

"I think whoever dumped the body here also hit the dumpster. Too bad it's white, the most popular color in the city." He stood. "The only thing that helps is the height of the paint. It's most likely a utility van of some sort." He took his leather glove off and scratched his chin. I noticed this was something he did when he was thinking hard about something.

"You can't be sure it's a van. It could be a truck or something. Basically we've narrowed it down to a higher vehicle, so truck, van or SUV." I walked around to the other side of the dumpster. I didn't find anything suspicious that I wouldn't expect in an alley.

"Alright, so we're on the hunt for a large white vehicle. So, basically, a needle in a haystack." I pushed my hair back from my face. "We also don't know what actually killed him."

"I told you I'll know more at the lab." Laura called out. "You are welcome to join me at the autopsy. I know you love spending your free time in my office."

I rolled my eyes. "It's so weird that you call the morgue, your office."

"It is my office, and I'll see you there. I've got one body to get to first. Then, your guy is up. I should be ready around midnight." She waved before heading to her car.

"Wait, was there any identification or anything on him?" I caught up to Laura before she left. Miller and Elliot were making their way back to us and heard my question.

"Nothing," Miller answered. "We thought robbery may be the motive, but considering he was dumped, we're not so sure." I thought it was funny how Miller always referred to both of them when speaking, as if they had one mind.

"Yeah, robbery wouldn't make sense since he was dumped here. It looks like our perp didn't want us to know the identity of our victim." I looked up at Elliot and Miller. "So, you had another body already?"

"Yeah, we finished up at that scene and came over here. It looks similar. Another body dumped in an alley on the South end by Lake Street. Not sure what's going on, but they could be related." Miller answered.

"We should compare crime scene photos when we get back to the office."

They both nodded. "Yeah, we're heading back so we can be there for the first guy's autopsy. See you back at the precinct." They strode past us and went to their car.

I looked back to Reed who was studying the ground. "What's up with you? I thought you had your own thing to do." I didn't buy the whole him being in the area bullshit.

"Well, I do have another reason for finding you." He tucked his gloves back into his pocket. His eyes stayed fixed on the ground.

"Okay, what would that be?"

"The council wants to see you." His head rose, his eyes were fixed on me.

"Well, it's about damn time."

CHAPTER 2

R eed pulled up to the front of a large brick building. He hurried around to open the door for me. I furrowed my brow and looked him up and down. I hadn't noticed at the crime scene that he wasn't wearing just any suit. He was wearing an Italian suit that had been perfectly tailored to him. I was in my black suit with my black pumps. Compared to him, I was underdressed. I hated that he decided now was a good time to visit the council. I could have used a little bit of notice so I could dress the part. Although, they had to know I didn't walk around in the evening gown I'd worn my first time here.

"You could have given me a little notice to prepare. You obviously knew you would be coming here." I waved my hand indicating his tailored suit.

"I come here every day." He smirked. He knew image was important to me.

"You could have given me a chance to go change." I glared at his hand holding the door open for me. I was baffled by his sudden gentlemanliness.

"You look fine. You always do." He waved his hand for me to go in. I pressed my lips together.

"Fine? You think I always look *fine*." I rolled my eyes. "I certainly look better than *fine*." I said as I strode past him.

"It's not that big of a deal." He commented. He nodded to the man standing near the door. The room we entered was dark, a dimly lit chandelier hung from the middle of the room. Older art pieces covered the walls with different macabre images. I wondered if it was a vampire thing to enjoy seeing such dark art.

"Says the guy who dressed me in an evening gown before forcing me to come here the last time." I turned on him. "What exactly am I doing here?"

"Could you keep your voice down? We're among vampires. Anyone in the building could hear you." His words were clipped, spoken between clenched teeth.

"Oh, do they not know I was forced to come here last time? Is that some kind of secret you're trying to keep?" The man standing by the door glanced up at us, his interest piqued. My smile widened. He didn't want them to know. That was one hell of an ace up my sleeve.

Reed grabbed my arm and yanked me off to the side. I hated that he was stronger than me. "Stop, you can't let them know about your making. Some of the council know, but not all of them. You're not going to win any points with them by speaking out against me. It's actually against the law and could end your eternal life before it even starts." His words were hushed, but I understood.

"It's not my fault you haven't taught me the laws or that you turned me against my will." I glared back at him. I thought they should know about the circumstances behind my becoming a vampire.

"What do I have to do to convince you it's in your best interest to not speak of that again?" The pressure on my wrist increased, and I glanced down.

"Are you threatening me?" I challenged.

"No, but you will die by the council if you speak against me. They won't care what you have to say. They will kill you." He growled out.

"Fine, help me become part of the Ravens. I'm tired of being on the sidelines."

"No problem, that's why we're here." He dropped his hand from mine.

"What?" I glanced over to the statue at the door. He must be security. Like vampires actually needed security. The smirk on his face let me know he could hear every word.

"The council called you because I let them know I thought you were ready for the next steps for becoming a Raven. You have been training hard. There are some things you still need to learn, like knowing when to keep your mouth shut, but I think you're as ready as you can be for what's next." He had a self-satisfied look on his face. I really wanted to wipe that smugness away, but he'd said what I wanted to hear. I've been waiting long enough to finally be a part of the Ravens. Reed had told me shortly after I'd been turned that I had been chosen for my work as a detective. He knew I was the best in the department. He'd recruited me. I just sped up my timeline when I was too close to one of his cases. I didn't actually believe that was why I'd sped up his timeline. He was supposed to ask me if I wanted to be part of something bigger. He actually gave me the whole spiel after I'd been changed against my will. I didn't trust Reed, but I was forced to live with him, to learn from him. I hated it. I hated him for changing my life so irrevocably. But since it was already done, there wasn't much I could do. I had to make the best of it. To me, the best was getting to be a part of the Ravens and hunting other vampires.

I smoothed down my suit. "Well, it's about time." I glanced to him expectantly.

"Only you would think they took too long to ask you to be a part of the group. It's only been six months. Most recruits have to wait several years before even being considered."

"Well, I'm not most people." I squared my shoulders. "Are you going to lead the way, or do I need to ask this gentleman to show me? The council awaits, after all."

Reed rolled his eyes. "It's not the entire council. You are being invited to show them what you've got. Consider it a trial before you're taken into the fold." He explained as he slipped around me and began down the hall. He knocked on a silver door at the end of the long hallway.

"They have offices like anyone else?"

"Yes, we have something similar to the station, but everyone's office is closed. We need to keep things a little more private here. Most of the offices have been sound proofed. Nothing in or out." He knocked again.

The door swung open and a woman with long hair pulled up into a simple roll stood at the door. Her suit was tailored to her curves, showing a hint of cleavage underneath. It was elegant yet still business attire. An energy emanated from her that let anyone near her know she was dangerous. I could almost feel the power of age radiating from her. She had a straight nose and long face. Her skin was alabaster and the picture of perfection. A slight pink blushed her cheeks. She was nothing short of magnificent. It took me a minute to recognize she was the woman who spoke the day I was changed. I wondered if she was the head of the council.

"Ah, Reed, it's good to see you." She lightly rested her hands over his and kissed both of his cheeks. "And Hope," her eyes grazed down my body. "Being a vampire certainly suits you." Her eyes focused on mine. "You look magnificent."

"Thank you, ma'am." I bowed my head unsure of the pretenses here. I knew she could be thousands of years old. I had no idea what the custom of greeting would be.

"Oh dear, call me Cassandra." She moved out of the door and around to her desk. "Please, do come in."

I walked behind Reed into the room. I was surprised at how large her office was. On one side was a Victorian style couch with inlaid gold around the edge. It was a rich burgundy. Two tall chairs sat across from the couch with a claw-foot table between. I liked the gold touches in the table and on the chairs. Cassandra motioned to one of the chairs and Reed took a seat next to her on the couch. His body angled toward hers, and I wondered how close they actually were.

"Thank you for having us today, my dear, Cassandra." Reed smiled.

"Well, of course, you have a bright young pupil here. I look forward to seeing what she will accomplish with us." She turned her focus on me, her long lashes blinking. "Reed believes you are ready to join our ranks in the Raven League."

"Yes, I believe I have done excellent in training and have been a decorated police detective for years. I believe I would be an asset to your organization." I spoke quickly, moving to the edge of my seat. I slid back, not wanting to seem too eager.

"As I've heard. Reed speaks highly of how dedicated you've been in your training. He believes it would be in our best interest to move you along faster than any other vampire trainee who's joined us before." Her voice deepened and her eyes focused back on Reed. "I'm not so inclined to give any new vampire special treatment." Something passed between them. I wasn't sure what was really going on here, but I knew they weren't talking about me.

"I believe I can prove myself to you if you give me the chance." I crossed my legs.

"Oh?" The way her voice rose was irritating. "Reed, do you believe she should be given the chance? You know the trials can be dangerous if she isn't prepared." Her voice was thick and her eyes never left Reed. I had no idea about any trial, or what I would have to do to be considered. Of course Reed would leave out anything important before bringing me here. I hated how he threw me into these situations without so much a s a heads up. He was a shitty partner if I ever had one. I wished there was some way to go back to having Carson. He was the only partner who both put up with me and never let me down. Reed hadn't done either in the time I'd known him.

"I believe she is ready to be given the chance. You know I wouldn't bring her here if she wasn't able to handle the danger." He rested back on the sofa, stretching his arm behind Cassandra's back. I narrowed my eyes on his hand. He skimmed his fingers over Cassandra's back. There was something more between these two.

"Well, I believe you would know her best." She stood, running her hand over her jawline. "How about we give her the chance to prove herself?" She turned to face me. "You say you've been a good detective. We're going to need your investigative skills. There's a vampire who's suspected of breaking the rules." She paused, sharing a look with Reed. "He's connected to someone here on the council. We haven't been able to officially investigate him because it would need to be cleared with the council. With his connections, we haven't been able to bring it up. If *you* were to investigate him, let's say, as a little trial, I may be able to move up your official entry into the Ravens." Her eyes lowered. "If not, no one would be the wiser." The smile that curled her lips sent a shiver down my spine. She was letting me know I was expendable.

"So, you want me to find out if this guy is breaking your rules without being discovered. Should be easy enough to pull off. How fast will I move into being a Raven if I succeed?" I wanted some assurances since it was obvious I was about to put my life on the line for it. This woman didn't strike me as the type to get her hands dirty.

"I can have you as a member in two years. That's much faster than any other recruit we've ever had." She tapped her finger to her lips like she was thinking something over. "Although, you'll still have to compete against others who've been turned in the city, but with your talents I'm sure you'll have no problem with that."

"Wait, you want me to do this undercover for a chance to compete a year early against the other vamps. No way, I want in as soon as I finish." I clenched my hands into fists. There was no way I was risking my life against a vamp with who knows what kind of strength and powers for a measly year earlier.

"Oh, well that's just unheard of, others would be suspicious if I let you move up that soon." She shook her head. "No way, I will not jeopardize my reputation like that for you to join any sooner. One year early, that's what I'm offering."

I leaned back, crossing one leg over the other. "You must not want to catch this guy bad enough. You know what. I think I'll just wait. One year isn't enough of an incentive for me to put my life on the line for you. Have someone else do it." I was calling their bluff. I bet I was their only option. They couldn't have Reed investigate him because he was an official member of the Ravens. I doubted there were any other recruits willing to do it. I was their only shot. I bet it pained her that I knew that. I wished I could read her thoughts as easily as I could the humans.

"Fine, you will get the chance to compete this year, as long as you complete this assignment. At least that way, you will show the others you deserve to be there early. That is if you are as good as you say you are." She folded her arms overlap, peering over at me.

"Oh, I am." I cocked my head, thinking it over. It was probably the best I was going to get. At least I would be free of Reed much sooner. I felt a slight bit of relief at that. "Fine, I finish this assignment and I compete. I agree to that." I held my hand out.

She let out a chuckle. "Oh honey, we don't do that." She walked to her desk pulling out what looked like a small letter opener. "We swear a blood oath." She pricked the end of her finger and glided over to stand before me. She handed me the opener. "Prick your finger."

"Um, what are we doing with our blood?" I asked, staring at the blood now forming a small bubble on the tip of her finger.

She smiled. "We drink the blood of each other and to swear to keep up our end of the deal. There's magic in our blood. We will have to uphold the pact we've made here today."

"What happens if either of us break the pact?"

"It's a blood oath. If either of us break it, that's the same as dying. But this seems pretty simple. Why would you worry about such a thing?" She held her finger out.

"What does that mean." I asked.

Reed stepped up. "She's saying if you break the blood oath you'll die. Once you drink the other's blood, your words become binding. You don't want to break a blood oath." She held her hand and finger out to me.

"How will you even know? I don't understand." I shook my head. I didn't want to drink her blood. There was something about it that seemed vile. I knew that was the human in me since I had no problem drinking blood when I was hungry. I just didn't want to drink her blood.

"It's a simple oath. You find me the killer, and I allow you early entry into the trials. What more do you need to understand?" She rolled her eyes and held out the bead of blood on her finger. "If you agree, you simply need to suck the blood off my finger. Unless you're backing out." She blinked like she was feigning innocence. I knew better. I grabbed her hand and jerked my finger forward. I sucked the blood off her finger and took a good pull, just for good measure. I looked at Reed as I swirled my tongue around her finger getting every last speck of blood. I watched as Reed's eyes hooded with desire. His look made me even more curious about their relationship. If I didn't know any better, I would say he was just as into Cassandra as he was me.

Cassandra smiled crookedly. "Good, now Reed make sure she has everything she needs." She waved us both toward the door.

"You don't want to tell her about the assignment yourself?" His voice rose in surprise.

"No, I think you can fill her in on everything. Please make sure you aren't overheard." Her eyes lowered and Reed nodded. Was she really worried that others would overhear us? I hadn't seen anyone other than the guards.

"You don't think they heard us in here?" I asked.

"Oh darling, the walls are soundproofed. No one heard a single peep out of this room." Her laugh was boisterous and fake. I hated it. I wondered how much of what she showed us was real. She seemed like she was always performing. Maybe it had something to do with the politics of being on the council. I would be sure to ask Reed as soon as we were away from here.

"Okay, partner, we have an autopsy to get to." I winked as he led me out of the door.

"Oh no, I am not going with you to see Laura. I think I'm already on her shit list." He stopped to open the passenger door of his car for me. "I have my other case to get to."

"Oh, so this wasn't the case you were working on?" I asked.

He closed the door on me quickly. He got into the driver's side and pressed his finger to his lips. "No, I have my own investigation. I'll need to get back to it. We'll talk when we're home. I don't want to chance anyone hearing us."

"So, are you going to drop me back at the scene? My car is still there. Hopefully, it didn't get towed." I looked out of the window as he drove.

"It didn't get towed. You know Kyle would have watched it like a hawk. He'd find a way to get it back to the station if you asked." Reed's voice was playful, almost taunting.

"What are you talking about?" I asked. "We're not that close." I shook my head. I watched as a man sat in one of the doorways to a closed shop. He was probably making himself comfortable. Many of the city-dwellers like to take up residence in shop doors for the night.

"It has nothing to do with being close. He likes you. He'd do just about anything you'd asked." The corner of his mouth curved into his devilish smile.

"What? No way." I shook my head.

"You don't see how beautiful you are?" He questioned.

"Well, of course I know. That doesn't mean my co-workers are going to do anything I ask." He was being ridiculous.

"Oh?" His eyebrow rose. "You want to wager a little bet?"

"No, take me to my car."

"Ha, it's because you know I'm right."

"No, it's because I have a job to get to." I rolled my eyes and continued to watch out of the window. Minneapolis was one of those cities that didn't sleep. There were always people on the streets walking, especially in the warmer months. It was like we were trying to make up for all the time we had to spend indoors. Even more so now considering it was coming to the end. The sumac trees started to change earlier this year, signaling the coming of fall and colder weather. Reed finally pulled up behind my car, which was still parked along Broadway. The cop from earlier was still stationed at the end of the alley. It would be up to us to finish and clear the scene if the crime lab hadn't cleared it. "It wouldn't hurt to take a look around while we're here." I glanced over at Reed. He was gripping the top of the steering wheel. It looked like he might be stressed based on how hard he was gripping the wheel.

"You go ahead. I have that other case to get to. I'll meet you for training at around four. I have to fill you in on the guy you're going after." He was all business.

"Were you like this before?" I asked. "Or is it because you have me now?"

"What are you talking about?" he asked, his eyes flicking over to me in annoyance.

"I mean with your cases at the station. Were you always so lax when it came to them or are you more absent now that I can cover for you?" I turned in my seat to look at him. I'd been wondering about that since he'd been pushing more and more off on me since I changed shifts.

"No, I glamored others into saying I was there and doing the work. You are convenient, but I've been doing this for years." He pressed his mouth into a hard line. I wondered what it was that bothered him.

"Hmm, alright, I'll see you at four. I may be a little late considering I'm investigating this case alone." I moved for the door. He reached over me and grabbed the handle to close it so fast I hadn't noticed right away.

"Do you have something you want to say to me?" He growled.

"Ah, yeah, I want a new partner. It'd be nice to actually have a partner at the station. It's bullshit that you made me switch shifts, and now I don't even have anyone backing me up. I'm not here to do your job for you." I spat.

"I made you strong. You should be thanking me. You don't need back-up." His eyes lowered. "You cannot ask for another partner, and I can't neglect my duties with the Ravens. You're going to have to get over your petty annoyance. You will do what you're told. You're still my progeny." He shook slightly as he spoke. Damn, he was pissed. There was something pleasing about that.

"So, should I start calling you master then?" I curled my lip.

"If it suits you, yes." He smirked.

"Go to hell, maybe I'll see you at four." I jumped out of the car before he could stop me. He peeled away from the curb, and I laughed. It served him right. He didn't get to tell me what to do and I was sick of doing his job for him.

CHAPTER 3

Kyle's smile was bright as I made my way to him. "Hey, having issues with the new partner?" he asked.

"Yeah, you know, it'd be nice if he were a gentleman." I rolled my eyes. "Too much to ask for, I guess." I stopped next to him. "I can see you're nothing like that. Did you keep an eye on my car for me?" I fluttered my lashes. Maybe Reed was right and I did have something going for me.

"Yeah, I made sure no one touched it."

I rested my hand on his arm. "Thank you so much. I could use a gentleman like you as a partner." I smiled. "Did the crime lab say when they would release the scene?" I asked.

"Yeah, they had some things to finish up. I'm here until they do or day-shift relieves me. You going to take another look around?"

"Yeah, I have to meet Laura for the autopsy, but I thought I'd take another look while I was here. Have you heard anything else?" I asked. I glanced down the alley. One of the guys had an MCSU jacket on and was taking pictures of something near the dumpster. I figured I would go talk to him next.

"Not really, it looks like a robbery gone bad. But I wasn't really listening to what the crime lab guys were saying." He shrugged. "I'm on grunt duty after all. It'll be a bit before I can make detective."

"Hey, maybe I can help you with that. When you get into the station, find me. I can give you something to do to get your name on the case." I smiled.

His face lit up. "Really? That'd be great. Thanks, Matthews."

"Anytime, Kyle. You can call me, Hope." I winked and headed toward what was left of the scene. I stopped next to the guy taking pictures. "You find anything noteworthy?" I asked.

"Ah, maybe, I'm thinking it's strange that there wasn't any blood at the crime scene. We don't know the cause of death yet, but based on the evidence it doesn't read like a typical robbery." He stood, clutching the lens of the camera.

"I didn't even think about that. There wasn't a wound or anything?" I bit my lip. I couldn't help but think about my previous case. It was staged to look like a robbery, but again there wasn't any blood, no outward wounds. It made me wonder what Laura would find at the post.

"No, I thought maybe it would be a shooting, but there weren't any wounds, no casings, nothing. If it were a robbery, you'd think they would have a gun or a knife or something. There wasn't any indication of a weapon at all." The guys brows furrowed.

"I guess I'll go chat with Laura to determine the cause of death. Maybe she's got some insight from the body." I ran my finger over my bottom lip. "When do you think you'll release the scene?" I asked. He was the last crime scene tech left.

"I just wanted to make sure we got everything. It's a weird scene, so I didn't want to miss anything." He glanced down to where the body had been.

"So, you're very thorough." My eyebrows rose.

"In this job, it's a requirement." He said matter-of-factly.

"It is," I waved as I headed to my car. "See you at the station, Kyle." I jumped into my car and looked back at the scene. Kyle was watching me in the car. I couldn't help but smile and wave as I pulled away from the curb.

I parked in the lot and headed straight for my office. I had about an hour before I would be able to go see Laura. I could check the system for any similar cases. I had a gut feeling this case was going to be similar to the other two I'd worked earlier. My bet was the body was drained of blood. I was starting to wonder if the assignment I'd gotten from Cassandra and the body in the alley were connected.

Running the search through VICAP, I found three similar cases. All the bodies were found dumped in an alley. All three had been drained of blood. That meant, if I was right, this would be the fourth victim. How likely would it be that some sicko was doing this? I'd put money on it being a rogue vampire. I bet this was exactly what I was recruited for in the first place. Reed had hinted that there were people in the force who were Ravens. They were tasked to keep anything supernatural under wraps. I couldn't imagine how that was possible considering all the evidence that would be left behind. He explained that they had insiders all the way up to the capital. I didn't believe him at the time. The more I learned, the more I wondered if he wasn't telling the truth. There was no way everything would be completely covered up. Some humans had to suspect something. Yet, I never once thought about anything supernatural. Now that I'd been turned into a vampire, I had a whole new outlook. I was only one of many types of supernatural creatures that roamed the Earth. It was almost mind blowing to think about, so I often didn't. Yet, this case had me questioning how well things were actually covered up. How many cases had I worked where the perp disappeared or a case was unsolved. I had a stack of files on my desk as glaring proof. There was much more to the world, and I'd only gotten a taste of it. Being a Raven would change that for me. I was sure of it.

My phone rang. "Matthews," I answered. "Oh hey, Laura." I smiled. Laura was the only one who hated being called by her last name. I didn't know what the big deal was. Oglvie was a perfectly good last name. She confided that she'd wanted to change it back to her maiden name but hadn't yet. Apparently she'd been married for an entire six months. Her marriage and subsequent new last name was something she didn't talk about. I didn't understand why she hadn't just changed it back already.

"I'll be right down." I hung up the phone. Laura was ready to do the autopsy. I was surprised she called considering I would be down there in thirty minutes. She must be eager to start. I was half surprised she wasn't taking a lunch break between bodies. I hurried down the stairs to the coroner's office. It took up one whole floor of the building on the South side, with a loading dock for all the trucks. They didn't call us Murderapolis for nothing.

When I entered her "office," she was lounged back eating her sandwich, her feet resting on the desk. "Why did you call if you were eating lunch?" I asked.

"Because I wanted company. Besides, you should take a break once in a while." She beamed. Laura thought I worked too hard, but she had the same affliction.

I sat in one of the chairs, kicking my own feet up and crossing my ankles. "I believe I've connected this case to three others." I sighed.

She narrowed her eyes. "How could you have connected them? I don't even have the cause of death." She took a bite of her sandwich.

"Just a hunch I have." I rested my hands on my stomach.

"I don't do hunches." She rolled her eyes at me. "I do facts, evidence, what the body tells me. They all have a story to tell, you know." She popped the last bit of her sandwich in her mouth, followed by taking a long drink from the pink straw floating in her orange soda can. To say that Laura was peculiar was a bit of an understatement.

"Well, then, hop to it. I could use some evidence to go with my hunch." I snapped my fingers at her.

She scowled at me. "Did I mention I'm on my lunch hour? I thought we could discuss the situation with you and Reed. He doesn't seem like a very good partner from where I'm standing. He barely even made his appearance known at the crime scene today. And that's the third crime scene where you've shown up alone." She dropped her legs from the desk and sat forward, her elbows on her knees. I knew she was going to get into her serious voice. "You need to transfer back to Carson. At least he was a good partner. Good for ya, too." She pressed her lips together and sat back. "I know he misses working with you. It wasn't right the way you switched without so much as an explanation. You owe him that much." Her eyes were steady on me.

She was right. Laura was always right, even when she was diving into more personal matters. She had a way of seeing beyond the obvious, but she'd never admit it without some sort of proof. "Laura, you know that's something I don't want to get into. Can we focus on the body and our current case?" I couldn't talk to her about why I couldn't exactly switch back. Although, I had been thinking the exact same thing lately. Reed didn't need me to cover for him. He'd been doing a fine job without me for this long. He could certainly go back to whatever he'd done before he changed me.

She stared at me so long I shifted under the weight of her gaze. "Fine, have it your way. But I will have you know, that Carson has been talking about it. If it's something you don't want getting out, you better have a little chat with him."

I nodded. "I will keep that in mind." I walked over and stopped in front of the man waiting on her table. A white sheet covered him, and I pulled it back down to his waist. "So, cause of death?" I knew that the minute Laura started doing her autopsy, she would become consumed. It was almost endearing how serious she took her work.

"Jeez, hold your horses, would ya? I just finished my sandwich." I heard the distinct slurp of her emptying the rest of her orange soda.

"I would like more than anything to get back to work. I have a case to solve. And since you so cordially pointed out, I can't go any further without knowing what happened to him." I pointed at the man's face. He was distinctly pale. The kind of pale you would be if you were drained of blood. But I needed Laura to confirm my suspicions before I continued. She knew that as well as I did. So, why was she stalling? "If I didn't know any better, I'd think you were stalling. Normally, you don't call me until you're nearly finished. Why did you call me so soon?" I narrowed my eyes at her.

"Because, I thought someone should tell you about Carson. No one else around here was going to do it. But he's suspicious. He has every right to be. If I didn't know you so well, I'd think you were hiding something big. But that's none of my business of course." She waved her hand dismissively before finally making her way over to the body. She slapped on her gloves and began examining the marks on his wrists. "He was bound with some kind of plastic." She grabbed a tweezers and pulled something out of the wound. She put it in one of the clear dishes on her table. She put it under the microscope. "It looks like plastic with ridges. If you find where he was bound, I can connect the fibers." She moved back to the body, continuing her examination. I was surprised that there weren't more marks beyond those on his wrists. If he were held, there should be more marks.

"There weren't any marks beyond those left by the zip-ties? Is there anything to show how he might have died?" I took a step closer to the body.

"I've only just begun." Her irritated tone made me smirk. I always got ahead of her. I wasn't great with having patience. Her focus returned to the body. I knew not to interrupt.

I waited for her to finish examining for other injuries, knowing all her attention would be on the man before her. She was not one to be distracted easily from something she admired so much. She pulled out the scalpel and got ready to make the incision. When the blood congealed from her cuts, I swallowed hard. Maybe I should have fed before coming down here. I was stronger than most when it came to my hunger, but I hadn't tested being around blood.

"Can I come back after you finish the bloody parts?" I didn't think about how difficult it was going to be. The smell of the blood from the cut overwhelmed me. I could hear the steady beat of Laura's heart as it pushed blood through her veins. I licked my lips involuntarily, focusing entirely on the artery in Laura's neck. My bloodlust wasn't strong, but it was growing uncomfortable. I worried I would do something regretful as the sound of her heart grew louder in my head.

She narrowed her eyes at me. "Really? Usually you want details as I work. You said that the details can lead to your next suspect." She pursed her lips as she studied me.

"Yeah, I'm just not feeling so well. Watching you work on the body may be a little much." I turned away and swallowed. I needed to breathe out of my mouth. I hadn't realized how much of my day-job would change as a result of being a vampire. "Can you call me with the results?"

"Yeah, sure."

I nodded and headed out of the room. I needed to pull it together.

I hit the elevator button and waited. Homicide was on the third floor, but I was heading for the parking garage. I needed to hit the streets, find out what people in the neighborhood might know about the homicide. I knew the other officers would have taken witness statements, but I wanted to hear it for myself. I wasn't good at sitting back and waiting. It would be hours until I heard back from Laura. The others would be running the evidence and entering it into the database. I probably wouldn't know much until the morning. I had a meeting in the morning, so I would have to prioritize. It's good I didn't really need much sleep.

I drove back to the scene. The officers who were there earlier had left. It looked like the scene had been released. I parked in a spot half a block down from the alleyway. I was in my car, hoping no one would peg me as a cop instantly. I certainly wasn't wearing a police issued uniform. My heels would certainly throw them off. I glanced in the doorways of the nearest shops. I was hoping one of the homeless men would have returned to their spots after the police left. It looked like I was in luck. I saw a huddle of newspaper over a body in the third door down from where I'd parked. I could see scuffed brown shoes sticking out beneath the paper and black plastic. I stopped at his feet.

"Are you okay under there?" I asked.

"Go away, this is my spot. I ain't a movin'," he pulled one piece of newspaper further up his body. The plastic rustled with the movement. The nights were still relatively warm. For anyone who lived in Minnesota year round, they were downright balmy.

"I'm not here to take your spot. I wanted to know if you saw anything earlier tonight?" I kept my voice calm. This man would probably know more than anyone else who lived around here.

"I ain't seen nothin'. Now go away." He moved again under his makeshift bed.

"Did you see something, for say, twenty bucks?" I pulled out a crisp bill from my pocket. I kept cash in my pocket for these such occasions. A twenty would buy this guy a hot meal or a fresh bottle. It wasn't my business what he spent it on.

His head popped out from under the paper. His eyes scanned down my body. "You ain't look like any cop I ever seen. What you think I done seen?" His eyes fixated on my mouth.

"I was hoping you could give me any information about the man they found in the alley tonight. Did you see anyone around eight tonight, maybe a little before?" I asked. I fluttered my lashes and gave him my best damsel look. Men really liked to help women and I could tell by the increase in his heart rate that I was having an effect on him. I knew I could charm him for information, but I could spare the twenty, and he would tell me either way.

He stumbled as he stood. He grabbed up his hat and floundered as he slid it on his head. He could have been considered a handsome man at some point. His hair was thinning in the middle making what was left look like a halo around his head. Wrinkles marred his brown skin and formed jowls around his mouth.

He looked perpetually angry. The toll life had taken was etched on this man's face. The color of the sky shined through this man's eyes. "I seen a man stroll out of the alley about that time. He had dark hair and a nice suit. You don't see too many people wearin' suits like that around here." He shook his head. "He didn't look real suspicious though. Man walked cool as a cucumber, know what I mean."

I smiled. "I do." I would bet just about anything he was talking about Reed. I couldn't know for sure. Why would Reed bring me to Cassandra to investigate him. He would have to know I would figure out it was him. He couldn't be that stupid. There had to be a reason. I needed to bide my time until I figured out what motive was behind his actions.

"Is there anything else you can remember? Anything at all. Did you see what kind of car he got into?" I pushed. Seeing a dark-haired man in a suit wasn't all that definitive. It certainly wouldn't hold up in any court unless he could ID the man. I wasn't about to put Reed in a line-up.

The man scratched the scruff growing on his jaw. "Well, I didn't notice what kind a car he done got in, but I bet it was a flashy one. I was headin' down the next block by then. I had an important meetin' to get to a little ways down Broadway. Mrs. Lolita give me a burger at the end of her shift. She is such a nice woman. I walk her home every day after her shift." He smiled and there was a wistful look in his eye. If I didn't know better, I'd think he had a thing for her.

"Well, if you think of anything or know anyone who does can you give me a call?" I handed him my card with a twenty.

He chuckled. "What you expectin' I call you with?"

"You're a clever man, I think you can figure something out." I smiled and turned away from him and back to my car. I wanted to do more here, but I wasn't sure I was going to get much. My phone rang the minute I shut the door. "Matthews," I answered.

CHAPTER 4

"Hey, Laura, got anything good?" I asked.

"I've identified the body." She said matter-of-factly.

"Great, who is he?" I asked.

"Patrick O'Donnell, he's from Boston. No idea what he's doing here."

"Okay, I'm on my way in." I pulled away from the scene. At least I had a description. Not like I was going to tell anyone else on the team. As a vampire, I couldn't speak against my sire. It was the one law you couldn't break. Even something as minimal as slander could earn you a swift death. It didn't sound like the council took time to investigate those crimes like I did with my cases. The sire would only need a witness. Telling anyone in homicide the guy fleeing the scene could be my partner would be a death sentence. Although I wasn't thrilled about being a vampire, I wasn't wishing for my death just yet.

I strode through the department lobby. I knew the other homicide detectives would be upstairs. Miller and Elliot were standing in front of the glass board. "Hey fellas, any news?" I stopped in front of the board. All the photos were up from their crime scene. Next to it was a second board, with the photos from my scene.

"We picked these up from CSU and hung them up for you. We've been going back and forth about how they are so similar." He sat back at his desk. They were both newer detectives so they shared the main office space. There were eight desks in this room, most of them were for day shift. Miller, Elliot, and Reed had three of them in here. I was the only one lucky enough to have my own office. Although, I missed working in the pit on days. We'd be cracking jokes as Carson threw a ball at the wall. It was his way of thinking. I'd missed that working on nights.

I sat on the top of Reed's desk, my foot on his chair and stared at the photos. "Did your guy have his wallet on him?" I asked.

"No, nothing in his pockets. He looked like a body-dump, same as your guy." He pointed to the way the guy was positioned. "It almost looks like they dragged him by his feet out of the van. The second scene had the white marking on the dumpster. There was nothing at the first scene." He sat back in his chair, spinning in a small arch, his elbows resting on the arms of the desk-chair.

"Okay, so, hypothetically, if we are looking at the same killer, why would he dump the bodies in two different parts of town?" I turned to look at their board. "What time was your guy found?"

"Six-thirty, just after sunset." He pointed to the file. Everything we found is documented in there. I picked up the file and combed through the copy of their notes. After seeing that they hadn't found much, I said. "We have to find the crime scene. Has Laura identified your guy?"

"No, his prints weren't in the system. She's working on dental records now."

"Okay, the second victim's name is Patrick O'Donnell. I'm going to dig into his life. Good luck on the ID, and I'll let you know if I find anything that can connect to your case." I hopped off the desk and strode into my office. I needed to begin the report with my own notes so I could add it to the file. I also had to check the database for my victims address. If he was dumped there, his home could be the crime scene. I also needed to speak to his family members and see who'd seen him last.

Once I had an address, I called to get a warrant to search his house. It was good Judge Marley loved me. He would sign a search warrant for me no matter the time. I called CSU to meet me at the house. I wasn't sure what I would find. The victim lived alone. I walked out to the main office-pen. "Hey,.either of you want to join me at the victim's house?"

"Where's your partner?" Elliott asked. He hadn't said much tonight, but there was a tone I wasn't sure I liked behind his words.

"I figured I'd call him on the way. If you guys are too busy, I understand. I don't really need anyone keeping me company on the drive." I flipped my hair over my shoulder.

They both looked at each other. "We should probably stick around here in case we get a break on our guy. We need the ID so we can get moving." Okay, sometimes Miller speaking for them was endearing, sometimes it was annoying. Elliott was the better looking of the two with his sandy-blonde hair that fell in a ruffled mess around his head. I found it cute even though it looked messy.

I took a step closer to Elliot. "Are you sure you don't want to keep me company?"

He paled and looked at Miller. He cleared his throat. "No, like he said. We have our own case." Wow, it looked like Elliot did have a back-bone.

I waved my hand as I made my way to the door. "Okay, your loss." I didn't stop to see what they thought. I would meet the CSU guys there. Maybe the hot one from the crime scene would be there. I really wanted a drink before I continued and I liked getting my fix from strong men. It would have been easy to take a little drink from either of them once I got them in my car. Maybe I would be able to catch one while I worked at the scene. Damn that stupid autopsy for making me so thirsty for blood. I wasn't so obsessed that I was going to run out and drink someone dry. It was more of an uncomfortable tickle in my throat that reminded me I wanted blood.

I made it over to Patrick's apartment quickly. He lived in the top floor of a duplex on Bryant. I wasn't sure what he would be doing on the North end, but so far none of this case made sense. A black Explorer pulled up behind me. It was probably the crime scene tech. I hopped out of my car and turned. The dark-haired tech from earlier was pulling his kit out of the backseat. He smiled when he saw me waiting by my car.

"Hey, fancy meeting you here," he said.

"Are you the tech working my case?" I asked. I hadn't recognized him, but I honestly hadn't paid too much attention to night shift.

"Yeah, I got both cases tonight. You were the first to need me." He tapped his hand against the case. "So, where to?" he asked.

"Well, aren't I lucky." I held out my hand. "I'm Hope Matthews, and you are?" I felt bad for not having asked his name earlier.

"Shaun McCarthy, I actually started here a few weeks ago, so I don't know too many people in town." He smiled. "Shall we?" He held his arm out toward the sidewalk. It wasn't smart that we were both standing on the street next to our cars.

"Oh yeah, Patrick lived on the third floor of the duplex. We didn't find keys on him so I'm hoping one of the other tenants has a key." I strolled forward toward the house. It was one of those older homes that had been split into three living areas. It had a massive pitched roof, with elongated windows. I should have looked up who owned this property, but I figured I'd let myself in either way. I wasn't expecting to have an audience. "So, did you just move here?"

"Yeah, I lived out East. I needed a change." He followed behind me to the door. "Are you going to just knock?" he asked.

"Yeah, he may have a girlfriend staying here or something." I rapped my hand on the door three times. "Minneapolis police, open up." I shouted loud enough so anyone in the house would be able to hear me.

A woman with cropped red hair threw the door open. "What?" her raspy voice called out.

I blinked. "Is this the home of Patrick O'Donnell?" I hadn't actually expected anyone to be here.

"What's that shitebag done now?" She popped her gum and continued openly chewing it in her mouth. I wanted to shake my head in disgust, but I also had to be a professional.

"How do you know Patrick?" I didn't want to tell some random person he was dead. I wanted to know who she was and what she was doing here.

"Patrick and I have a little thing going. You know the on again off again types. Never want to settle down. If I knew what was good for me, I'd leave the cheap bastard. Can't even come home for a dinner he asked me to make." She rambled on as the gum continued to smack around in her mouth.

"What is your name, Miss?" I asked.

"I'm Jenna." She stopped snapping her gum and gave me a once over. "You lookin' to arrest Pat?" she asked, her lips pursing like I had the best gossip in town.

"No, ma'am, I'm sorry to inform you that Patrick is dead. We found his body this evening." I dropped my head.

"What?" her eyes widened before she let out a ridiculously loud wail. She clutched at her chest and wailed again. "Oh, my sweet Patrick." *And best actress of the year award goes to...*

"I'm sorry, is there someone I can call?" I tried to mask my humor at her sudden change of heart. "Do you live here with Patrick?" I needed her out of our way to search, but I was trying really hard not to be a heartless bitch in the process. *I love my job.*

She sniffled and walked into the room. I was amazed at how fast she'd recovered. "Please, come in." She stopped at the table. It was set for two, but one of the plates had been smashed against the counter. It looked like she had been pretty pissed off that he hadn't shown up.

"When was the last time you spoke with Patrick?" I asked.

She plopped down in the chair with the empty plate. "He texted me at lunch. He said he had a surprise for me. I offered to make dinner at his place." She sniffled. Shaun handed her a tissue from a box on the counter. "Thank you," she smiled. "He was supposed to be home by seven. I just thought he was running late. After waiting here an hour, I got a tad upset." Her voice was low as her eyes flicked to the plate of food that was now scattered across the floor.

"Do you know anyone who would want to hurt Patrick? Anything he might have been involved in that we should know about? Any detail helps." I pressed my lips into a thin line. I was waiting for her to tell me Patrick was a saint. It was always funny how people changed their story after they found out their loved one was dead.

"He was involved with a guy named Tommy. I didn't know his last name. Pat wouldn't tell me much about it, but they often met at night. No respectable meeting happens after dark, ya know." She fluttered her lashes up at Shaun. "You are such a nice man. Are you single?"

Shaun coughed. "Excuse me?" the shock in his voice was evident.

I smiled as I turned to look at him. "You heard the lady. Are you single?" I pressed my lips together to keep from laughing.

"I'm not sure how that's relevant to the case." He glared at me. My smile grew wider. I knew I was evil. No respectable man should be dating this woman. She still popped her gum.

"Okay, Jenna?" I looked down to my notebook. "I didn't get a last name. Can I also get a number where you can be reached?" I asked. "In case we have any questions later."

"Oh yes," she walked over to a drawer and pulled out a card. She scribbled something on it and handed it over to Shaun. "You can call me anytime." She fluttered her lashes, and I about choked with laughter.

"Great, we're going to need to search the property. Is there anywhere we can bring you?" It was the nicest way I could think of to ask her to get out.

"Oh no, my car's downstairs." She smiled up at Shaun.

"Great, we'll be in contact if we have any more questions." I smiled as I held the door open for her. Her eyes widened at me, but quickly recovered. She grabbed her purse and phone off the counter and headed out of the door. At least she took the hint. She couldn't exactly stick around when we had a search to do. After I shut the door, I smirked at Shaun. "Looks like you've got a hot date waiting for you. Don't leave a lady waiting."

He held the card out to me. "Very funny, here's her number. You're the one who will have to do all the important questioning." He wiggled his brows and held out the card.

"Oh yes, I really hope I don't have any more questions." I licked my lips. I had him alone. It wouldn't hurt to take a little snack before we got started.

"Alright, I guess I'll get started. Do you think it happened here?" I glanced around the apartment, but it didn't look like a crime scene. The place was pretty clean considering it was a bachelor pad.

"I doubt it. It's way too clean in here to be a crime scene. Unless Jenna cleaned up after she got done." Shaun knelt next to the food. "It's still warm. I doubt she'd have time to clean up while making dinner."

"I thought she said she was expecting him at seven. How would the food still be warm? Unless she was lying about the time. It's been hours." I opened the oven to feel for heat. It was cold.

"Maybe she kept warming it up?" He shrugged. "Although, that is odd."

"I'm going to check out the bedroom." The layout was easy enough. The kitchen was small with an area in the center where the table was. Straight ahead was the living room. Off the living room were two doors. My bet was the one on the left was the bedroom and the one closest to me was the bathroom. It was a tiny apartment, but since he was living alone, it didn't seem so bad. I began checking his drawers. Everyone hid their secrets in the bedroom so I was hoping to find something that could tell me why someone would want good ol' Patrick dead. Although, I thought I had a pretty good idea already.

I opened the top drawer and scoffed. His boxer briefs and socks were neatly organized. There wasn't anything else. I began opening other drawers, but each were meticulously organized. *Who was this guy?* He didn't keep much beyond what he needed. I searched his closet. I was disappointed that I didn't even find a sex toy or anything. This was the most boring bedroom. This guy had to be hiding something, but where?

"Any luck?" I asked as I entered the living room. He turned off all the lights and was using a black light to search the furniture of any fluids. The couch was lit up like a damn Christmas tree. I shuddered. "So, good ol' Patrick had a thing for the couch."

"Yeah, I'll collect samples. There are also some receipts in the kitchen you may want to take a look at. They might give some insight into the daily life of Patrick." He rummaged in his kit. "This guy is pretty organized. I'm surprised those receipts were still there. Everything in here seems to have its place. There also doesn't seem to be a lot of personal stuff here. Have you noticed the lack of pictures?" he asked.

I glanced up at the walls. Shaun was right, there wasn't a single picture on the beige walls. I understood not wanting to hang things if it was a rental, but there wasn't a picture anywhere. I walked back into the bedroom. There was a simple lamp on the nightstand. There were cufflinks and a watch on a pad on top of the dresser. It was incredibly plain. It was lacking a human touch. It felt almost institutional in its plainness.

I walked into the bathroom. There were a few towels under the sink along with some cleaners. I eyed the large bottle of bleach suspiciously. Why would this guy need a gallon of bleach? He couldn't exactly do laundry here. Behind the blue shower curtain was just soap and a bottle of shampoo, Dove 2 in one shampoo and conditioner for men. Ugh, people actually used the two in one. I guess if you didn't have much hair, it worked. I shuddered. I couldn't imagine.

"I'm starting to think, he either hasn't lived here long, or he's using this as a second home. I can't find anything personal." I watched as Shaun was bent looking under the sofa.

"I have to agree. The apartment is rather simple with the exception of the couch." Shaun stood. "I took the samples. I'm not sure what else we'll find here."

"Do you find this strange?" I asked.

"His apartment?" he asked.

"Yeah, I didn't find anything personal. There wasn't anything beyond clothes and even those were limited. Is this a guy thing?" Reed's place was super clean but he paid people to clean it. I couldn't imagine this being anyone's bachelor pad.

"I certainly have more personal items in my place." He closed the kit and set it on the kitchen table. "What did you think of the girlfriend?"

"She's one crayon short of a whole box." I glanced down at the food. "I don't think she'd kill him though. It's one thing to throw a plate because he didn't show. It's another to escalate that to murder."

"So, you wouldn't murder someone for standing you up?" His eyebrow rose.

"I don't know. It's never happened to me."

"Seriously? You've never been stood up? Not even once?" The shock in his voice kind of hurt my ego.

"No, not a single time. I take it you have been." I smiled coyly.

"Ah, yeah, I think it's a dating rite of passage." He looked at the floor.

"Oh, well, I guess I missed that one." I stopped at the door. I went back to grab the receipts Shaun mentioned. It might give me an idea into the victim's timeline. "Will you let me know what you find out from the evidence at the scene and here?"

"You'll be the first call I make." He winked at me. That reminded me. I turned around and stopped in front of him. I locked onto his dark eyes. I felt like I could swim in their depths.

"What are you doing?" he asked.

"Shh, I just want to try something." I stared waiting for the familiar click when I knew I could manipulate his mind. It never took this long.

"Are you trying to charm me?" he asked.

My mouth dropped, and I stepped back. "What? No, I wouldn't do that." I shook my head. How in the hell did he know about charming people?

"I'm a vampire. You can't charm me." He smiled, and I watched as his fangs descended. "It's one of the reason's I transferred here. I'm a Raven but things weren't working out in Boston, so I came here." He retracted his fangs.

"What? Why didn't you say anything?" I asked.

"I figured you could tell. You must be newly made. Most vampires can easily identify each other." His knowing smile bothered me. "I take it you're hungry or do you make it a habit to drink from your co-workers?"

I huffed. "I went to the autopsy and it made me want a snack. That's all. I don't make it a habit to drink from co-workers." I flipped my hair over my shoulder. I hated what he could be insinuating.

"Ah, yeah, that part is hard to get used to. One tip, try not to breath out of your nose when you're around blood. We don't have to breathe at all, so just make it looks like your breathing, by moving your shoulders. I've found that helps." He shrugged.

I narrowed my eyes. "Thanks." I shouldn't be so suspicious of someone helping me. After Reed turned me into a vampire, it was hard not to be a little on edge anytime anyone offered their assistance.

He handed me a card. "You can call me anytime."

I looked down, it was his work card. "Why are you helping me? I would have charmed you if I could have?" I wasn't any less suspicious.

"I have a feeling you might need friends in our world." He pressed his lips together into a smile that looked more pitying then genuine.

I squared my shoulders. "Thanks, but I think I can handle myself." I strode out the apartment door. I certainly didn't need anyone pitying me. I've been fine on my own for my entire life. That wasn't going to change because I was a vampire.

"I'll call you when I've processed everything." He called after me. I didn't stop. I got in my car. It was time to work on a timeline and figure out who might want this guy dead. So far I'd gotten nothing but dead ends, but the night was young. I was also gearing up for my morning with Reed. I was ready to be a Raven. I also wanted to ask where he'd been before he showed up to the office. There was a gap in his timeline. I wanted to know if he had enough time to drain my victim and get to the office. I knew I couldn't outright accuse him of the murder, but I could ask him where he'd been.

CHAPTER 5

I hated how many holes were in my timeline. I couldn't exactly go question anyone at his job in the middle of the night. I would need to get there before close tomorrow. I couldn't stare at this stupid board anymore. Elliot and Miller went home a few hours ago. I hated how I hadn't learned much tonight. Laura hadn't even called me back about the autopsy which wasn't like her. Well, to be fair, I usually stay for the entire autopsy. I planned on using Shaun's tips the next time I had to be around a body. Being around bodies was a big part of my job. Not being able to stomach it, wasn't an option.

My phone buzzed. It was almost four. I needed to get back to find out who I was going after for the Raven's. I couldn't wait to have the opportunity to kick Reed's ass. He'd been leaving me to do everything at the station. He would expect me to fill him in and I wanted to tell him to shove it. He didn't listen anyway. Today, I wanted to ask him where he was when the victim died. My witness had seen a dark-haired guy in a flashy car.

Not that his information narrowed it down at all. His description could fit half the damn city. It was enough to make me suspicious of Reed. It added to the suspicion I already had. It was too convenient that he turned me at the crime scene of another body who'd been drained of blood. He conveniently dismissed the topic anytime I brought it up. But it was certainly the reason I was standing here, as a vampire.

"Well, it's about time. You're late." Reed was leaning against the kitchen counter, an empty glass next to him. He'd already changed into a pair of jersey shorts and tank. It looked like he'd been waiting for a while.

"It's only five after four. I'm not that late. Besides, you left me to investigate a case by myself, again." I strode past him to go change.

"Where do you think you're going?" He grabbed my arm before I even made it to the hallway. I rolled my eyes and glanced at his grip on my arm. His hold tightened.

"I'm going to change so we can train." I waited for him to let go of my arm. He didn't.

"Nope, you are training in what you are wearing since you're already late. You need to learn about discipline and the importance of being prompt. When one of your colleagues needs you, there is no room for tardiness. There are many things you need to learn before you can be a Raven. Don't make me regret recommending you early." He dropped my arm and stormed toward the stairs that led to the basement training room.

Shit, this is how he reacted after only being five minutes late? I slipped off my heels and reluctantly followed him down the stairs. At least I wasn't in a skirt. I couldn't imagine trying to fight him in a tight pencil skirt. Today, I had worn a stylist suit. I slipped off the black pinstripe jacket and folded it neatly in half and carefully laid it over the back of a chair. There was no way I was going to mess it up. That jacket was dry-clean only. I should slip my pants off too. It'd serve Reed right to have to fight me in only my bra and panties. It would certainly serve as a distraction in my favor. After all, I had to stare at his perfectly toned biceps. Despite how much I hated Reed, my libido didn't always agree with me.

Reed stood, his right leg slightly in front, in his fighting stance. "Aren't you going to tell me about the job for Cassandra?" I folded my arms over my chest.

"Are you saying you can't fight and talk?" His eyebrow rose. I hated all the ways he liked to challenge me. Apparently today was about taking in information while fighting. Just another one of Reed's lessons.

"No, I'm not saying that." I strode forward, stretching my arms across my chest more out of habit than any real need. My muscles never got sore. Having super vampire strength helped.

"Good, because there will be a time when you have to battle while also taking in information quickly. I need you to be the best." He held his hands out in front of him. He was ready.

"Why is it that I need to be the best? You already seem to have Cassandra's favor. Why do you need me?" I dropped low, ready for him to inevitably strike. He was always the one to make the first move. I was stronger at playing defense rather than being the aggressor. It was probably because I still held onto my very human female instincts. It was hard to think of myself as the one making the first move on a target. It hadn't been my style. I had a feeling that was one of the many things Reed was trying to drill out of me.

"Because you are my progeny. You will not be second best. Now how would you attack?" he asked.

I blinked. He usually went for the blow, and I deflected. I studied his stance, noticing a slight weakness as his steps were slow and deliberate. I wondered if he'd injured his left ankle recently. I didn't think vampires could sustain injuries. "I would go for a weak point." I lunged, and dropped down, sweeping his legs out from under him, going from the left to right to take advantage of the weakness I'd noticed. He landed hard on his back, but instantaneously flipped back up.

"Good, always take your opponent by surprise, but you should have immediately continued attacking once you had me down. You gave me a chance to regain my stance. Use the element of surprise in your favor. Do not stop until you've debilitated your opponent." He circled me again.

"Okay, Mr. Miyagi, I didn't realize you actually wanted to get your ass kicked today." I circled, looking for another weakness. I'd been training with Reed for months. He didn't have many weaknesses. I dropped again and went to sweep my leg around, but this time he jumped, pushing me back as he did. I wasn't expecting it and landed on my back. He landed a punch next to my head. He straddled me, holding my wrists to the side of my head. I bucked and kicked him, but couldn't get far enough to do any damage.

"You are distracted. I need you focused. Tell me about the case."

"No, you tell me first." I glared at him. I'd stopped struggling because I knew it was pointless. I was surprised he hadn't gotten in a few blows while he had me down. I knew he wanted to take something out on me. It was in his behavior the moment I walked through the door. I wondered what he was so frustrated about. I'd learned in our time together when it was a normal training session and when he was taking something out on me. Today it was the latter. "Who am I targeting?"

He hopped back and held his hand out to help me up. I took it and let him help me, even though I didn't actually need his help.

"How about I give you the file on the vampire you're targeting, you give me the one on our case at the station." He smirked.

"You know I didn't take the file home." I shook my head.

"That would be a first." He narrowed his eyes on me.

Damn, he knew me too well already. "Fine, it's in my bag upstairs. Does that mean we're done training for the day?" I asked.

"No, it means we both have some reading to do. I will not fight you again until you are one hundred percent present and ready to fight. It's pointless when you're distracted." He threw a towel at me and headed up the stairs.

"Seriously, normally you'd be making it a lesson about how I had to fight during the distractions or some such nonsense." I narrowed my eyes as he continued to walk away from me. Something must really be bothering him to not even comment.

I trudged up the stairs. I grabbed the file out of my bag and held it out. He'd grabbed his own file. "You can't leave the house with this. Once you know everything in here, you'll need to return it. We're not allowed to keep files, but since you're new, I brought this one for you. It's everything we have on your guy." He pressed his lips together, shaking his hand in annoyance. I took the file from him, and he took mine.

I turned and headed down the hallway to my room. "Where are you going?" he asked.

"To my room. I don't want to read with you hovering. I like to do my work alone." I continued until my door clicked shut behind me. I seriously didn't want to be around Reed right now. He seemed frustrated, and I knew how easily he took that shit out on me. Maybe he just needed to get laid. It's not like he didn't have the opportunity.

He seemed pretty cozy with Cassandra today. I wasn't sure why that bothered me. The way he looked at her caused a sharp jab in my chest. Maybe it was our sire bond or something. It certainly couldn't be jealousy. I hated Reed. Biting my lip, I thought back to the night I'd been turned. He'd made me come harder than I ever had. My whole body shook.

I couldn't help but think about what more he could do. It was a nagging thought in the back of my mind. Too bad he ruined that by kidnapping me in the first place. He hadn't shown himself to be a gentleman. I wouldn't settle for anyone who didn't treat me like the queen I was. Although, a good fuck wasn't out of the question. He'd taunted me since that night. Damn, maybe I was the one who needed to get laid.

A few minutes later my door opened. With file in hand, Reed leaned against the door jamb. "What if I have questions?" he asked in his gravelly voice.

I rolled my eyes. "Do you?"

"I don't know, but I think we should go over these together. We are partners after all." He sat next to me on the bed, moving one of my pillows up on the headboard. I couldn't believe the audacity he had to just make himself comfortable in my room.

"Oh, so now we're partners?" I turned and stared at him. I couldn't believe him.

"Well, yes, although I do have my Raven responsibilities. I will try and do better on investigating murders with you at the station," he said through gritted teeth.

I laughed. "It was very hard for you to say that, wasn't it?"

"No, I'm serious." I could tell he was working to make his voice sound less strained.

"Okay, I'm going to hold you to that." I pressed my lips together and studied the photo in front of me. "How about we talk through each of our cases. What do you know about this guy?"

"He owns club Medusa downtown. He's got a close circle, and we've been having trouble getting eyes on him. He's selective of who he even lets into his club." Reed explained. "I think that's why Cassandra is making this deal. We need someone to get close enough to him. We've struck out." He stared at the photo of the vampire outside his club.

"Is that why the photo is of him getting into his limo. No one can even get into the club."

"No vampires can get in. We haven't tried anyone who was female yet. None of the males we've sent have made it past the bouncer." He sighed.

"Got it." I flipped through the contents of the folder which included a home address, the address of the club and the name of his sire. That was it. "This seems kind of light. Is this really all you have on the guy? What crime is he being accused of committing?" I asked.

"We believe he's been using his club to lure in victims. It's why he keeps all vampires out who aren't in his immediate circle. We've had a few mortals and other supes go missing after attending the club. We have enough to suspect it's him or one of his men. We need you to get in the door and find out for us." He looked away from me. I suspected he didn't actually like the idea of me going after this guy.

"Supes?" I asked. I hadn't heard that term before.

"Supes is short for supernatural beings, like vampires." His tone turned playful.

"So, why don't you just say vampire?" I didn't understand why we would need more than one name.

"Because there are more super naturals than vampires." He shook his head. "I should have shared this with you already. Ravens are in charge of handling those who break the laws of our world. We're mostly vampires because of our strength and skill. But we're not the only monsters out there." He winked.

"Monsters? You're the only monster I've met." I was only half kidding. He'd taken my life away, and I wasn't going to forgive him for that. I was able to continue my job but it wasn't the same. He saw being a vampire as a gift. I saw it as a curse.

"Har, har, I suppose Laura already told you she's a Svanti." He shook his head. "Considering they're the secret keepers, you'd think she'd be able to keep one from her friend."

"What?" My mouth dropped as I looked over at Reed.

"Oh, I thought for sure she'd told you."

"No, she left that out of the autopsy." I bowed my head. "I didn't actually stick around very long." Biting my lip, I didn't want to admit my weakness to Reed.

"It took me a while before I could handle being around blood. You'll get there." His kindness surprised me, and I stared at him again. I wasn't sure what to make of him. One minute he was scolding me for being late, the next he was being kind, empathizing even.

"Shaun, the CSU tech gave me some tips." I stared at the photo. Vincent Moretti was my mark. I would need to figure out how to get in the club and get close to Vincent. I wondered how old he was.

"Shaun?" Reed's voice rose in question.

"Yeah, he's a Raven. He gave me some tips for dealing with it." I closed the file. There wasn't anything else I could glean from it. I needed to get on the inside to learn anything new.

"Did he now?" His tone changed. I stared across the room. I'd put up a bulletin board and a small white board next to my desk. It was an old habit of taking my cases home with me. I often spent long hours at the office, but I liked having a space to work once I was home. Reed's place was big enough that I could have a separate office, but I kept everything of mine here instead. I hadn't exactly been happy about living with him. Although, his house was nicer than mine. I wanted my own place. I continued to pay my bills and had only moved over a small fraction of my wardrobe. Reed wasn't aware I hadn't ever fully moved in.

"Yes, is that a problem?" I asked. I wasn't sure about his tone. Was he worried I would say something about him to Shaun? I couldn't imagine why else he would be worried.

"No, no problem. I'd just be careful who you make friends with in our world. You haven't been in it long, so you don't know how dark it can get." There was an authority to his words. Working as a detective and seeing some of the worst of humanity, I could only imagine how a dark it could be.

"So, Laura is a what again?" I asked. I hadn't been able to comprehend the fact that my friend was a supernatural being, and I didn't know about it.

"She's a Svanti, they are the ones who keep our secrets and histories. They pass knowledge through the blood to future generations. We like to think of them as the librarians so to speak, although somehow the knowledge is passed through their DNA. If anyone knew more, it would be Laura. Although, I'm not sure how much she'd divulge. They are the keepers of secrets after all."

"I'm going to have to ask her next time I see her." I pressed my lips together. "Anything else I should know?" I asked.

"Let's take it one day at a time, alright? What can you tell me about the case here?" He held up the file in his hands.

"Well, first where were you at between seven-thirty and eight tonight?" I turned, tucking one leg under me as I stared him down.

"You know where I was." He narrowed one eye. "Why, Hope, do you think I'm a suspect?" He chuckled. I waited. He wasn't with me at that time. After the silence stretched between us, he furrowed his brow. "I was at the house with you. Then we went to the station."

"No, I went to the station alone. I left at six." I crossed my arms.

"I left a few minutes after you did. I had to check in at the council. I was at the station shortly after. Do tell, why are you suspicious of me?"

I wasn't sure I wanted to tell him what had me suspicious. "The victim was drained of blood. He was one of several that have been drained over the last six months. If you remember, I was investigating one of those scenes when you decided to kidnap me and make me a vampire. You don't find that at all suspicious?"

I stared at his cobalt eyes. His dark hair fell slightly over his bronzed skin. His tongue slid slowly over his full bottom lip. I waited for the lashing I knew he was holding back. It was illegal to speak against your sire. I'd basically just accused him of murder. I wanted to know how he'd react. I'd been in hundreds of interrogation rooms. I was one of the best at reading people. I wanted to get a read on Reed.

He tipped his head to the side and stared at me for what felt like several long agonizing seconds. "I guess I could see how you might be suspicious. I had nothing to do with those bodies, but they may be connected to the guy you are charged with investigating. We have a feeling he's been draining the missing people and dumping them around the city." He was all business as he spoke. I wasn't sure what to think. He hadn't given me a reason not to believe him, but why the secrecy?

"Why didn't you mention that when you gave me the file?" I asked.

"I wasn't supposed to lead you in one way or another. You are supposed to investigate him as an unbiased party. Cassandra didn't want you corrupted. She fears you'll give yourself away if you know too much about this case." He shook the file. "So, now are you going to tell me what you know?"

"I can handle myself against a simple bar owner." I rolled my eyes. I hated how they thought so little of me. I was one of the best detectives in the city. I would argue I was the best, but I couldn't be certain because I hadn't worked with all of them.

"How many have you connected to this case?" he asked. His tone let me know he was becoming annoyed with my delay in answering his last question. It wouldn't hurt to fill him in. I certainly could use another set of eyes. I hadn't come up with much.

"I believe there are at least four. The guy I investigated when you turned me, a woman, and another man besides this guy. I thought the woman might be out of character for him, since before this they all were similar looking men. But her body had been drained of blood, so I'm keeping her with the others. All of them were drained, but there wasn't a drop of blood at the scene. Some at the scenes have described a man in a suit and dark sedan leaving prior to the incident.

But as you know, we found white paint that indicates the bodies were dumped out of a van. The only problem, it's the most popular color. The only thing that narrows it down is the height of it on the dumpster. Not much to go on. I'm waiting on a few reports from the autopsy and Shaun said he'd let me know as soon as anything came back." I set my file on my nightstand.

"So, you're thinking vampire based on them being drained of blood. Considering there wasn't anything spilled it is more than likely. Vampires typically lick the wounds to seal them. Did you find any puncture marks on any of the bodies?" he asked. He was flipping through the notes I'd typed up and added to the file about his apartment. There hadn't been much to find and Jenna wasn't helpful. She mentioned a Tommy, but tracking down someone based on their first name could be difficult. I figured I'd work on that tomorrow.

"There weren't any puncture wounds. Laura mentioned a few abrasions on his wrist like he'd been bound but that was it. I didn't stick around to hear the full autopsy report." I stared down at my hands clasped in my lap. I was rubbing my finger over my thumb nail. I hated to admit any weakness, especially to Reed. He had a tendency to use that information later.

"You should have her swab the neck. We might be able to match it to one of our investigations." He flipped another page. He crossed his ankles together as he read my notes. I hated the butterflies in my stomach. I knew he would find something I missed. I was the best, but it was hard to compete with a vampire who'd been alive for many years longer than I had.

"I didn't think they kept things like DNA. Wouldn't that cause problems with keeping our secret?" I asked. I couldn't imagine a DNA database for supernatural beings.

"We have a database. It's highly guarded." He flicked his eyes up to mine for the briefest of moments.

"You guys aren't worried about hackers?"

He looked at me again like he was appeasing a child. My eyes narrowed. "No, we have our own skilled team. Anyone who even tried would be hunted and killed."

"You guys don't mess around, do you?"

"No, Hope, you should think about that before joining. I know you are anxious to join the Ravens but we are a strict group. You should not be in such a hurry to sign your immortal life away." He closed the file in his lap. He must've decided he'd read enough.

"What? You seem so devoted to being a Raven. You've spoken highly of your position. What's changed?" I asked.

"I didn't become a Raven for years after I'd been turned. Once you are one, you are signing your life over to them. It is not like being a detective. You cannot go back once you have taken their oath. I want you to be certain this is what you want. I know you don't see what I've done as a gift, but someday you may change your mind. I don't want you to regret the decisions you've made. You are so young, you don't know enough to make an informed decision." He turned to look me in the eyes as he spoke. I could almost feel the weight of his words as he spoke.

"I signed my life away as soon as I became a detective. Hunting down criminals is what I'm good at." I paused. "You were the one who recommended me early. Why are you changing your mind now?"

"I just want you to fully know what you are getting into. This is not something that should be taken lightly." He shifted so he was sitting with his back to me.

"So, why did you recommend me to Cassandra?" I was confused. He'd pressured me to think about joining the Ravens. Now, he was saying something completely different. What changed?

"I recommended you because of how much you wanted it." He paused, the silence stretching between us like the dense fog of an April morning. "I did it for you." He got up and left, closing the door behind him.

What was that? I thought. *Why would he do it for me?* I couldn't comprehend Reed doing anything for me. I know he saw turning me as a gift, but I saw it as him stealing my life away from me. He took away so many things when he made that decision for me. It would never feel like a gift. He had to know that. He stole all the possibilities of my life. I couldn't ever forgive him for his actions. One action wasn't going to wipe away the other. You couldn't fix the paper once it was crumpled. You could try, but it would never be the same. I would never be the same.

CHAPTER 6

I strode through the door of the morgue. Laura was leaning back in her chair, a set of images on the computer screen in front of her. "You coming to bail on Saturday, already?" She shoved a salsa filled chip into her mouth. The crunch was loud to my sensitive ears.

"No, what did you find out from the body?" I asked.

"Oh yeah." She closed the images on her computer. She reached over and grabbed a file from the counter next to her desk. "Here's the report."

She filled another chip with salsa and jammed it into her mouth. I flipped open the file. Again, the victim died of exsanguination. He had bruises around his wrist. I noticed the pictures Laura took of the cuts. It looked like he'd tried to pull against the zip-ties to escape. "Did you swab the guy's neck?" I asked.

"What? Why would I swab his neck?" She asked, a bit dumbfounded.

"So when were you planning on telling me?" I asked. I hadn't forgotten about the conversation I'd had with Reed about her being a Svanti.

"Telling you what?" she asked, as her eyes shifted around the room, not once meeting mine.

I arched a brow. "Really? I know you're a Supe." I used the word Reed had used. I was too new to this world to even begin to understand half of it.

She shoved another chip in her mouth. As she slowly chewed, averting her gaze, I wondered if she didn't actually want me to know. She brushed her hands together and finally looked at me. "So, how exactly did you find that out?" she asked. Her eyes kept shifting between the large window and the open door. I rolled my eyes and walked over to close the door.

"Reed told me this morning." I pulled over a stool and sat down.

"Oh, I guess you are a Supe, too then?" Her voice lowered.

"Yeah, Reed turned me a few months ago. How could you not tell me? Didn't you notice I was different? You are the one who was guilting me into going back to days when you knew why I'd changed." I took a breath. It wasn't her fault I was a vampire, but she should have told me.

"I didn't know for sure that was the reason you changed. You could have been having some kind of life crisis." She held her hands out and shrugged.

"Since when do you know me to have life crises?" I cocked my head. She knew better.

"Aye, there's a first time for everything." She reached for another chip. I grabbed her wrist. "Can't a girl even enjoy her dinner, jeez, what'll you be asking me next? Why didn't I tell you about the Easter Bunny? Seriously, Hope, it's my job to keep the secrets, not blabber them on to just anyone. I couldn't tell you until I knew for certain you could be trusted." I dropped her wrist, and she dipped another chip in the salsa.

"So, what are you exactly?" I asked. "Reed told me some of it, but I'm still new to all of this." I rested my hands in my lap, rubbing my finger in a circle over my thumb nail.

"Reed should be the one filling you in on everything. It's not the kind of conversation you have just anywhere." Her eyes moved back up to the door.

"Oh, I guess I didn't realize."

"Reed should have filled you in on the importance of the secret. We have laws that are strictly enforced. You don't want to be on the wrong side of the Ravens." She shook her head.

"I am actually trying to work for them. It's why Reed changed me in the first place. I was recruited." I tucked my hair behind my ears. I was proud of them noticing how skilled I was at my job. I loved being a detective, but I thought my skills would be put to even better use if I could work for the Ravens.

Her brows furrowed. "I don't know if that's such a good idea. You don't even know what I am let alone what the Ravens actually do. Why would you want to jump into that line of work without knowing too much about 'em." Some of Laura's Boston side came out when she got flustered. I could tell she wasn't happy to be having this conversation. I wondered if it was because of where we were having it.

"I know what I'm doing." I stood up from the stool. "Have you gotten any calls tonight?" I wanted to get off the topic of me becoming a Raven. I fully planned to begin my work with her on Saturday. She just wouldn't know what I was doing. She would think we were having a night out at the club. I would be working my way into Vincent's good graces.

"No, it's been slow." She looked over to the two clear autopsy tables. "Did you notice anything else about my guy?" I asked.

"Not much. He was obviously bound around both wrists. I'm waiting for the tox report and the fiber analysis. I analyzed the stomach contents. He'd eaten a burger within a few hours of dying. Everything's in the report if you bothered to read it." She rolled her eyes.

"I'd much rather hear it from you. Were there any other ligature marks or punctures that would explain how he was exsanguinated?" I asked.

"No, I couldn't find anything beyond the abrasions on his wrists. They had a specific marking that makes me think he was bound with zip-ties. Nothing else would leave that specific marking on the skin." She popped another chip in her mouth.

"Would you do me a huge favor?" I clasped my hands together and blinked at her.

She heaved out a sigh. "What is it Matthews?" She only used my last name when I annoyed her. I heard it often enough that it no longer bothered me. Annoying Laura was becoming the highlight of my nights at work.

"Could you swab the victim's neck so I can compare it to DNA in the database?" I smiled.

She narrowed her eyes. "You think you're going to find the killer's DNA in our databases?" Her eyes narrowed on me.

"Well, not exactly." I bit my lip. "Reed said he could check the database at Raven headquarters." I waited patiently for her to berate that decision.

"Okay, I guess it wouldn't hurt. I'd rather get whoever this is off the street before he drains any more people." She strode over to a metal cabinet and grabbed out one of the swabs we use to collect DNA. She opened the locker and pulled out the metal slab. I shivered. I didn't actually feel cold since I'd changed but there was something about the way the bodies were stored that gave me the chills every time she opened the doors. Maybe it was that I'd seen so many bodies brought through here. Not as many as Laura, but enough to believe this place could very well be haunted.

"So, if supernatural beings exist, does that mean there are ghosts too?" I asked. My mind was beginning to see all the possibilities of what could be out in the world. How many other supernatural beings were there?

"Yeah, I guess. I haven't seen one in person." She stopped, rubbing her finger along her jawline. "Which is surprising considering the work I do. I tend to stick with the scientific side, although each body has a distinct story to tell. I am their final voice after death."

She stopped and stared off into space like she was caught up in her own thoughts. "I've seen records of ghost sightings and some of the history in our records. Svanti are the keepers of supernatural history. I have access to everything we know about the supernatural. Although, we had found new species all the time. Similar to the scientist in the rainforests or marine biologists studying the ocean. There could be beings that we don't have any written record of in the world. It's an awfully large world. Not to mention the universe beyond our own. It seems like it'd be an awfully big waste of space if something else wasn't out there." Laura rambled on. I waited patiently, knowing that once she got on her kick, it was just easier to wait it out.

"Isn't that from a movie? Something with Jodi Foster in it?" I asked.

"Yes, but I tend to agree with her. Don't you think it'd be a waste?" she asked.

"I guess I have enough trouble with catching the bad guys here. I don't want to think about ones that could be beyond our world." I shrugged.

"Aye, Hope, always so literal. I'm not surprised Reed chose to turn you. You certainly could use a few eye-openin' experiences. It's an awfully big world out there." She paused. "Speaking of, are you absolutely certain you want to be handin' your life over to be a Raven? You've barely been a vampire, after all. You've got much to experience in this new life. Maybe it'd be better if you waited a few more years before you decide." She held out her hand with the swab.

I sighed. "You and Reed should get together on the anti-Hope bandwagon. I'm good at what I do. They must have recruited me for a reason. I know what I'm doing." I tucked the swab away so I could give it to Reed later.

"If you say so..." Her voice trailed off. "If you don't mind, I'll be gettin' back to my dinner." She walked over to her chair. I swear Laura was always eating. How in the hell did she stay so thin? Maybe that was part of her magic or whatever.

"Okay, I'll see you later." I turned toward the door. I kept the file she'd handed me. I planned on adding the report and any other pertinent information to the board in the den.

I slipped my phone from my pocket and called Reed. "Hey, can we meet up? I have the swab." I waited. "Yeah, I can be there." I hung up. I liked how Reed got to the point when it came to business affairs. There was no muss. I hadn't spent a lot of time with him since he'd left my bedroom last night. I was still thinking over what he'd said about recommending me to the Ravens because I wanted him to.

I knew he'd wanted to sleep with me. He'd made that very clear the night he'd changed me. A part of me, mostly my libido, wanted me to give in to that desire. The rational part of me wouldn't give in. He'd betrayed me, lied to me, kidnapped me, and took away my life. It wasn't something I could just forgive. I also wasn't someone who slept around. If I gave you my body, it was because you'd earned it. Not because I gave into some whim or spark of desire.

I'd been unable to help myself when Reed's vampire blood was coursing through my veins and I didn't feel guilty about that. From what I understood, it couldn't be helped. Now that I wasn't under that compulsion. I wasn't going to give him any part of myself. He certainly didn't deserve it.

Part of my desire to join the Ravens so soon was to gain my freedom from him. He certainly didn't know that was the reason. He had to sense my distrust of him. He wasn't oblivious. I'd told him such many times over our time together. He couldn't think a few small actions were going to change my mind. He'd said that night that I would beg for him.

He'd be waiting a hell of a long time before I ever begged anyone for anything. I didn't need him. The Raven society was my ticket to freedom. He must have known that was the reason. But why would he help me obtain my goal faster? I thought he'd wanted to break me down enough to sleep with him. Maybe his motives changed. Maybe what he had with Cassandra was enough to make him give up on me entirely. One could only hope.

Now, I just had to impress Cassandra with my skills. There was no way they'd deny me my chance once I got close with Vincent. I would get them the evidence they needed, I was damn good at getting what I wanted. And right now, what I wanted was my ticket into the Raven league. I wanted my ticket to my freedom.

CHAPTER 7

R eed's black car was parked outside a small-town bar. I had a soft spot for the greasy spoons and The House of Coates boasted that they had the best burgers. Despite what others thought, I had a thing for a good burger. It looked like that was something Reed and I had in common. He sat with a steaming cup of black coffee in front of him.

"What made you drive all the way out here to meet?" I asked. "There were certainly places closer to the station we could have met." I hadn't understood why he'd made us both drive this far into the suburbs. We were twenty minutes outside of the city. Neither of us had time to waste on frivolous driving.

"I didn't want anyone hearing our exchange. Besides, I like their burgers." The corner of his mouth lifted. There was something in that smirk that let me know there was more to it, but I let it go for now.

"You drive all the way out here just for a burger?" I slipped off my jacket and set it next to my purse on the seat. I took in the typical bar feel. They had booths lined along the far wall with a few high-top tables in the middle. Two pool tables were in the back with green lanterns hanging above them. There were more people than I would expect in here this late on a weeknight. On the other hand, it was the only place to go in this town. Well, other than the gas station and the strip club across the street. I was half-expecting him to suggest I meet him there. The bastard enjoyed making me uncomfortable.

"There aren't that many places that serve late. I also like to get away from the bustle of the city once in a while." He took a drink of his coffee. A buxom blonde made her way over to our booth.

"Hey honey, what can I get ya?" I enjoyed her southern charm.

"I'll take a coffee, black." I smiled.

"Comin' right up, sugar." She smiled and hurried off to get my coffee. I couldn't help but notice the way Reed watched her as she sidled away from our table.

"Are you sure it's the burgers you come out here for?" I smirked. I had a feeling it had more to do with Dawn our waitress than the burgers.

"Of course, it's the food. They don't have the same waitresses here every night." My smirk grew at how defensive he became. It was the waitress.

"And you know this how, exactly?" I rested my chin on my clasped hands and blinked.

"So, did you get the swab?" he asked.

I nodded my head. "I said on the phone I did. You do know I'm good at what I do, right? It's the reason you turned me." It was annoying how he would go from praising me one minute, then berating me the next.

"It's not the only reason," he muttered, as he stared down into the black coffee. The light from the jukebox caught my attention as a woman in leather chaps tapped her foot in front of the glass. Doves Cry by Prince filled the dim-lit room. I watched as the woman pressed a few more buttons before deciding it was time to call Reed out on his cryptic messages.

"What does that mean?" my voice rose just as the waitress came back over with my coffee. I leaned back in the booth and smiled up at her.

"Can I get you something to eat, darlin? We've got the Quarterback burger on special, but I can rustle you up a salad if that's what you're looking for." I had to admit, Dawn had a megawatt smile. I could admire a woman who used her assets to get what she wanted.

"I'll take the burger, medium rare." I stared straight ahead as I ordered, never taking my eyes off of Reed. Maybe Dawn and I would go for a little walk after I ate.

"Okay, sugar, anything else?" she asked.

I turned to her. "What time do you get off tonight? You seem like my kinda girl." I flashed her a wide smile. A growl rumbled from across the table, but I ignored it. I was used to Reed's tantrums by now.

"Oh dear, I'm afraid I'm here all night." She rested her fist on her hip. Her look turning from gleeful to suspicious in an instant. I wondered how many creeps asked her the same thing.

"Don't mind her. She doesn't have many friends. She's a little too forward." Reed flashed her his own charismatic smile, and I hated watching the blood rush to her cheeks. He had that effect on most women. It was hard not to be heated when he flashed his pearly white teeth and dimples. Damn him for looking so delectable. I pressed my lips together and averted my eyes. As Dawn walked away, Reed glared at me. "What exactly do you think you are doing?" he asked.

I licked the corner of my mouth. "I thought I'd go for a little snack after my burger."

"Have I taught you nothing?" he fumed.

"No, not really, Laura pointed out how lacking your education has been. It's not the only thing you seem to be lacking." I flicked my eyes down to the table and back to his eyes, a smile stretching across my lips. I don't know what I found so enjoyable about riling him up. But I could see him trying to calm himself. I could almost see the smoke coming out of his ears.

"Oh? What else did Laura tell you?" he asked through gritted teeth.

"She just mentioned how you should have filled me in about all the supernatural beings by now. She thought you were shirking your responsibilities as a sire. I guess there's an expectation for that sort of thing." I rested my head on my knuckles, feigning disinterest. "At least Cassandra sees my potential. I'm sure she'd love to know how you're not fulfilling your responsibilities." I glanced down at my blood-red polish. I'd chosen it last night after the conversation I'd had with Reed. Something about it made me feel better.

"You're on dangerous ground, Hope." His eyes were scorching.

"Am I?" I smirked. "Why don't you actually fill me in on everything I need to know. I'm tired of you piecemealing information as it suits you. I want to know what I'm getting into. You hinted last night that being a Raven was something I shouldn't strive for, yet you've spoken nothing but the best of them and your position. What is it that I should be concerned about? Isn't that the reason you changed me in the first place, or was it something else?"

I paused, taking a breath. "I think I deserve to know the truth. All of it." My gaze stayed steady on his cobalt eyes. He didn't break eye contact for a long time. When a throat cleared at the bar, Reed shifted his gaze to the side. It was hard to remember to act human when we were around others. It's not like we couldn't erase any suspicion, but it was easier not to cause any in the first place.

"We'll discuss this later," he ground out.

Dawn sauntered up with two plates in her hand. "I give you credit. Not many order their burgers bloody. I hope you got an iron stomach." She set the plates in front of us. "Anything else I can get y'all?" she asked.

"No, that will be all. Thank you." Reed reached out and lightly clasped Dawn's wrist. She looked down at his hand on hers. "Dawn, I do appreciate your attentive service. Would you like to meet us outside when we're finished eating?" I could hear the layer of charm over his words.

"Yes," her voice took on a dreamlike quality.

"Good, that will be all." He sat straight and rested one hand on the table next to the red basket in front of him. "I do love a good burger before dessert."

"Oh? I thought you came here for the burgers." I shook my head. I wondered how many times he'd been here to drink from the locals. The town was legitimately one strip off the highway. No one lived here. It was the place everyone passed through. He couldn't really think no one would notice his presence out here. I glanced over to the bar where several men had their eyes trained on us. By the looks they were giving us, they had an excellent idea of what we were and why we were here.

"What was the real reason you called me out here to join you?" I asked, growing suspicious of the atmosphere. The guys at the bar hadn't taken their eyes off of us. I recognized a murderous glare when I saw one. Tonight I had four eyes trained on me.

"Let's call it training. You said you wanted to get out more and apparently I haven't instructed you well enough on the other Supes in our world. Well, tonight we're in shifter territory." He smiled as he bit into his burger.

"What the fuck does that mean?" I asked.

"You might want to eat up. You're going to need your strength in a few minutes. It's not best form to fight on a full stomach, but the burgers here are damn good. Nice touch ordering one medium rare. I bet they don't get that too often. Humans are too weak to withstand the bacteria." He took another huge bite. Mustard stuck on the corner of his mouth, but he hadn't bothered to wipe it away.

I stared down at my burger, my appetite gone. How was I supposed to eat then go fight those guys? I didn't know anything about shifters. "You seriously brought me here so we could fight those guys?" I asked. "I have cases to work. You're wasting my time." I sat back, stretching my arm across the back of the vinyl booth.

"Training is not a waste of time. You have to be ready to battle to become a Raven. It's not only the case you have to work, but you have to prepare for the trials. They will not be easy. That is part of the reason many wait before applying. You are far too new so we have to speed your training for you to have any chance at survival."

He stuffed the last bite of his burger in his mouth. I glanced around the bar. There was a family sitting in a booth by the door. I assumed they were traveling. No respectable parent would have their children out this late unless they had to. The boy was frantically scratching his crayon across the table in angry arches. The mom was shaking her head at him.

The only other people who were here were the guys at the bar. I didn't look their way, but I could feel their eyes on me. I could always play the cop card. They wouldn't go after a cop, would they? I hated how Reed found these surprises entertaining. I didn't believe this was to speed my training. He was getting me back for the things I'd said. "So, you planning on eating that?" he asked.

"I've lost my appetite." I stared at him.

"Suit yourself." He waved Dawn over. "Can we have the check, please?"

"Certainly, sugar." She pulled a group of slips out of her pocket, checked them and set one on the table face down. "Now you two have a good evening, ya hear." She turned and walked back behind the bar.

"I thought she was joining us?" I asked. He'd charmed her a few minutes ago. "She will, we just have something to take care of first." He set a few hundreds down on the table and slid out of the booth with a primal grace that should be illegal. He held his hand out to me. "Shall we?" he asked.

I rolled my eyes. "If you insist." I took his hand and got out of the booth. I noticed two of the guys shifted, ready to follow us out of the door. Damn, this was going to be a night to remember.

CHAPTER 8

Four burly men stared me down in the House of Coates parking lot. We'd moved toward the back, but I could still hear the steady hum of traffic from the highway. Reed had his arms crossed, his black V-neck t-shirt hugging every line of his muscled body. I should have noticed he'd dressed down for the occasion. He wore his fancy suits anytime he was headed to the council. Tonight he was relaxed in a t-shirt and jeans. I, on the other hand, was in my black Louie Vuitton's and a pinstripe suit. I unbuttoned the jacket letting it fan out to the side. I needed to be less restricted to fight, but I wasn't about to drop a thousand dollar suit coat on the muddy parking lot. The men's eyes were trained on the two of us, but Reed was behind me, taking a dismissive role.

One of the men snarled. "What are you doing in shifter territory, Vamp?" he growled.

"Thought we'd go for an evening burger. Didn't realize you were so protective of the place. That Dawn sure is a looker." He flexed his bicep and licked his lips. He was instigating the fight.

The man with the dark beard and almond shaped eyes glared. "Looks like we need to teach these Vamps a lesson about manners." He cracked his knuckles.

I took a step closer to Reed. "I thought you said they were shifters?" I asked.

"Yeah, they are technically Loup Garou's. We have a file, and these guys have been making others without permission. I'm here to stop the problem before it gets out of hand." He said in a low voice.

"So, what do they shift into?" I asked.

"Werewolves, not the cute and cuddly kind either." He smirked.

"Are there cute and cuddly kinds?" I asked.

"I've seen the books you read." He shifted his right foot in front of the other but his arms were still crossed. I recognized he was getting ready to fight. I looked at the four men and marveled as the air shimmered around them. In place of two of the men were two very large, very hairy, werewolves. Their snouts stuck out, and they were hunched forward. Their legs were those of a dog's but longer, and they didn't seem to need to stand on all fours. Long, black claws extended from their front paws to match the elongated teeth in their snout. Holy hell, I didn't want to get any part of my body between their teeth. I reached for the holster on my hip.

Reed chuckled. "Your bullets won't work on them."

"Seriously, how are we supposed to fight them?" I asked.

"The old fashioned way. I hope you've been brushing up on your technique." He smirked. One of the wolves charged at him. He sidestepped and then jumped, his elbow cocked in the air and coming down hard on the back of the wolf's neck. I was so distracted watching him, I hadn't realized the other wolf was gunning for me. I had two seconds to dodge his mouth before it chomped on me. I felt the scrape of its claws along my forearm and cursed.

One of the men, who was still in human form, laughed. "Not so tough are you, sweetheart? I can't wait until we get to have our way with you." My skin crawled at the insinuation. I would die before I ever let that happen. I shifted my stance and waited. I concentrated my senses on the one wolf. I could hear the beat of his heart, the shift in his footing. He was readying himself to charge again.

I held a blade tucked in a strap around my ankle. You could never be too careful as a cop. That was one thing Reed didn't know about me. I had at least four weapons strapped to my person and only two of them were guns. I was curious what he meant about my gun not affecting these guys. Was that because they were like the actual werewolves? Did I need to start carrying silver bullets in my gun?

The wolf charged, instead of moving out of his way, I leapt into the air, flipping and maneuvering my arms to his neck. I slashed my dagger out and cut across his throat before landing on my two feet behind him. I turned quickly and stabbed the wolf in the back, aiming for where I could hear the racing beat of his heart. The wolf dropped to the ground, lifeless. I wiped the blade of my knife along the course fur of his back. I heard a clap behind me. Reed had already finished his wolf and one of the others who'd shifted.

The man who'd commented about having his way with me stood stock still. His eyes wide as he stared back at us. "Have these guys never fought vampires before?" I asked.

"They were expecting you to be weak because you are a woman. That is something you should always capitalize on. Men will not see you as a threat. They will see you as something to be conquered. Use that to your advantage." He folded his arms over his chest.

"What's wrong with that one?" I asked. It was weird how he was still just standing there, motionless.

"I charmed him to stay still until you called. I didn't appreciate what he'd said to you, so I thought I would give you a chance to, *have your way with him*." His eyebrow rose.

"Now where's the fun in that?" I asked. I wasn't an angel, but I wasn't sadistic either. I had no desire to kill this man just because I could.

"Fine," He walked up to the man. "You are free," he said in his soothing voice. You could always hear the magic behind his words when he was charming someone. I was sure I had the same, but I didn't pay as much attention. "You can do whatever you want." Reed turned his back on the man and walked to the car.

The man glared at me. "I'm going to kill you, bitch."

I shook my head. "You guys really need to expand your vocabulary. I've heard that one too many times." His body shifted, the air swirling around him until a snout elongated from where his mouth had been. His long black claws struck out at the air between us.

"You're really going to make me kill you." I rolled my eyes. I wondered if Reed had already known he would kill all of these men. He'd haphazardly mentioned Ravens having a file and that they were making others. Was that an offense punishable by death? I had to admit. I didn't know enough about Ravens. Maybe Laura and Reed were right. I needed to learn more about what I was getting myself into.

The werewolf dropped low and charged. I dodged, but he was expecting that. His paw reached out and slashed across my abdomen. I cried out at the sudden pain. The wolf turned and growled, heading for me again. I swallowed down the pain that was threatening me and readied for his next attack. He wasn't going to go down easy. With my dagger held in my right hand, I waited for his charge again. He ran at me, and I leapt into the air, ready to finish him like I had the last time.

He grabbed my ankle and yanked me down. I landed hard on my back on the asphalt, the air rushing out of my lungs. He went for my throat, and I rolled out of the way, slashing out with my dagger. I sliced across his chest. The gash wasn't deep, but it was enough to make him flinch. Werewolves' skin seemed to be tougher than ours. My wound had already healed. I wondered if werewolves had the same healing ability. I jumped up, ready for another strike. His arms whipped out, thrashing at the air. Fighting with emotions like anger made you weak. The angrier he got, the sloppier his attempts became. He stopped swiping, and his attention focused on me. I needed to go for his weak spot, but as a werewolf, I wasn't sure he had any.

We circled each other. In training, I always waited for Reed to make a move, and I played defense. He always told me I needed to learn when to be the aggressor in a fight. This was my moment to learn. I scanned his body. He had to have a weakness. The other went down when I cut his throat. Did that mean, they bled and died like anything else?

I noticed his left leg was weaker than his right. I charged, but at the last second I swung left, using my foot to propel myself around him. He wasn't expecting it, and I slammed my dagger into his back. I aimed again for his heart, and when the dagger pierced it, I knew I'd hit my mark. He clutched at his chest and fell to his knees. I yanked out the knife and plunged it in again for good measure. He dropped lifeless.

I turned to the sound of Reed clapping. "You're finally getting the hang of being on the offensive. It took you a bit too long, but you are improving." I hated the self-satisfied grin that was plastered on his face.

"Thanks," I looked down to the blood on my suit pants and cursed. Now I would need to change before going back to work. "Dammit, how am I going to go back to the station covered in blood?"

He chuckled. "You should probably keep a change of clothes in your car for these occasions." I stuck my hand in the pocket of my jacket. I pulled out the swab and held it out to him.

"Maybe next time you shouldn't waste my time on bullshit and call it training. I have my own cases to work. Last I checked, I wasn't a Raven. You shouldn't be involving me in your cases." I glared at him. "Call me as soon as you have anything on that swab."

I spun on my heel and strode to my car. I didn't have time to fight werewolves. This had been one of Reed's cases, and I didn't learn anything in the process. I slammed the door to my car, and the wheels spun as I hit the gas too hard. If the suspect wasn't a vampire, I needed to do some actual police work. Plus, I needed to go check out Club Medusa. I wanted to take note of any of his patterns and who he trusted to have around him. I didn't understand how Reed didn't have his own cases to work.

I parked across from the club. Tonight wasn't the night to go in. I just needed to get a read on what to expect when I made my move on Saturday. I took out my laptop to check out anything about this place on social media. I sifted through pictures taken of the place from the many patrons. I took note of the people I noticed around my mark. I saved pictures of the ones that kept coming up. After searching through all the pictures, I could place at least four men who he was closest to. I had to figure out why these men, and how they got close.

After hours of watching and waiting, I decided to head back to the station. I wanted to check with Shaun. He should have called with an update about my case. The lab doesn't take this long to analyze evidence. I checked my phone. He hadn't called. I decided it was time to see what was going on.

I headed to the lab. Shaun was spinning around in a chair, his hand pushing off from the desk with each spin. "What is it that you're doing instead of analyzing my evidence?" I asked. I cocked my head to the side and watched. Who was this guy?

"Waiting for the results. Haven't you ever spun in your chair when you were bored?" he asked, a goofy smile plastered across his face. I couldn't help but focus on his disheveled hair and dimples. There was something rugged and sexy about him. I couldn't help but smile at his child-like enthusiasm for life.

"I can't say that I've stayed in my chair long enough to need to spin in it." I smirked.

He stood, wobbling a little. "Would you like to take a spin?" he asked.

"I came here to check on my evidence. Did you find anything useful?"

"I'm not giving you anything until you take a spin." He held his hands out toward the chair. When I didn't immediately sit in the chair, he sagged.

I shook my head. "I'm not spinning in the chair."

"Well, then I don't have any information for you." He pressed his lips together in a tight lipped smile. I huffed out a breath and crossed my arms.

"You can't keep the evidence from me. Maybe I'll have to call Jenna and give her your personal number." I cocked my head. There was no way I was spinning in the chair. I also wasn't leaving this office without the information.

"You wouldn't." His eyes narrowed.

"I absolutely would." I smirked. Although it might be fun to play with Shaun, I had things to do. There was something wonderful about his playful spirit. I had to admit, my playful side seemed to be muted since I'd met Reed.

"Hope, you need to learn how to have a little fun in your life." He sat back down and pulled himself closer to the computer. After a few keystrokes, he was pointing to the screen. "I ran the fibers from the scene. It looks like it's a high end cashmere wool. My bet is your murderer was wearing Armani." He scratched the side of his cheek. "How many rich guys do you know who go around killing people?"

"I don't know many rich men, period." I bit my lip. "Anything else?" I asked.

"Coming from the girl wearing Louis Vuitton's." He smirked.

"Shoes are one of my passions." I cocked my hip and rested my hand on it. "So, anything else? I have a witness who saw a dark-haired man leaving the scene. He described him wearing a flashy suit."

"Not much, the samples I collected at the house was what you would have expected, although there was more than one female sample. Jenna may not have been the only woman our victim was seeing." The light in his eyes was mischievous.

"Good to know. I may need to track down the other woman. She may have insight into who would want him dead. Maybe she found out about Jenna or any other women he may be seeing." I patted Shaun on the shoulder. "Good work."

He covered my hand with his. "For you, anytime." He winked. "How's the appetite? You aren't planning on sipping on any other unsuspecting crime scene techs?" His smile grew.

I shook my head. "I don't plan on seeing any other crime scene techs."

His eyebrow rose. "Is that so?"

My eyes narrowed. "But if I was, they would be more than willing to do anything I asked. Trust me." I slipped my hand out from under his and sauntered out of the room.

"I bet they would." I heard him say before I left. Shaun might be a nice distraction. I could certainly use another vampire on my side. I couldn't really trust Reed. He'd made me, but he chose when to dole out information. Shaun seemed to tell me anything I wanted to know without pretext. Shaun was definitely going to be someone I needed to get to know better.

CHAPTER 9

Laura tapped her toe as I took one last look in the mirror. "So, when are you going to tell Reed you're keeping this place." Her eyes swept around the room.

"I don't plan on ever telling him. I love my condo." I slipped the necessary card into my sleek black clutch. I didn't want much to hinder me this evening. I wore a sleek black key-hole dress. A diamond tennis bracelet dangled from my wrist. I dressed to impress, always. Tonight was important. Vincent needed to see me as important and uncatchable. Men liked a little mystery and my bet was, Vincent liked a challenge. I planned to give him both. Laura wasn't aware of my real intentions for the night. She was happy I was joining her on a night out. It'd been months since we'd gone out on the town. We were due.

"Do you really think that's a good idea? You should just tell him." She'd rested her hand on her cocked hip. Laura had a style all her own. She was wearing black rimmed glasses with flames on the tips. She had on a black halter dress with red plaid in the center and a large silver buckle in the front setting off the black pleats at the bottom of the dress. The studs on her belt matched the ones that lined her platform Mary Jane's. Her red knee socks even had small back bows in the back which matched the black bow hanging from her choker. I appreciated her unique style. I was going for simple and sexy.

"Reed doesn't know everything. I'm planning on separating myself from him sooner than later. I'm going to need my own place as soon as I have my freedom." I looked to the door. If she didn't like me keeping this from Reed, she certainly wouldn't like that I was keeping my agenda for tonight from her.

"What if you don't make it in the trials?" she asked, her head down like she felt ashamed for even saying it.

"Not making it is not an option. I am skilled and I will learn everything I need before then. Failing has never been an option for me." I squared my shoulders.

"Now, no more of that dastardly talk tonight. Are you ready to go have some fun?"

"I thought you'd never ask." She fluttered her lashes and tucked her arm in the crook of my elbow as we made our way to the car.

I pulled my car up to the valet in front of the brick building. The valet quickly opened my door and I stepped one long leg onto the pavement before giving the boy a dazzling smile. "Take good care of my baby, now."

"Ye..ss, ma'am," he staggered as he spoke. I tended to have that effect on people since I'd become a vampire. My skin was flawless to begin with, but the vampiric blood had given me a whole new luster that I could appreciate. I tucked my clutch under my arm and joined Laura on the sidewalk. She turned to go to the back of the line.

"Oh honey, I don't wait in line." I smiled and pulled her next to me and went straight for the bouncer. When I noticed how human he was, I inwardly celebrated. You would think a vampire would know not to leave a human at the door. I could charm my way in easily. I squared my shoulders and stuck out my chest with an aura of authority as I met the large man. "Hello darling, would you mind letting a lady inside?" I fluttered my lashes and added the extra charisma to my voice to charm him into submission.

His mouth thinned. "Are you on the list?" I blinked. How was he not affected? It was good I had already assumed I would be facing another supernatural at the door and had made arrangements for a VIP area for myself and Laura. I figured I'd pick up a few more friends along the way. I planned on having my fill tonight. What fun was being a vampire if you couldn't enjoy yourself from time to time.

"Aurora McCartney," I sighed as though this was an utter inconvenience. The burly man scanned his list, his bicep flexing as he flipped the page on the clipboard. Laura narrowed her eyes at me. We were coming here because she had a friend who could get us into VIP. I wasn't going to take the chance that she couldn't, so I booked a space upstairs where I could get a full view of the club. I also didn't want anyone here connecting me to the precinct. I was here on another mission entirely. He paused, and tapped the clipboard.

"Ah, here you are Miss McCartney." He moved the rope aside for us to get in. I flipped my hair behind my shoulder as I passed him. I needed to play the part here. I had no idea where Vincent was, but I was sure he was aware of everything that happened at his club. I needed to make the right kind of impression to draw him to me. Money spoke volumes to men like him. I would be his greatest challenge. I could feel the beat of the music through my whole body as we entered the club. I wondered if that was one of Vincent's vampire deterrents. I swayed my hips as we made our way to the bar.

"What are you doing?" Laura asked. She'd pressed herself against my side to speak directly into my ear.

"Tonight, I'm going to pretend I'm free, if only for tonight."

"Jaysus, did you get that out of some sappy love song?" she cursed. "I know you got something up yer sleeve, but I'm going to let it go for now. Don't think we're not talking about this later though." I heard her Boston accent come back a little which meant she was yet again frustrated with me.

I winked. "We might be even after tonight." She'd kept a big secret from me. I wasn't sure how big this secret would become tonight considering what I had planned.

She shook her head. "Then I take it, you'll be buyin' me drinks, then?"

"Of course," I purred. I rolled my eyes at the sheer number of people at the bar. I crooked my finger, "Come, I have a place reserved upstairs." I took her hand and lead her to the stairs. I had to give my name yet again, but he motioned us passed quickly. A tall woman, with the dark brown hair and complexion led us to a private section with a booth overlooking the dance floor.

I wanted the best view of below. I smiled at the woman who had an amazing complexion, it was flawless. I couldn't sense if she was a vampire, but I doubted it. She was just unnaturally beautiful, which was something I noticed about the club. All of the people who worked here were gorgeous by any stretch of the imagination.

I wondered if that was how Vincent liked it, to be surrounded by such beauty. His club was certainly beautiful with the blue and silver seating and purple icicle lights that dangled over the floor. Even the intricate infinity lights were breathtaking. Everything was etched with gold or silver accents.

The different sections were split off by different lights and designs making you feel like you were almost in a different place entirely, but they all blended into one magnificent theme. I loved every inch of this place. I could see why he would like it. No amount of money was spared in the design.

"What can I get you ladies?" she asked.

"I'll take a martini, dry." I stared out over the dancers. I couldn't wait to get my fill of them tonight. I could already taste the salty sweet blood. I couldn't stop watching as their bodies flowed to the beat from the speakers. I felt my own pulse match pace. It was hard not to be swept up in a place like this.

"Do you want to go down and dance?" Laura asked from next to me. I hadn't even heard her step next to me. I needed to sharpen my ears. I wanted to know where Vincent was at all times. This show was for him after all.

"I want to take it all in for a few more minutes first." I closed my eyes, focusing my attention on his name. Someone in here would give him information at some point. I needed to know where he was. I figured this place had back rooms only for him. I could only imagine the nefarious things that occurred in those back rooms. I slid my tongue over my bottom lips as my fantasies ran away with me. I snapped my eyes open when I heard his name. It came from behind me in one of the corners. I knew he would have his own section roped off for the night, but I lucked out in that it was so close to mine.

The waitress appeared with our drinks. I sipped on my Martini as I watched the crowd below. I wondered how soon he would approach me since I was breaking his rules. Vampires weren't allowed. I planned on using naivety and power to convince him I was someone he wanted in his club. I could feel Laura scrutinizing me. I heard him ask the waitress what I ordered. I grabbed Laura's hand. "Let's dance." Her eyes widened. I pulled her next to me and looped my arm in the crook of hers.

"Well, it's about time. We came here to have fun." I appreciated she wasn't commenting on my strange behavior. I knew she had already figured out I was up to something. She was a Supe so she certainly knew there were others around us.

I pulled her into the middle of the floor, swaying my hips to the music the entire way. I was ready to have some fun. I glanced around. So many possibilities to enjoy myself. I moved so freely, Laura dancing in front of me. I turned, a dark-haired man caught my eye. His hazel eyes were striking as he took a step closer. I crooked my finger, beckoning him closer. He placed his hands on my hips and danced with me.

Laura had found another man to dance with. I closed the distance between the man in front of me. I wrapped one hand around his neck and dipped my head to his neck, my other hand roaming over his back. His hands gripped my hips, our bodies moving against each other. I inhaled the sweet scent of his blood and licked a trail up the artery, feeling the pulse quicken beneath.

I sunk my teeth into his neck and sucked a few mouthfuls. I delighted in the taste on my tongue and the thick liquid sliding down my throat. I moaned before swallowing another mouthful. I licked the punctures on his neck, sealing them closed. A quick run of my tongue over my mouth cleared away any evidence of my misdeeds. My hands trailed down to his hard pecks, feeling the taut muscles. I turned, giving him my back and shimmied down, feeling him press against me. I turned, giving him a peck on the cheek as a new song came on over the speakers.

"Thanks for the dance," I winked before sliding between two dancers and finding another partner. Drinking was such a sensual act and the beat of the music and the sweat on the bodies around me brought my body to a new level of ecstasy. I wanted more. I found one after another to drink from on the dance floor, Laura forgotten in my own pursuits.

My eyes flicked up to our table and I could see Vincent watching me on the floor. My tongue traced a slow trail over my lips so that I knew he would be able to see. My eyes locked on his as I danced to the hypnotic music. I pressed against the man I was dancing with. A ginger with a mess of hair tied up at the back. I ran my hands over his chest, feeling the sinewy muscles beneath. I did love a ginger.

I turned him so Vincent would see the moment I drank from him. I kept my eyes focused on the other vampire as I licked the ginger's neck. I kept my eyes locked on his as I sank my fangs into the man's neck. I closed my eyes, enjoying the moment his blood filled my mouth. I wanted so much more, but I couldn't weaken these men too much. I drank down two more mouthfuls before I licked the wound closed. I wasn't filled with bloodlust, this was just fun. I wanted to feel their excitement through their blood. The humming of my body had me lifting my arms and swaying.

I felt a cold hand pull my back to his front. I draped my arm over him, expecting to feel the ginger's man-bun. I blinked when I felt the gel of slicked back hair. The kind I'd seen on Vincent. His lip pressed against my ear. "Having fun in my club?"

"Mmm, I am." A smile spread over my lips as I swayed my hips against his. His hands held me against him.

"We need to have a talk upstairs," he growled against my ear.

I turned and pulled him by his collar towards me. "I'm not ready to stop dancing, yet. Don't you ever have a good time in your own club?" I held firm as I continued dancing, pressing my front closer to him.

"I'm always having a good time." He smirked, his onyx eyes seeming endless.

"Oh, we both know that's not true." I bit my lip, showing him my fangs. I splayed my hand over his chest, admiring how hard he was beneath. "Have fun with me. You know you want to." I fluttered my lashes. I wanted him to let loose a little. I also wanted to know how far he would go for me.

"I think you've been having enough fun for the both of us." He bent, licking my neck. "How many was that, six men?" A shiver ran down my body when he licked along the artery in my neck. It was so sexy, I wanted him on this very dance floor. The people around us be damned.

"Do that again," I breathed. He licked up my neck. I knew I had him. I leaned back, my eyes heating under his gaze. "Are you sure you want to talk?" I could feel his hardness pressing against me. I knew he was as aroused as I was.

"You like breaking the rules, don't you?" His voice was filled with a gravelly desire that sent a twinge in my core.

I smiled. "I don't know what you're talking about."

"Don't you?" He wrapped his arms around me again, pulling my front flush against him. "No one drinks from my customers. Vampires aren't allowed through the door." He backed up, his eyes skating down my body. "Although, I understand why my guys let you in."

"Oh?" my eyebrows rose. "I didn't see any signs posted."

He chuckled. "It's also against the law to drink so publicly. What if one of the Ravens saw you so devilishly breaking their laws?" His tone deepened. His hands dipping to the bare skin of my thighs, he inched my dress up a bit, splaying his hand against my thigh.

"I didn't see any Ravens." I covered his hand with mine. "Would you like to take this somewhere more private." At this point, I wanted him. I didn't care that he was supposed to be my mark. I wanted to feel his body against mine. I hadn't gotten a release since the night I was made. I was a sexual creature and the blood heightened all of my senses. I wanted to have some fun with Vincent. I was supposed to get close to him. So far, I was succeeding in my mission.

His eyes flicked up to the balcony. "I'll be seeing you later. Save me another dance." As soon as he'd appeared he was gone. I wasn't sure what made him leave so abruptly. Something had him spooked. I glanced up to the balcony and saw him talking with a burly man with tattoos wrapped around both arms. His crew-cut reminded me of the cuts men got in the military. Vincent's eyes met mine for a second before he crossed his arms and scowled. *Shit, did he find out who I am?*

Chapter 10

Laura clutched my arm. "I need a drink." She wiped a stand of hair back from her face. "Let's go back upstairs." She grabbed my arm and practically dragged me back to our spot. This time the man didn't even ask our name but moved the rope and stepped aside for us, his eyes downcast. I wondered if that was because I'd danced with Vincent.

Laura plopped down on the blue leather seats. I sat across from her, crossing my legs. I waved my hand to get the waitresses attention. She hurried over.

"Another round ladies?" she asked.

"Yes, make sure the next is top shelf." I narrowed my eyes on her.

"Oh yes, of course, same for you?" she turned her head to look at Laura.

"Yeah, can you bring a glass of water, too, please?" she smiled.

"Of course, anything else?"

"That will be all, thank you." I turned my attention back to the corner where I'd seen Vincent. There was a group of men and women who looked like they were having a good time, but Vincent wasn't among them. I wondered where he went. Was someone informing him of my true identity? I doubted anyone here would know me as a detective, but I couldn't be sure.

The waitress brought our drinks quickly. I needed the relaxation alcohol promised. I thought alcohol wouldn't affect me, but I was wrong. I didn't get drunk as fast as I did when human, but it still had an effect.

"We have to come here again." Laura commented as she sipped her drink. "I love the atmosphere, especially all the purple lights hanging from the ceiling. Aren't they beautiful?"

"It does have a certain je ne sais quoi." I took another sip of my drink. I listened for Vincent but I didn't hear the sound of his voice anywhere in the building. Was he out killing another? Disposing of yet another body? The possibilities raced through my head.

Her phone buzzed. "O'Connell," she answered.

"I thought you were off for the night." I scolded under my breath. She'd been drinking. There was no way she could go into the office now.

She held a finger up. "Yeah, send Josh and Shaun. I'll take a look over it tomorrow."

She hung up and looked to me. "Looks like we have another one." Her eyes scanned the room. "We can talk more about it when we go. Tonight is about having fun." She leaned back in her chair, her eyes focusing on something. I looked over my shoulder and noticed a long-haired blonde guy with a black button-up watching her. Maybe we wouldn't be able to talk tonight.

I glanced back to the corner where Vincent had been earlier. He was still missing. I found the timing of him leaving me on the dance floor to be suspect now that there had been another murder. At least I'd done what I planned. I made an impression. "It looks like you might not be telling me anything tonight." I flicked my eyes over my shoulder at the man who was more than a little interested in her.

"Would you be terribly upset if I didn't leave with you tonight?"

"You did say tonight was about fun. I bet he'll be a lot of fun." I gave her a knowing smile.

"You're the best." She barely finished before she got up and sauntered over to where he was staring at her. I was pretty sure I noticed him dancing with her earlier. They must have made quite the connection. I relaxed back in my seat and watched the dancers move on the floor. It was mesmerizing to watch such a crowd all dance to the rhythm as the DJ spun the track. My mind drifted and I hadn't noticed him take Laura's seat.

"Do you like to watch?" There was a seductiveness to his words.

"Them? I guess it feels so different now." I didn't take my eyes off the dancers. Vincent could think whatever he wanted about me.

"Are you newly made?" he asked.

I laughed. "Is it that obvious?"

"Not in the least, you have the skill of an elder. I enjoyed watching you work on the dance floor." I finally met his gaze. "I couldn't take my eyes off of you."

My smile widened. "I bet you couldn't."

"Would you like to join my party for a drink?" he asked, indicating the group who were drinking in the corner. I glanced over to the women who were laughing loudly and throwing themselves all over the other men. I remembered the way he made me feel on the dance floor. I didn't want to be another one of the women who threw themselves at him. I was here to make an impression.

"Maybe another time," I stood up from my seat. He stood after me.

"Is there nothing I can do to change your mind?" I knew that if I joined his group I would be another one of his groupies. I was no one's groupie. I had no intention of being just another notch on his belt. I needed to get into his life. The only way to do that was to leave him wanting more.

I leaned in and spoke into his ear, running my fingers down his chest. "I don't like to share." I patted his chest. I slid a card with my fake name and the number to a burner phone in his pocket. I turned on my heel and searched for Laura. She was still talking to the blonde. I wasn't sure about leaving before her. We always had a system. We left together, or we knew who the other was leaving with. It was part of the girl-code. We took care of our friends. I paused next to her. "Are you sure, you're good?" I needed to check in with her before I left.

"Yeah, I'll see you tomorrow." She winked.

"Okay, have fun." I locked eyes with the guy sitting across from her. I wanted him to know that I was trusting my friend with him.

I left the bar and gave the valet my ticket. I wanted to check out the new body. I knew she sent Shaun. He'd fill me in on everything if I asked. I drove to the station and headed to the lab. Shaun was standing over the mass spectrometer. "Hey, find anything interesting?"

He jumped. "Damn, Hope, I wasn't expecting you."

"You seem a little jumpy tonight." I stopped next to him.

His eyes heated as they made their way down my dress. "Well, aren't you looking fancy for the office. What are you doing here? Aren't you off tonight?" he asked. "I thought you were out with Laura."

"I was. She went home with a sexy blonde. She told me about the call so I thought I'd stop by and see what you found." I glanced to the machine.

"It was another body dump. There were fibers on the body that didn't match his clothing so I'm running those against the ones from previous scenes. There were also a few samples that I'm testing now to determine their chemical make-up." He looked back at the machine.

"So, there was actually evidence this time. That's interesting. Is he getting sloppy?" I asked. I thought back to the club. If it was Vincent, he wasn't gone long. That could explain the reason for his missteps.

"I'm not sure. The body was in the alley like he'd been pushed out of a van. We won't know more until Laura performs the autopsy. This guy had the same markings around his wrist as the others. We still believe they're connected." He explained.

"Okay, so what's his motive? Why is he just dumping bodies? If it were a vampire, wouldn't he be doing everything to keep from getting caught." I tapped my finger against my lips. "Laura mentioned the Ravens tend to instill fear in the supernatural. Why would one of them be leaving bodies this haphazardly knowing they would be hunted. I assume punishment is swift. It doesn't make sense."

"Unless they want to get caught. Some of the older immortals want to die but aren't keen on doing it themselves. Maybe they are hoping to get caught so we kill them. It wouldn't be the first time." Shaun shrugged.

"Hmm, I guess I hadn't thought of that. But then why is he not leaving more evidence behind. If he wanted to get caught, you'd think he'd leave behind more to help us track him. No, something else is going on here." I didn't know what to make of it. Vampires were skilled. I easily took blood from many tonight without anyone being the wiser. This was what we did. There was no reason to kill anyone when you could drink so freely and charm the humans into thinking they were just tired. None of this case was making any sense. Without a motive, what was the reason for any of this.

"You have a peculiar look," he commented.

"I don't get it." I looked up into his dark eyes. "Why? There has to be a reason behind all this." I stared at the computers. Everyone had a reason, especially when it came to their actions, right?

"Maybe there isn't a reason. Maybe this person just likes to kill people. He could be leaving them behind so that we find them. There doesn't always have to be a reason." He paused. "You'll find that as a Raven, immortals don't live the same way people do. You have too much of your humanity left in you. Immortals will do something just to cause chaos. They don't always have a motive behind their actions."

"How long have you been immortal?" I asked, curious as to how long someone needed to live to no longer have their humanity. Should I expect my thoughts to change so drastically that I no longer acted without motivation? Everyone had a reason for everything, otherwise what was the point of all this? What was the point of living?

"That's a fairly personal question." His eyes narrowed on me.

"Oh? People ask about their age all the time, what's the difference?" I asked.

"You can tell a lot about a person by when they were born. We tend to hold on to many of the customs from our specific time period." He shifted his weight from one foot to the other.

"And why wouldn't you want me to know more about you?" I quipped.

"I'm not sure if I trust you just yet, little Raven."

"What do you mean? If anyone shouldn't trust anyone here it would be that I can't trust you. I have no idea why you had to relocate here from Boston. Maybe you're the killer and that's why you're here in the first place. You do know that most killers try to insert themselves into the investigation." I rested my hand on my hip, not liking what he was insinuating about me.

"I'm not the one who tried to drink from me on our first meeting, or did you forget that little occurrence." He narrowed his eyes and pressed his lips together. Even angry, he was sexy.

"How was I to know you weren't just any crime scene tech? I had no idea there were even other super naturals at the time beyond vampires. Besides, if you had been a regular it wouldn't have mattered anyway. I would have left you with a happy memory of our time together." I winked.

"Oh, so now you're planting false memories. Remind me again why you're the trustworthy one?" His smile was more playful than serious. I loved our little word battles. I could only imagine how this would play out later. I didn't mind Shaun. He had a fun side that was lacking in my current consort. Not that I would ever let Reed touch me after what he'd done.

"Okay, okay, so maybe neither one of us is trustworthy. Maybe we should stick to the work." I licked my lips slowly and watched as his eyes tracked the movement.

"Yeah," his voice came out a little breathy, "maybe that's a good idea."

"So, did the mass spectrometer spit out whatever that substance was?"

He blinked. I knew I had gotten him a little worked up. I did enjoy that power I had on occasion. It was part of the reason I had so much fun at the club. My body was a weapon as much as anything, and I had no problem using it to get what I wanted.

He grabbed the report from the printer. "Looks like it's a compound for champagne, combined with the samples collected from the couch, I'd say our victim enjoyed a little bubbly before a rendezvous on the couch. Considering there were numerous samples, maybe that was a ritual for him." He paused. "I ran the other female samples and haven't found any matches yet for our second victim. It will be up to you to dig up the other possible contributions." He winked.

"Has anyone ever told you there is something seriously wrong with you?" I shook my head. "I'll see what I can dig up. Jenna obviously wasn't his only companion. I'm still stuck on where his second residence may be. I'll check his phone records and credit to see if I can dig anything more up." I paused. "Who's assigned to the new victim?"

"Miller and Elliot, you night shift folks get the brunt of the work."

"Have they found anything on the first guy found?" I asked.

"You'd have to ask them. I wasn't the one on their scene. I think that was Andrews. He's off tonight. I haven't had time to ask about any evidence he's run. You could ask Karla. She's been running DNA for days." He set the report on the desk. "Now if you don't mind. I have more work to do."

"Oh, I'm sorry to have inconvenienced you on my day off." I folded my arms across my chest.

"You don't have to be here. It is your day off after all." He smirked. "Unless there's another reason you wanted to see me."

"Don't flatter yourself. I'm here for information on the case."

"So, you wouldn't want to join me for dinner tomorrow night?" he asked.

"Is that your way of asking me out?" I asked.

"I believe I just did." He smiled, "So…"

"Dinner tomorrow sounds good." I smiled. "See you then." I strode out of the lab. It would be nice to see Shaun away from the office. Maybe then I would stop fantasizing about Reed. I went back to my apartment. I wasn't ready to see Reed and he had his own stuff going on anyway. The only thing he knew about tonight was that I was going out with Laura. He had no idea that I was going to the same club Vincent owned. He didn't need to know everything going on in my life. He would be more than happy once I found out what Vincent was up to at the club. How many more bodies would be discovered before whomever was committing these murders was stopped?

CHAPTER 11

I slipped off my heels and plopped down on the couch. It was nice to be alone without any expectations. My phone buzzed. I figured it was Laura telling me she was okay or Reed telling me what I should be doing right now. I wanted to ignore it, but I knew better. I looked down at the illuminated screen. My hand flew to my mouth. Laura was bound to a chair and gagged. Blood was running down her lip and head. She had bruises on her face and arms. The text read, *Stop investigating me or else.*

I dropped the phone. They had Laura. I never should have left her alone at the club. We shouldn't have been there when the vampire who owned it was under suspicion for killing people, especially other super naturals. I thought Laura could take care of herself. I didn't think for a second that anyone would take her.

I closed my eyes, finding the calm strength that I needed to save Laura. I picked my phone back up. *If you hurt her, I will kill you.* I hit send and grabbed the keys to my car. I couldn't do this on my own. I drove to Reed's apartment. I wanted to find Shaun but I wasn't sure if I could trust him yet. Reed was my sire. He would have to help me save her.

Except his apartment was empty. I didn't think about the fact that he was probably working his cases for the Ravens. I called him, which I should have done immediately.

"Where are you?" I asked as soon as he answered.

"Well hello to you too." His voice was far too upbeat for my taste.

"I don't have time for pleasantries. Someone took Laura from the club. I got a text saying to stop investigating them or else. You need to come home, now." I hung up the phone. I was not negotiating with him. I needed him to help me, now.

I paced the length of the open living room and kitchen as I waited for Reed to get his ass here. I didn't know where to begin. Do I go back to the club? Do I confront Vincent? If it's not him, then I give up my identity and any chance I have at finding out what he's doing will be lost. I can't waste what I've already started with him, so I'm going to need to figure something else out. Unless it is Vincent and he knew the entire time what I was doing there.

I could go to the lab and try to figure out where the text originated. Not that I thought it would do any good. The number was probably to a burner phone. I called Shaun anyway.

"Hey, couldn't wait till dinner?" he asked.

"No, hey someone sent me a text of Laura. I'm going to forward you the information. Will you see if Mac can triangulate where the text came from and anything he can dig up on the number?" My words were rushed. I couldn't help it. Laura was being held by a demented murderer.

"What kind of text?" he asked.

I tapped my phone and forwarded him the message. "That kind of message." I said after it went through.

"Holy shit, did you leave the club together?" he asked.

"No, she was going home with the blonde, remember? I left her because I thought she would be okay with him. Other Supes have been going missing after visiting the club." I cursed. "I should have never left her there."

"Hey, it's going to be okay. We'll find her."

"Let me know as soon as you have anything." I didn't need lies. He didn't know if it was going to be okay, but I appreciated the sentiment.

"I will," he paused. "Where are you now?" he asked.

"Reed's apartment. He's on his way here now. Find the number, Shaun. We have to get her back." I could hear the desperation in my voice. I didn't like feeling helpless. I needed to be doing something.

"Who are you talking to?" Reed asked.

"Call me as soon as you know anything. I have to go." I hit end on the phone and turned to face Reed. "I called Shaun, the crime scene tech. I have him searching for information on the number. We need to know where the text came from so I can kill whoever thought they could go after one of my friends." I waited for him to challenge me.

"What do you know?" he asked. I handed over my phone.

"This is what I received. I left Laura at Medusa. She was with a blonde guy, long hair, thin, a little over six foot. He was wearing a blue button up and black pants." I tapped my finger to my lips. "He had a snake tattoo on his arm. I only know because the head was just below where his shirt sleeve stopped. That's the only thing I can think of that would distinguish him from someone else."

Reed's eyes narrowed. "You brought Laura to Medusa?" he growled. "Then you left her there? You were there because supernaturals have been disappearing after attending that club. What the hell were you thinking?" I could hear grinding as he spoke between clenched teeth.

"I needed a cover. I have Vincent on the hook. Laura said she was going home with the guy. I didn't think anything of her leaving with him. He seemed nice enough." I shrugged. I was already beating myself up. I had gone against everything I knew as a woman out with friends. You never left your friends at a club, never. Being a vampire, and knowing she was Svanti had skewed my interpretation of our safety. I knew I could take care of myself. I thought Laura could too. "This is partially your fault. I don't know anything about her abilities as a supernatural. Can't she protect herself like we can?"

"Oh, so now you want to turn this on me." He turned away from me. "I told you Svantis keep our secrets. They are the historians and healers. They can't defend themselves. That's why vampires are the enforcers. We're the strongest of the supernaturals. I can't believe you just left her to go home with some guy. Is that something you would do as a human?" he asked.

I dropped my head. He had a point. "No, I wouldn't." I clenched my fists at my sides.

"There's nothing we can do about your egregious mistake. We just need to find her before she ends up on her own autopsy table. Did you find out anything useful at the club? You are the only one who's been able to get past the bouncers and into the club." He folded his arms, waiting.

I scanned through what I'd learned. "I have Vincent on the hook, or at least I thought I did. He has the number to my burner phone, which is different than the one I got Laura's picture on. Vincent got called away from me on the dance floor and he was gone for about an hour at around eleven. The body was found in the time that he was gone."

If it wasn't Vincent, it was definitely someone at the club. But why would they send the message to stop investigating them? I doubt he would have sent that message.

He would have taken me out to dinner and gotten rid of me. Who else could it be?

"What else happened at the club? Were there other vampires there?" Reed asked.

"None that I'd noticed, beyond those who are with Vincent. The guy who interrupted us on the dance floor certainly could have been." I pressed my lips together, cursing that I hadn't paid more attention to the other people at the club. I was solely focused on Vincent, whom I assumed was my prime target. I didn't even think to get to know who else may have been there. I'd gotten tunnel vision.

"You don't know?" Reed's mouth fell open slightly before he righted it. I could see the anger flashing in his eyes. "I thought you were the best. You didn't notice if anyone else at the club that you were investigating was a vampire? What exactly were you doing there?" he asked.

I didn't want to look at him. I knew I'd screwed up and now my friend's life was hanging in the balance. "I was having fun with my friend. I kept a keen eye on Vincent. I thought he was the suspect." I clenched my hands at my sides trying to stop them from shaking. "I had tunnel vision, alright. I was only watching him."

"So, someone at the club could have been watching you. Many perps go back to the crime scene. He probably saw you there and at the club. He put the pieces together and as soon as he had his chance, he took advantage. Now we have to clean up your mess." He threw up his hands pacing away from me. "I can't believe I recommended you. I knew you were too green for this."

"The only reason I'm too *green* is because you refuse to teach me the things I need to know." I charged toward him, stopping an inch away from his face. "Is that because you want to keep me here, with you?" My eyes narrowed and my heart pounded in my chest.

He gripped my wrists and held them together forcefully. "No, it's because you have no idea what you're getting yourself into, but you're too damn stubborn to listen to anyone." He tightened his grip. "I care what happens to you, okay. Is that so fucking hard to believe? I care about you, Hope." He dropped my hands and turned away from me.

"What? If you cared so much about me, why didn't you give me the choice every other vampire gets to make? Why didn't you let me choose to end my human life?" I spat back. There was no way I was going to let him off the hook with more bullshit. I knew better. He could say he cared but every single thing he'd done showed me otherwise. Caring was about actions, not words.

"I couldn't give you the option." His voice lowered.

"Why not?" I asked. I didn't believe him.

"Because then you could have said no, and that wasn't an option. There is more at play here then you know. I am trying to keep you safe, but you are making that impossible," he growled.

"Keep me safe, from what? You are the only one who's done anything to hurt me." I was reeling. He was so good at spinning things to make it sound like he was the good guy, when in reality, he was anything but good.

"I can't explain it right now. Will you please trust me? You are more valuable than you know." He closed the distance between us. His eyes blazed as he gazed down at me.

"What? You're not making any sense." It was hard to concentrate with him so close. I could smell his cologne mixed with the manly scent of him and my head spun for a second. I closed my eyes and tried to regain my composure. "Why can't you just tell me? I don't understand why you need to keep this from me."

"Because if you knew, you would put yourself in even more danger. Please, Hope, can you please just trust me for once. I can't give you the explanation now, but I promise, as soon as I can, I will." There was such sincerity behind his words.

I swallowed hard and nodded. I really wasn't giving up this argument, but I had a friend to save. "So how do we find Laura?" I asked.

"We figure out where that call came from and find out who at that club was watching you." His eyes darkened. Reed was a dangerous man. Whoever took my friend was going to find out just how dangerous we could be.

CHAPTER 12

S haun called. "Can I meet you somewhere? I'm not sure we should be having this conversation over the phone."

"Really?" I glanced over to Reed. "Can Shaun join us?" I asked.

"You want to invite him to our home? Do you honestly trust him?"

I wasn't sure how to answer that because I hadn't actually known Shaun that long. I had that same fear the other day. "Sure, how about the bar on 38th and Cedar?"

"I'll be there in fifteen. We may want to go for a walk from there. Don't get comfortable." He hung up the phone.

I knew he had something to share that wasn't for others to hear. "Reed, I'm meeting him at the bar. I'll be back as soon as I can."

The corner of his mouth lifted. "So you don't trust him to know where you live, yet." I was sure he was filing that information away for later. I was forced to trust Reed since I lived with him and he was my sire. I still didn't really trust him. He was keeping too many secrets from me.

I drove to the bar quickly. Instead of going in, I leaned against my car. He said the conversation needed to be private, so I figured we'd leave as soon as he got here. It wasn't cold yet, not that either of us would notice. Others might notice two people walking around outside if it were winter.

On the other hand, this was Minnesota, we grilled outside in the winter. We were crazy bastards when it came to withstanding the cold. Much like Canadian's I presume, in that respect. In Wisconsin, they just drank until they couldn't feel anything. It was a different world here in winter.

Shaun pulled up a few minutes later. His strides were purposeful as he made his way to me. His head moved like it was on a swivel before he stopped in front of me. "Are you sure we can talk freely here?" he asked. I wondered what was making him so suspicious.

"Let's go for a walk." I suggested.

"How about we go for a drive? We can head out to Fort Snelling. It should be deserted this time of night." His eyes darted around like he was growing increasingly nervous.

"Okay," I took a step toward the front of the car and he grabbed my arm.

"I'll drive. I have some things you need to see." He pulled me behind him to his car without waiting for me to answer. I was a little nervous by his behavior, but I was a vampire. I'd been trained in combat. I could handle myself if this meeting went south. He held the passenger door open for me, and I got in. The gentlemanly gesture put me at ease slightly. He probably wouldn't open my door for me if he was planning to take me out.

When he got in, he handed me a file. "I think the person who has Laura is a vampire."

"I kinda knew that already." His head snapped to look at me. I hoped he had more than that to share with me. Reed and I already knew that whoever was taking people from the club was probably a vampire since they were draining people of their blood and leaving them dumped all over the city. I still had yet to find a primary crime scene for any of the bodies we'd recovered.

"Did you know that they are probably a Raven?" he asked, his eyes flicking over to meet mine. I averted his gaze. I didn't like lying, but I knew I couldn't share what I already knew with him. That was part of being a Raven. He wasn't my partner in this. I couldn't tell him.

"No, that I didn't know." I said slowly. "What makes you think it's a Raven?" I asked.

"Because, the call pinged from near the council headquarters. The only people in that area are Ravens. We also pulled the call log. They didn't even try to hide who they were." He paused. "I think they want you to find them. The numbers are for other Ravens including Reed." He gave me a serious look. Shit, Reed was on the list. What had he gotten me into?

"So, would you have told me if Reed were here?" I asked. I wondered how he was involved. If the killer called him, he would have known him, right? Was Reed playing me or was it a coincidence?

"I'm not sure. I'm glad you came alone." He raced down the highway, turning off toward the abandoned homes that once held soldiers of long days past. I always thought it was interesting how they hadn't actually torn them down. On the other side of the highway, they were homes for veterans. Here they were abandoned. Baseball fields filled the open space and Shaun pulled into the parking lot for the light rail. There were a few cars that looked like they may have been left here overnight. Not many would notice cars in the transit parking lots. The cops would drive through at some point.

He turned to look at me. "You have to be careful if you are trying to hunt a Raven. They will kill you. They are trained to kill supernaturals." He took my hand. "How did you get involved in this? You aren't a trained Raven."

"I can't talk about all of it. I was investigating the bodies we'd found. I think there are at least five connected to one killer. I believe they are all connected to the club I went to tonight." I sighed. "I should have never left Laura there. They won't hurt her, right? She's too high profile. Cops will be all over her murder. It's too public. I'm counting on that to find her before anything happens to her." I knew I was rambling. I was trying to convince myself more than Shaun that she was going to be okay.

"You can't blame yourself. These guys are very good. We're trained to be. Whoever took her was probably watching you. Looking for their chance to get to you. Laura just happened to be an easy mark." His voice softened.

"I thought because she was also supernatural, she could take care of herself. I assumed she would be leaving with the guy she met." I glanced out at the streetlights. "She was with a blonde with a snake tattooed on his arm. I could search the tattoo database."

"Do you think it was him? I doubt he would be so open about taking Laura. He knows you saw him." He stopped to rub his jaw. "Unless he wanted you to know it was him. He could be playing you." Shaun looked at me. I wasn't sure what to think of that idea. Could he be playing me? I doubted it.

"Anything else from your search?" I asked. "Anything to help find Laura. He could be hurting her." I knew as a cop I needed to control my emotions. I needed to focus on the task. Emotions would only get in the way. It was hard knowing my friend was in danger.

"I'm not sure if this helps, but there was dirt in the treads of the victim's shoes. In both cases, it was the same make-up. It had flakes of aluminum, which makes me think it is near the southside of Inver Grove Heights. There's a factory over there that would leave this specific compound in the soil." He took my hand. "We're going to find her."

"Okay, so champagne, dirt that connects to the southern suburbs and a phone pinging near the council headquarters. Jenna said he was supposed to meet her at seven. The cameras at his office complex have him leaving at six-thirty. He was found two hours later. That doesn't leave much time in between to murder him, clean-up, and dump the body without being noticed. It makes sense if he's a vampire." I stared at the softball fields. "Is that why we came here?"

"I thought it would be good to be close if we figured something out. During that time, it wouldn't be hard to get into the city but nearly impossible to get out. So, I'm betting they have a place near where the soil would have been. But how did they get the guy from his work during rush hour?" he asked.

"Reed had me meet him at House of Coates the other day. It seems like an awfully big coincidence considering the things we know now." Reed hadn't given much of a reason for being in that area other than his own supposed case.

"What were you doing there?" he asked.

I wasn't sure what I should tell him. "Reed likes the burgers."

"Do you expect me to believe that?" His eyebrow cocked as he watched me.

"Yeah, I didn't believe it either. Now I think there may be something more to why we were there, but I don't know what. There's something we're missing." I wasn't sure if I should tell him the real reason we were there. I wanted to be a Raven, and one thing I'd learned was that you didn't talk about Raven business.

"Reed didn't tell you why you were there?" Shaun asked.

"Any other calls on the list that could help us? Knowing that it's a vampire and possibly a Raven doesn't narrow it down much. I don't even know how many vampires are in this city." I knew I was letting the frustration get to me. I needed to think clearly to figure out how to save Laura.

He handed me a few sheets of paper. "These are all the numbers with the names I pulled for the phone. Whoever this is, they want you to find them." He gave me a meaningful look. "Why else would he have used his actual phone to send you that picture? It doesn't make sense."

He was right. I studied the list of numbers. I needed to show this to Reed. He would know who everyone was on this list. "Okay, so why would they want me to catch him?"

"I can think of only one reason."

"And that is?" I asked.

"It's a trap to get you. The person who took Laura knows that you will go charging in to save her. That's probably what they're counting on." He stopped waiting for me to say something. I thought about it. He was right again. I can't think of any other reason, but why would they want me? I'm just a detective. Whoever this is, they are a Raven and a vampire. I'm nobody compared to him. Was this what Reed was mentioning earlier? He kept saying he needed to protect me. I just didn't understand from what. "So, who wants you?" he asked.

"I have no idea."

"Well, we better figure that out before you go rushing off to save your friend. Whoever it is, wants you pretty badly."

I stared at the lights outside. It was time to go talk to Reed. "Start the car. We're going back to my place." I smirked.

He winked. "I thought you'd never ask."

CHAPTER 13

S haun followed me up to the door. I stopped and picked up my car before going back to Reed's house. The drive felt long considering everything that was running through my head. Reed turned when I entered. His ear was pressed to the phone. "I think it's about time you star—"

Reed held up his finger to stop me. He nodded his head. "Yes, I want to know as soon as possible." He hung up the phone without a goodbye. That was strange. I wondered who he was talking to.

"So, you decided you trust him, now?" Reed glared at Shaun.

"I do. We have some things to show you."

"Well, by all means have a seat." He moved to the loveseat, leaving a wide space next to him. I knew he was looking for me to sit by him. I wasn't going to play his games. I handed him the printout with the numbers.

"Any of those look familiar?" I was tired of only getting information out of Reed after he was backed into a corner.

He took the paper and flipped through the pages. "This is from one of ours." His eyes narrowed. "Is there something you'd like to ask me?" His gaze held Shaun's. "Please, do tell our young detective here what happens to vampires who speak against their sires."

His eyes narrowed. "That depends entirely on the sire. A good man wouldn't be threatened by some simple questions if he didn't have anything to hide."

I smiled. I knew there was a reason I liked him. "Do you know who that phone number belongs to?" I asked.

He set the papers on the table next to him. "You already know I do." He slowly licked his lips, his eyes steady on Shaun. This display of dominance was getting ridiculous.

"You need to start telling me what's going on. Why would someone take Laura to lure me to them? You mentioned keeping me safe. Why?" I asked. Obviously Reed knew what was really going on, and I was tired of being kept out of the loop.

"We can have this conversation as soon as he's gone." Reed stood and made his way to the liquor cabinet. He poured himself two fingers of whiskey, swirling it around in the glass before taking a drink.

"Are you serious? He's helping me, unlike you apparently." I sat on the arm of the chair and crossed my legs. "He got me the numbers. Now, who do they belong to?"

"Another Raven, he's an older vampire. You are going to need me if we have any chance of going against him." Reed took another drink from his glass.

"Why does he want me? The only reason I can figure he took Laura is to get to me. It has to be a trap. I just don't understand why." I waited. Reed was the only one who could give me the answers I needed. By the tightening muscles of his jaw, he knew he was going to have to tell me.

"They wants you because of me. It's the same reason they took Laura. They knew she would get you to come. If they get you, they will force my hand. They can't take you." The command in his voice made me flinch, and Shaun took a step forward.

"Why do they want to get to you?" Shaun asked. His hands were clenched at his sides.

"I can't talk about that with you. It's confidential Raven business."

"Well, your confidential business is threatening the life of your progeny. It's your responsibility to keep her safe." He turned away. "Call me when you want to talk." His eyes met mine.

"Wait, Reed stop being so damn territorial. We need him. He's an insider just like you. The difference is, the guy who has Laura doesn't know Shaun. He knows you. We need to get Laura away from him." I tilted my head to look at Reed. "Shaun is here to help me, not you. He can stay as long as I'd like him to." It was time I started taking my life back. Besides, Shaun seemed to be the only one who actually gave a damn about me.

"How do we know it's not Shaun here instigating this entire thing to get on your good side?" Reed set down his glass. "You may trust him, but you need to ask me before you bring strangers into my home. Shaun, it's time for you to leave."

"I will respect you as her sire. But know this, if anything happens to her, I will report it to the council. You know what happens if your progeny dies due to your negligence." He paused. I could feel the tension radiating from both of them. "I'm leaving her life in your hands." Shaun took one last look at me. "I'll see you tonight." He smiled at me before he closed the door behind him.

I whirled around on Reed. "What is your problem?"

"You can't be serious about him." He held his hand out toward the door.

"I don't know, but we needed his help, and you just kicked him out of the door."

"We don't need him. He already got us what we needed." He sat back down on the loveseat, a newly poured drink in hand. The self-satisfied smile made me even more pissed.

"Oh yeah, did you know the cell phone was pinging near the council's headquarters. Are you ready to tell me what the hell is going on now?" I asked. "I knew you had something to do with those murders. I just knew it." I paced behind the couch. I couldn't believe how stupid I'd been.

"I didn't have anything to do with them, but I suspected. It's why I went out to Coates to take care of his lap dogs. He was using the Loup Garou to help him. I believe they were the ones dumping bodies for him." Reed explained.

"Then why the hell didn't you tell me?" I asked. "You could have filled me in on everything while we were there." I walked over to the window and watched as Shaun got into his car. He looked up to the window and smiled when he saw me. He made a motion like he was tipping his hat and got into the car. Disappearing into the night.

"No, I couldn't. You've been watched since the moment I turned you." Reed took a drink.

"Wait, What?" I whirled on him. "You didn't think that was important for me to know?" I shook my head. "This whole time I've been a target. You sent me to crime scenes on my own, knowing there was someone after you and following me. What the hell, Reed?"

"Don't worry, you've been protected." He took another drink as if nothing important was going on. He was so fucking irritating.

"What the hell does that mean?" I asked.

"Was there not another Raven with you at every scene?" The way he said that spoke volumes. I thought back to him showing up the first time. Then, when I returned, Shaun was there. He was also at the lab with me. I took a deep breath.

"Shaun, you're the reason he's here from Boston." I felt like a real idiot.

"Precisely, Shaun is an old friend. He transferred here the night I introduced you to the council." He paused. "I didn't think you'd hit it off quite so well. I may need to have a little chat with your new friend." I couldn't believe this. Every part of my life since that night had been a fucking lie. What else didn't I know?

"Are you serious? You hired him to protect me." That felt like it was out of left field. He'd been nice to me and suspicious of Reed. What the hell was that show of masculinity if they were working together this entire time? "Why couldn't you just tell me?"

"I didn't want you to know. There was more to me changing you then you know. I wasn't ready for you to know everything just yet." He poured another drink.

"Are you going to get drunk while Laura is being held by some lunatic?" I grabbed the glass out of his hand. The growl he made after was satisfying. "You are going to get Laura back since you're the reason she's in danger."

"He's not going to kill a Svanti. He needs her too much." He took his glass back.

"So, what? You're just going to sit around drinking while she's suffering God knows what. If you don't get her back now, I will." I stormed into my room. I'd only had my police issued gun, but I didn't want to use that against a vampire. Maybe silver bullets would work on this guy. Plus, after Reed mentioned how the Loup Garou's' were helping him, I wanted silver bullets just in case.

Reed stopped in the doorway, his hands folded over his chest. "What do you think you're doing?" he asked.

"I'm going to find my friend. This guy is in the southern suburbs. I need a name or I'm going to trace Laura's phone to find her." I rested my hand on my hip and waited.

"You can't go after her alone. I won't allow it."

"I love that you think you get to tell me what to do." I glared back at him.

"Last I checked, you are my progeny. I do get to tell you what to do." He closed the distance between us. I could smell the whiskey on his breath. His hands gripped my hips, holding me in place. "You will not go after your friend. I have others working on her rescue. I need you to stay safe." His fingers dug into my hips. I stared back into his blue eyes, defiant.

"Who? Who do you have going after Laura? I need to know she's okay." The corner of his eyes turned down, and I could almost see sympathy.

"I wouldn't let anyone hurt you or Laura."

"Reed, I'm going to need more than that." I stared into the depth of his dark eyes. It was hard to look away from him. I could smell his cologne mixed with the whiskey. It was a heady mixture that spoke to a place deep inside of me. I had to remember my friend was in danger because of the man before me. I hated how I responded to Reed when he got this close to me.

"You have my word, what more do you require?" he asked.

"Your word doesn't mean much." I couldn't help it.

"When have I ever broken my word to you? There may have been times when you didn't like what I'd said, but I do not break my word." I could feel the intensity in his words.

"Are you trying to charm me?" I asked.

"No, that doesn't work between us." I saw a flash of pain cross his eyes before he stepped away, his eyes drifted to my bed. The blood rushed to my face. I hated how I reacted to him. What did he think I would let him fuck me to forget about my friend? Fat chance. Not that I wasn't thinking about it when he was that close to me. It was hard not to. My body was drawn to his. I blamed that fateful night when he'd turned me into a vampire. It was hard to get that kind of pleasure out of my mind, or my body. It was like my hormones remembered every fleck of his talented tongue when he was close to me. I hated it. I felt like I was being betrayed by my libido.

"So why did I hear the tell-tale sound in your voice? Reed, when are you going to be honest with me? You say you care about me, but not once have you trusted me enough to actually tell me what's going on." I strapped my guns to my belt. "I'm not going to wait for you. I'm going to find my friend. If you want to keep me safe, I guess you'd better come with me."

"Where do you think you're going to find her?"

"I'm going back to the club. If you're not going to help me, maybe Vincent will." I pulled my hair back and twisted it. I clipped it in place and pulled a few loose strands free. I went to the vanity and touched up my lipstick. We'd had a few moments at the club earlier. The last place I saw her was his club.

He'd want to help me find my friend. The damsel needing his help desperately would be an easy play to make with him. If he wasn't the vampire behind this, he would want to help me. It was in a male's DNA to help a damsel. At least it seemed that way for how often that shit was played out. I hadn't met a man unwilling to help me when I let them know how much I needed them.

Reed grabbed my arm before I could walk through the door. "You are not going back to that club." His gravelly voice was probably supposed to sound commanding. I was sick of this song and dance.

"I am. It's my job to find out what Vincent is up to, right? If he had anything to do with Laura, I'm going to have him begging me to just kill him."

"No you are not." His grip tightened.

"Well, then you better get my friend." I glared. "And I don't mean later, I mean, right fucking now." I yanked my arm out of his hand. "You may have some control over me, but I will do what I need to when it comes to my friends." I strode past him and into the living room. I needed a drink after dealing with all this bullshit. Reed better not test me. I would go back to that club, with or without his permission.

CHAPTER 14

I groaned. What the hell happened? My head was pounding. Could vampires even feel pain? Obviously considering the knife that felt like it was being repeatedly punched into my skull. What the fuck was even happening to me? I lifted my eyelids and instantly threw my arm up to block the light. Why did everything hurt?

"It's the drug. It will wear off in a little while." Reed's voice sounded like it was muted, like he was speaking underwater.

"Drug? What drug?" I mumbled.

"The one I gave you. I knew you would go for a drink so I spiked the rim of your glass. I couldn't very well have you go after Laura and put yourself in danger." His voice was getting a little clearer. I still couldn't sit up. My limbs felt like they were filled with lead. Every part of my body felt heavy. My muscles and joints ached.

"Are you some kind of masochist? What kind of drug does this?"

"It's a special blend made by a witch practitioner friend of mine. She's been very good to me over the years." He made a little hum in the back of his throat after he'd said that. It made me wonder what kind of relationship they'd had. "It will wear off, but the effects are a bit off-putting at first. Try to breathe through it."

"How long have I been out?" I asked.

"Two days." There was a lightness to his tone that infuriated me.

"Two days?" I tried to lift my head, my legs, anything to charge at the bastard. "How the fuck did you keep me drugged for two days? Where's Laura? Where's Shaun? How did no one notice?" I asked.

"Well, the station thinks you skipped town. You might not want to go there anytime soon. The Captain is pretty pissed you skipped out on your cases." I hated how easy going he sounded as he destroyed every aspect of my life.

I felt an angry tear slide down my cheek. "How could you?" I asked through clenched teeth. "I thought you needed me at the station." I didn't understand.

"You wanted to be a Raven. I figured you'd want to focus more of your time on that." I lifted my eyelids to look at the bastard. The light hurt, but it wasn't unbearable.

"Where am I?" I asked.

"In a secure room in the basement. Don't worry, no one will hear you down here. The whole place is sound-proofed." he chuckled. "Well, you know that already. The gym is next door." He stopped and came closer to me. It was still hard to move, and I had a feeling he knew that. He ran his hand up my arm. "It's really a shame you weren't more cooperative. Now, I may need to make things more unpleasant for you." He ran his hand up my bare arm. "I am surprised you never found this part of the house."

"What are you going to do with me?" My head was still spinning, but I knew I needed to focus. I was in some serious trouble here.

"Did you know your parents?" he asked.

"What? No, they died when I was young. It was a car accident. I was adopted." I shook my head. "Why does that matter?" None of this made sense. I hadn't thought of my birth parents in years. A couple adopted me when I was a baby. They explained that they hadn't been able to find any of my family after my parents' death. I was told I was lucky I was so young. Not everyone in the system ends up with a nice family. I hated being told how lucky I was. They didn't know what they were really like. I was the only one who knew their true natures.

"They didn't die in an accident. They were murdered. You would've been next if I hadn't turned you. There are some dangerous supernaturals looking for you." He sighed. "I'm going to keep you safe."

I finally took in the room around me. I was in some kind of box. There was a bed, a toilet, sink, a desk and a chair. I could see through to Reed on the other side. "What the hell is this?"

"I told you. I am keeping you safe." He pressed his hand up against the glass. "Isn't it remarkable. It's a special material. Even with your vampire strength you won't be able to break through it." His self-satisfied smile made me want to vomit. He was proud of his fucking cage.

"You plan on keeping me in a cage, to keep me safe? Are you fucking demented? Let me out of here." I got up, still wobbly on my feet. My hand cupped my head as the world spun around me.

"You better sit back down. You shouldn't be standing in your condition."

"Fuck you," I spat.

"You don't understand now, but you will in time. I will explain everything." He smiled.

"Where's Laura? What happened to her?" I knew without help she was probably dead. With two days lost, there was no way I would find her now.

"She's been rescued. The vampire who took her has been dealt with, I assure you." He scratched his chin. "Too bad they know about you now. I was hoping it would be a little while longer before they came looking for you." He shook his head. "I was hoping we could have become better acquainted before this."

I glared at him. "There is no way you will ever be acquainted with me in that way. You are holding me prisoner." I clenched my hands into fists. I flew up from the bed and pounded against the glass. Any normal glass would have shattered.

Reed smiled, "See, isn't it remarkable?"

"I hate you." I stared back at him. He wasn't going to break me. I vowed that I would kill him. One day, I didn't care if it was against the vampire rules. I would be the last person he saw before his life was over.

"You don't know hate yet. I've only put you in a box. There are far worse things I could do. Remember that." He smiled and walked out of the door.

My fists pounded on the glass. "You can't keep me in here." My screams were met with silence. I dropped to the floor feeling defeated and still woozy. I thought I was a prisoner before. Now, I was in a fucking cage. How the hell did I end up here? Where was Laura? There was no way I was taking his word for it. How did I know she was really safe? Maybe Reed was the one who took her. How many other rooms like this were in the house? I didn't understand any of this. What was Reed's motive? There was no way he was really locking me up for my safety. Who the fuck does that?

I heard a door open. Reed was back, a bag of blood in his hands. "Here, you will need this to recover from the drug." He slipped the bag into a slot and closed it. When he did, it opened on my side. He'd thought of everything.

"Why am I really in here?" I asked.

"I told you. I need to keep you safe." he sounded so reasonable.

"Why can't you keep me safe upstairs?" I asked.

He chuckled. "You threatened to go after Laura if I didn't find her in two hours. You, my dear Hope, are a volatile woman. I cannot have you doing whatever you please. We have an order to things. Progeny are to listen to their sire. If they do not, they are killed. I do not want that to happen to you. So, for now, you are here." He waved his hand in a wide arch indicating the box. "These accommodations will suit you for the time being. I will decide when you have earned the right to your freedom."

"You're really serious." I stared at him. In some demented way, he thought of this as helping me. What world did he live in?

"Of course," he blinked.

"What about Shaun? I was supposed to go to dinner with him." Everything I missed was starting to come back to me.

"Oh, that has been handled. I hired Shaun to protect you. He wasn't supposed to date you. I have rectified that misunderstanding." He ran his fingers over his jaw.

"What does that mean?" I asked. My stomach clenched. Did he kill Shaun because he was interested in me?

"Don't you worry, Hope. I promised I would take care of you. Shaun was right. It is my job to make sure nothing befalls you. I take my job as sire very seriously." There was an edge to his words.

"Okay, psycho." I shook my head. He was seriously insane.

"I will leave you for the night. I have Raven business to attend." He turned.

"Wait, what about Vincent and the club? I was getting close to him. Has he called my phone?" I asked. I thought he might be willing to let me go considering Cassandra knew I was working the case.

"Don't worry, he will still be interested. Even if he has to hunt you down." He smirked before he left me alone again. I glanced around at the "room" I was in. Reed would have been thorough in making this box. I still had to see if there may be some kind of weakness in the design. I started with the seams, looking for any inconsistencies. Nothing.

I had to admire the construction, everything was sealed tight. I could see through the material but it was stronger than glass. I checked out the toilet and sink. There would have to be a hole out to account for the plumbing. I yanked at the sink. It didn't give. How was that even possible? I should be able to pull it free if it were attached with any adhesive.

I tried to push the toilet, but it was stuck, almost as if they were cemented in place. I hadn't tested my strength in any real way beyond training, but I should be able to move both of these. Reed went to great care making this damn cage. How many other women had he kept in here? I sat back on the bed. There wasn't much I could do if I couldn't get out. I made jokes about a damsel in distress. I never actually thought I would be one. Where was Shaun? How was he okay with this?

There was one thing I knew for certain, I would make Reed pay for this.

Chapter 15

It felt like days had passed before the door opened again. "Did you come to let me out of here?" I asked. I was hopeful that I would be able to leave. "People will notice I'm missing. No one is going to believe I just left town." Someone must have noticed I was gone.

"Oh Hope, no one is missing you. It's why you were so perfect for the change. Minus your other gifts, you've estranged yourself from everyone around you. Hope, dear, you made yourself the perfect mark. I only had to charm a few people at the office. Carson was a bit of a challenge, but he came around eventually." He stood in front of the door, the smile on his face made my blood boil.

"What did you do to him?" I asked. He was talking about my partner. I'd owed my life to Carson time and time again. I should have never abandoned him.

"Oh, nothing much, I had to scrub his memories of you. I hadn't realized how long you two knew each other. I may have done a bit of damage in the process." He slid his hand over his chin. "It's no matter. I couldn't have him off searching for you. I needed everyone to forget you exist for the moment. I was hoping I would have more time to ensure your cooperation."

"What does that even mean? I will never forgive you if you've hurt someone I love." I clenched my hands into fists.

"Oh don't be so dramatic. I swore I wouldn't hurt you or anyone you love. I meant it." He shook his head. I hated when he spoke to me like he was appeasing a child. It was then I noticed the laptop in his hand. "I wanted you to see that your friend is fine. She is working in the lab as we speak." He turned the computer screen toward me.

I trudged closer so I could see the screen. Laura was bent over a microscope. Shaun was leaning slightly over her shoulder. I couldn't hear what they were saying, but I could see his lips moving. It looked like they were in the lab adjacent to the examination room. Were they working the case together? A stab of jealousy went through me at how close they were to each other. When he brushed a piece of hair back from her shoulder, I turned away.

"How do I know this is current?" I asked, my voice strained.

"The date and time are in the corner of the camera." He tapped the top of the screen. "You're usually more observant than this. It's only been a few days since you've been in here. Have you lost your touch already? I thought you were a skilled detective." I knew he was bating me. I wasn't going to fall for his games. He stuck me in a fucking box. I was not going to be cooperative.

"So, what do I need to do to get out of here?" I asked. I wanted to know what happened but I also wanted to get the hell out of here. I noticed he was in a pair of black jeans and white t-shirt. It was a far cry from the suit he typically wore out. I could see a small smattering of chest hair under the V-neck shirt.

"Patience has never been your strong suit." He shook his head. "I am going to need some assurances before I let you out of here. As your sire, I do not want you to do anything that could jeopardize your life. Talking about this with anyone would put you on the council's radar in a negative way." He folded his arms over his chest.

"I get it. Don't tell anyone about you locking me in the box." I rolled my eyes. "I can't believe no one noticed my absence. Do I even have a job?"

He chuckled. "Hope, you have yet to accept your gifts as a vampire. You can charm the humans into forgetting your absence entirely. For now, you cannot leave. You are not safe."

"Will you please explain what is actually going on. You mentioned my parents being murdered. How does that connect to me becoming a vampire? Maybe if you tell me, I'll be more cooperative." I wouldn't, but he didn't need to know that. "What has you so dressed down today?" My eyes swept down to his tight black jeans. I had to admit, if I didn't hate him so fucking much, I would say he looked sexy.

He glanced down. "It's my day off."

"I've never seen you in a pair of jeans." My brows furrowed. He should dress down more often. He raked his hand through his hair.

"Are you trying to distract me? It will not work." He sounded so serious.

"No, I was being honest. Are you going to give me the same courtesy?" I asked.

"Fine, where should I begin?"

"Who took Laura?" I asked. It wasn't my most pressing question, but I couldn't believe that she was back at work like nothing happened.

"There is an older coven of vampires here. They had settled in Boston, but came here recently. These men have been tracking a special group of people who immigrated here from Europe. They've been tracking them because they are the only known supernatural to keep their power after the change." His head dropped. "One of the elders of the coven sent a man after Laura. He wasn't one of the elders, so he was inexperienced. It was too easy to track him and save your friend." His eyes lifted to mine.

"So, the evidence Shaun and I collected led you to him." I sat forward in the chair. I should have been the one to find her. She was my friend.

"In a manner of speaking. I already had a good idea where he was when I found the Loup Garou. See, not many know about their continued existence. They've been hunted to near extinction because of their uncontrolled blood lust. When they turn on the full moon, they kill indiscriminately. They have decimated entire towns in Europe, but it has been a long time since they've been spotted Stateside." He clasped his hands in front of him. "That was when I confirmed the redcoats were here. They tend to use the Loup Garou to do their killing since they have no remorse."

"So, how does this connect to me?" I asked.

"You are one of those descendants. It's the reason your parents were killed." He paused, letting the information sink in.

"My parents were supernatural?" I shook my head. Not that I knew for sure. I was a baby when they died.

"The redcoats believe you are an abomination, one that they have been trying to rectify. They believe one of their vampires mated with a witch. It's not supposed to be possible, but crazier things have happened in our world. The descendants of that union have been heavily guarded. The vampire who was involved in the birth, began the redcoats when he learned the baby had been carried to term. Babies rarely survived during that time. The witch had been whisked away for her safety. The vampires didn't believe the child should be born. The witch wouldn't let him hurt her child. It started a war between the groups. The redcoats have been hunting the descendants of that union ever since. It's a miracle you're even here. Your parents did their best to keep your existence a secret." He pressed his lips into a tight smile.

"So, how did you find out?" I asked. This was baffling. I couldn't really be who they were looking for. I didn't have magic or anything. He had to be mistaken.

"I've been keeping tabs on you. The descendants are part of my assignment with the Ravens. We do not wish to start the war again. No one is to know of your true existence. As long as you're a vampire, they shouldn't be able to figure it out." He explained.

"How long have you been keeping tabs on me? I remember you joining the unit a few years ago." I furrowed my brow. It was creepy to think he'd been watching me this entire time.

"Since you were young. I had to make sure you were protected after your parents died." He dropped his head. "I was supposed to be watching them. It's my fault they're dead." His voice was so low, I almost wasn't sure I heard him correctly.

"What?" I asked.

"It's my fault, alright. I was supposed to be their guard. I didn't know the redcoats were here, but it didn't matter. I was supposed to be watching out for them always. I let my guard down and they paid the price. I swore I would not let that happen again." His voice broke.

"So, your answer was to turn me into a vampire." I stood up and began pacing the small room. My head was spinning with all the information he'd just unloaded on me. He's been watching me forever. Like, he knew my parents. I was trying to stuff this all into the evil man that was before me. This couldn't be true.

"I wanted to make sure that if they ever got to you, you would have the strength to defeat them." His eyes sparkled under the lights as he looked up at me.

"Am I the last descendent?" I asked.

"No, there are more. I cannot tell you anything about them. They are protected by Ravens." He furrowed his brow. "You think I would change the last descendent." He let out a laugh. It was such a boisterous sound that I flinched in surprise. "Excuse me," he held out his hand. "You are always so full of surprises."

I continued to pace trying to wrap my head around all the information he'd just dumped on me. "So, there is an old coven of vampires who are here to kill me?"

"Correct, their goal is to kill all the descendants. I am not sure how they discovered your existence. I believe we have a leak in the organization." He nodded.

"Yeah, I think you also have a killer. Unless you were the one dumping bodies." I crossed my arms over my chest and stared at him.

"No, we connected the dumps to the club." One eye narrowed slightly. "Unless you've found something else."

"If you wouldn't have put me in the damn box, maybe I would have told you." I huffed out a breath. "It couldn't have been Vincent, but as Shaun and I told you, the calls pinged near the council. The killer has to be a Raven. That's the only explanation."

"I found Laura with one of the Redcoats. She wasn't with a Raven." He watched me.

"Are you sure they didn't have someone helping them?" I shook my head. "And you said I was losing my touch." I sat back down in the metal chair. "You could have at least given me something comfortable to sit in. How long are you planning on keeping me in here?" I asked.

"Have I not established that I was doing it for your own protection?" He sounded offended. Protection? He was holding me prisoner.

"No, you did it out of fear of repeating your same mistakes. I could have protected myself since I am a vampire. This," I pointed up to the box. "Wasn't because you were protecting me. It was because you were afraid." He glared at me. I enjoyed it. He needed to be called out on his bullshit. I didn't care what the consequences were. No one should be above reproach when it came to telling them when they messed up.

"I disagree."

"Fine, when are you letting me out? I hope you have realized I can help you." I got up and moved to the door expectantly.

"You are still in danger."

"No, I am an asset. If there are people after me, I am more vulnerable in here. I have no way to protect myself. If I am out, I can get to the weapons if I need to. I can also help you find out who the insider is."

"How do you figure you can help?" he asked.

"I can be the perfect bait." I held my hands out to the side, palms up.

He shook his head. "No, no way. You cannot be in danger. I won't allow it." He stood up and strode to the door.

"Come on, you need me. Admit it." I called. He had reached the door.

"I will admit no such thing. You are staying." With that, he closed the door. Leaving me yet again stuck in the fucking box. Damn him, now I was alone with my thoughts.

Chapter 16

I laid on the bed and stared at the ceiling. He could have at least given me access to the light. It was annoying being under the sharp light of the fluorescents all the time. What if I wanted to wallow in darkness. I had a lot of time to think about all of the things Reed said. I wasn't any less creeped out. He had a strange way of showing he cared.

I'd thought back to every time he'd told me he cared about me. It was starting to make sense in a twisted sort of way. Not that I liked being in this fucking cage, but I was beginning to understand the motive. It was what made me a good cop. I understood the bad guys more often than the victims. I wanted to ask my adopted parents about this, but I knew they wouldn't know. Reed was my best chance at knowing anything about my real parents. In some weird way, that was a comfort. He was my chance at knowing who they were.

I heard the crack of the door and footsteps. I didn't move. He needed to see how unaffected I was by his presence. I would not give him the power. He may think he did this to keep me safe, but it was out of his own fear. I hoped he had thought about that and come to his own conclusion. That was the only way I was getting out of here.

"You ready to trust me as an equal yet?" I asked. I didn't move to look at him.

"I brought you blood." I heard the compartment close.

"I think I'd rather starve." I crossed one ankle over the other.

"Hope, you need to feed. You need to keep your strength up." He used the tone that I hated. I may have been a child when he knew me, but I was no longer a child. I would not be treated like one

"No, I don't. You don't seem to need me. As long as I'm in this cage, I don't need anything. Apparently, you've given me everything I need." I clasped my hands behind my head and continued to stare at the ceiling. I refused to look at him until he agreed to let me out of here.

"If that's what you wish, I will leave the blood. You will give in to your thirst eventually."

"I'm a stubborn woman, so I doubt it."

He chuckled. "I can't let you out until I know you're safe. There are still Redcoats in the city. We have been hunting them, but they are proving to be more volatile."

"Wouldn't it be nice if they just came to you?" I asked. I hummed softly.

"I am not going to use you as bait. We will find another way." He sounded almost angry. He was getting frustrated. I loved it.

"Didn't think it would take this long, did you?" I smiled.

"Not exactly," I could hear the frustration again.

"How's Shaun? Is he helping you?" I asked.

"Yes, why?" I'd piqued his interest.

"Just wondering if he's okay with you keeping me caged? Does he even know I'm down here, or did you fill him with some lie?" I smirked.

"He doesn't know you are down here, no."

"Oh? Why not? Is it because holding people in a cage against their will is wrong? I can't imagine he would be on board with this. But whatever. You will realize you need me eventually." I crossed my other ankle.

"Hope, I am trying to keep you safe." He sounded desperate. Good, I bet Shaun was asking questions. Other vampires couldn't be charmed. Cassandra had also given me a case. She was probably asking for status updates. I knew he couldn't keep lying to them forever. He would have to let me out of here.

"You keep telling yourself that. Maybe someday you'll actually believe it." I mocked.

I heard his boots pound up the stairs. Good, I was getting to him. I needed him pissed off. Maybe I was lucky enough that Shaun was here and would see him angry. Would he ask even more questions? Someone would figure out I was down here. Either that, or Reed would realize how stubborn he was being by locking me up.

Another day passed in the box. I hadn't touched the blood, but I wanted to. I had to tamp down my thirst several times. He would not win. I heard footsteps again. I laid down on the bed, crossing my ankles. I wanted him to think I was as relaxed as possible down here.

"You win," he said. I heard the turning of a key and the door swinging open.

I snapped up. "Really? You're letting me out?" I asked. I didn't want him to change his mind, so I flew at vamp speed through the door and up the stairs. He was fast on my trail and tackled me in the kitchen.

"You can't leave the house yet." He held me tight against the floor.

"Hey, Hope," Shaun said. I saw his boots as he stepped closer.

"Seriously? This asshole keeps me in a cage for God knows how long and your response to me is, hey." I struggled against Reed's hold. It was pointless, I knew he was stronger than me.

"Are you going to be good?" he growled next to my ear.

"I wasn't going to leave. I just didn't want you to change your mind and lock me up again." I wiggled my ass, hoping to distract him enough to loosen his grip.

"You swear you are not going to run," Reed asked.

"I swear, now let me up." I pulled on my wrists. He stood. I rolled onto my back and stared up at the two men. "Were you in on this?" I glared at Shaun.

"I knew he was keeping you here. I was not aware you were in a cage." His eyes narrowed on Reed. "A little extreme, don't you think?"

"She threatened to leave. What would you have me do?"

"Um, not lock her in a cage." He shook his head. He held his hand out to me. "I'm sorry, Hope. He's not much of a people person. Something about being a vampire too long. Makes them unfit for humanity. I also believe he forgot how to be a gentleman long ago." He helped me to my feet.

"That's no lie." I brushed off my pants. "So, what's the plan? I assume you were failing without me." I smiled.

"Well, it looks like your ego is still intact so that's good." A coy smile spread up Shaun's lips. "We need you to go back to the club. We believe that Vincent knows something about the redcoats. He may be one of them, or he knows who they are. You're still the only one to have gotten past the doors of the club." He tipped his head to the side. "We asked Laura, but she refused to go back there. I can't really blame her."

"No shit," I glared at them.

Reed poured himself a drink and sat down on the loveseat. He crossed one leg over the other. "We need to go back to Medusa. Get close to Vincent. Cassandra has been calling for updates, and we could only stall her for so long. I need you to focus entirely on him. You have nothing else in your life beyond finding out what he's up to."

I could hear the threat behind his words. The only way I was staying out of the cage was to do whatever he said. At least before, I had the illusion of freedom. Now, I felt like a damn lap dog, doing everything my owner required. My stomach turned at the thought, but I didn't want to be in that damn box again. I would do whatever it took to stay out of there.

"Fine, whatever." I waved a hand dismissively. "I was planning on working the case anyway. You're the one who stopped me." I walked over to the liquor cabinet then paused. Drinking was how he was able to subdue me before, I wouldn't make that mistake again.

"There is nothing on the glasses. You may have a drink." He waved his hand before sipping his own whiskey.

"I don't think I'll take your word for it." I walked over and sat on the couch, as far as I could away from Reed. "Do you mind if I take a shower? There's not much I can do with only a sink."

"By all means. Join us when you are finished."

I glanced at Shaun. I wanted to trust him, but he knew Reed was holding me. How in the hell was I going to get away from these two? Maybe Vincent would be my answer. I left the room. I had to make my own plan.

I stepped into my bedroom after my shower, a towel wrapped around me. A throat cleared. I jumped, the towel dropping to my feet. "I'm sorry, I didn't mean to startle you. I wanted to apologize for listening to Reed. I should have known he was up to something." He walked over and stopped before me. He bent to retrieve my towel and handed it to me. "I believe I still owe you dinner."

"I'm not sure I want to go to dinner with someone who didn't notice Reed had me locked in a cage." I glared at him, securing the towel around me.

"I didn't know anything about that. I thought he'd convinced you to lie low for a while. I thought you knew what was going on and agreed." He looked to the floor. "I'm really sorry for not checking on you."

I could hear his remorse. It wasn't his fault Reed was sadistic. Who would have thought he was keeping me in a fucking cage? "You didn't think it was weird. I hadn't exactly been cooperative the last time you were here. You obviously don't know me very well." I turned away from him and went to my closet.

I pulled down a blouse and felt his presence behind me. "I would like to know you better," he whispered, his lips pressing against the crook of my neck. "How can I make this up to you?"

"I'm not sure you can." He swept my hair to the side. His lips trailed kisses down my neck and across my collar bone.

"Are you sure? I would really like to make this up to you." He nipped my shoulder, and I felt a jolt between my legs. Damn vampire nature had a whole new idea of what was sexy. I hadn't been into biting before. I was now. I could feel the scrape of his fangs against my skin. I wanted more. It felt like every nerve in my body came to life.

"I don't think this is a good idea." I breathed. I didn't even believe myself. I felt his hands on my thighs.

"Have you done this yet, as a vampire?" he asked.

"My first night," I dropped the shirt I'd grabbed. I didn't need clothes. His nails grazed up my skin. He was barely touching me but every part of me was alive under his touch.

"Let me show you how good it can be. Let me make up for hurting you." His nails scored my inner thigh. I shifted my weight, feeling lost under his touch. I wanted him so badly.

"Yes, oh God, yes." I was beyond reason. I wanted him. All of him.

He turned me to face him and captured my lips. His fangs grazed my bottom lip, and I could taste my blood. He latched onto my lip and sucked hard. He ran his tongue over my fang and his blood flowed into my mouth. It was delicious. I hadn't tasted any other vampires beyond Reed. I couldn't believe how amazing it was.

He growled and savored my mouth. Shaun was talented. He knew when to give and take. When he pulled back, he left me wanting, teasing me with his mouth. I gripped his shoulders, making him moan against my lips. The towel had dropped at some point and the chill of the air made my nipples hard. He lifted me into his arms. I wrapped my legs around him as he lowered me onto the bed. He kissed down my body before stopping and staring down at me.

His eyes twinkled in the dim room. "You are so beautiful."

I reached my hands up, begging for him. "Please," I felt bereft in his absence.

"Just let me admire you for one second. Your level of beauty should be criminal." His tongue slid over his bottom lip.

"Now, you're just being ridiculous." I rolled my eyes.

"Oh?" His eyebrow arched. He met my lips and kissed me again, pulling back as soon as I gripped his hair. "Someone is impatient." He chuckled darkly.

I narrowed my eyes. "Someone promised to make a certain discretion up to me." I ran my tongue over my lips.

"Oh, don't worry. I will make it up to you even if it takes all night." He dropped his head, taking one nipple and then the other into his mouth. When he scraped his fangs along the peak, I cried out as unexpected pleasure shot to my core. "You like that?" He did the same on the other side, and I moaned. I didn't know how heightened every sense and touch would be.

He dropped his head between my legs. His tongue stroked and licked. One of my hands was gripped in his hair as the other gripped the comforter. I cried out as my orgasm shot through me. It was unlike anything I'd felt before. He continued to work his mouth and when his fang pierced my skin, another orgasm rocked my entire body. I cried out, unable to hold back as wave after wave went through me.

"Mmm, I like when you lose control," I was sure I was panting. My hands flopped to my sides. "I'm not even close to done with you, He crawled between my legs and lifted me into his lap. He positioned me and slid me down onto his shaft. I moaned at the fullness of him. "Oh God, Hope, you feel so good."

"Yes," I breathed. I was proud that I could still use words. He began moving me up and down on his shaft as if I were weightless. My legs wrapped around him, and I used my legs to speed up. The door cracked open, but I didn't care. Shaun and I were racing to our next release. He felt so damn good inside me.

My eyes caught on a white shirt before I saw Reed's eyes. He had come in and sat down in the chair in the corner of the room. His eyes hadn't left me. When our eyes met, I shivered at the heat I saw there. His hungry look was filled with unbridled desire. His eyes stayed on mine as I rode Shaun's cock.

I didn't think I was into having someone watch. But as we stared at each other, I felt a new wave of pleasure spreading through me. I liked having him watch as his friend fucked me. I could feel the best orgasm of my life building in my muscles.

Reed licked his lips as he pulled his cock out of his pants, rubbing his thumb over the tip. He began moving his hand over his shaft to the rhythm of our thrusts. It was incredibly hot to watch him stroke himself as I fucked his friend. I wanted him to know what Shaun was doing to me. "Oh, God yes, harder, deeper." I begged. Shaun gripped my hips and shifted, going impossibly deep with the new position.

I stared at Reed as I continued to make little noises as Shaun fucked me. I stared at him, defiant. I would never let him inside me. This was as close as he would ever get to fucking me. There were no words spoken between us, but the message was clear. There was something primal about the way he watched me.

Shaun increased his thrusts and a few seconds later my orgasm barreled through my entire body. My head flew back, and I shook in Shaun's arms. He followed shortly after. I closed my eyes and wrapped my arms around Shaun's shoulders as the last quakes rocked through my body. When I opened my eyes. Reed had tucked himself away, but there was a sheen of sweat above his brow. He looked angry, yet satisfied. He stood up and exited the room.

Shaun kissed my shoulder. "Hope, you are fucking amazing." We were both out of breath despite being vampires.

"You're not so bad yourself." He laughed a full bodied laugh that rocked my body and reminded me that he was still buried to the hilt. Damn, I was sated, but a small part of me wanted to do it again. That was the best damn sex of my life.

CHAPTER 17

R eed was in the living room when we'd both emerged, freshly showered. Shaun hadn't been kidding about making it up to me. He held me tucked against him all night. I felt safe in his arms. He was giving me the comfort I'd lost after Reed had locked me away and betrayed my trust. Somehow, Shaun knew exactly what I needed to feel better after that experience. Reed sipped his espresso from one of those impossibly small cups. It was almost comical to see his large hands holding such a dainty mug.

"Please tell me there's real coffee." I moaned.

"Yes, it's in the kitchen as always." He set the cup down on the saucer and flipped another page in his book. His eyes hadn't even lifted from the page. I wasn't sure if he was actually immersed in his reading or trying to act like last night didn't happen. I was completely fine with that. It wasn't something I ever wanted to talk about.

I poured myself a cup of coffee and hopped up onto the counter between the kitchen and living room. "So, I'm going clubbing tonight." I took another drink.

"Yes, you will be going in alone this time." Reed's eyes met mine briefly. "Will you be okay with that?" he asked.

"It's kinda weird to just show up on my own. Most women travel in groups, especially out to a club." I drank my coffee and thought about who I could get to go with me. "You said there's no chance of Laura coming again, right?"

"No, she told us there was no way she was going back there." Shaun leaned against my leg, one arm wrapped around my hips, his finger absently tracing over the swell of my hips. It was too bad I was wearing jeans. I'd like to feel the presence of his hands on me a little more.

"Maybe I could ask her."

"You think she's going to go back with you even though you left her to get taken?" I could hear the absurdity of my suggestion in his tone.

"Why not? I know there are people after me now. I'll take better precautions. Besides, Laura is my friend." I hopped down from the counter. "I'm going to call her."

"I don't think that's such a good idea." Shaun grabbed my wrist before I got very far.

"Is there something you're not telling me?" I looked between him and Reed.

"She's not really happy with you right now. You might want to give her some space."

I furrowed my brow. "Laura always forgives me. This isn't a big deal."

"Hope, trust me. You might want to give her some space."

I rolled my eyes. "Fine, I will go through my phone and see who else I can ask to come with me." I began walking but stopped and turned. "Shit, I can't bring someone who doesn't know about the supernatural. So much for that plan." I glanced at the two men. "You wouldn't happen to have a female friend who already knows about us who would come, would you?"

"I can think of someone." Shaun gave Reed a peculiar look.

"No, you are not calling *her*." Reed growled.

"Color me intrigued, yes, Shaun, please call her." I smiled. "I would love to meet anyone who got Reed riled up." I went to change into something I could wear to the club. I would rather be in my closet at my apartment, but I didn't exactly have that option without alerting Reed to having it. I wanted a place to flee to if he ever tried to lock me up again. I had learned exactly what kind of person Reed was after he locked me in that damn box. He wasn't someone I could trust, ever.

I emerged from my bedroom in a champagne pink satin ruched party dress. The cowl neck hung low and it stopped mid thigh. I heard Shaun's sharp intake of breath from across the room when his eyes set on me. I'd chosen a pair of thin diamond drop earrings. I sat on the couch adjacent to the loveseat where Reed was still sitting. I slid on a pair of rose gold sandals. I secured the ankle strap on the heel, doing my best to give Reed a full look at my shimmering legs. I'd rubbed down my body with lotion to give my skin a nice sheen.

A knock sounded at the door. "That's Alejandra, would you let her in Shaun?"

"Are you planning to disappear?" Shaun rolled his eyes when Reed got up from the loveseat and headed in the opposite direction.

"I believe you two are more than capable of handling this." He waved his hand before disappearing around the corner.

"Oh no you don't." I rose from the couch and followed. "You are introducing me to your friend." I grabbed his arm and yanked. He slipped his arm from my grasp.

"Trust me that is not in our best interest." He pressed his lips together in a tight line.

"Oh, but you are going to do it anyway." I rested my hand on my hip.

"Reed, darling, I know you're here." A melodic voice called from behind us.

I smiled. "See, you might as well introduce us. You are my sire after all. Isn't that your job, to present me to other vampires." I crossed my arms over my chest.

"Alejandra is not another vampire. She's a panther." Reed stalked past me.

"A what now?" I turned, still shocked. "How could she be a panther?" I asked. I followed behind Reed, the curiosity getting the best of me. I stopped in my tracks when I laid eyes on her. She was beautiful. Her burgundy dress plunged between her breasts and looked amazing against her bronze skin. The slim hoop earrings added a nice touch. She looked sexy. Was this one of Reed's exes? That would be amazing. I looked up at her. She had to be six feet tall. Everything about her screamed dominance. She threw her clutch on the couch and brushed her hair behind her shoulder.

"It's about damn time, Reed. I thought you'd never get over that little incident." She tapped her nail against her teeth.

"Little incident? You blew up my Mercedes," he growled.

"Oh, this just got interesting." I strode over to Alejandra and held out my hand. "It's a pleasure to meet you." I smiled.

"I'm sure it is." She scanned me. "You are certainly his type." Her eyes flicked to Reed over my shoulder. "I do love your dress."

"How do you two know each other?" I asked.

"Oh darling, you haven't figured that out yet?" She stepped in front of Reed, running her hands over the collar of his shirt and wrapping around his shoulder. "I thought you said she was a skilled detective. I can smell her curiosity from here. Did you not tell her who I was before you called me?" Her voice stroked at some part of me and a pang of jealousy went through me. I hated it.

She whirled. "Oh, that's interesting."

"Actually, it was my idea to call you." Shaun stepped behind me, placing his hands on my shoulders. I looked over my shoulder at him.

"Oh? And here I thought Reed was ready to work things out." She turned back to stroke her hand over his jaw. "Apparently not, such a shame." She turned back to me.

"Are you really a panther?" I asked. I couldn't help myself. I was new to all of this, and I was curious about how that might work.

She chuckled and even her laugh had a silken tone to it. "Oh darling, I'm a Pantera. We're descended from panthers, but I do not turn into one like those mongrel shifters." She shook her head. "I can't believe he hasn't even taught you the basics, yet." She turned on Reed. "You are an awful sire. I guess it's true what they say about only being good at one thing." She strolled to the sofa and sat down, crossing her legs. "So, boys, do tell me why I'm here. Calling a girl and telling her to wear her party clothes is not enough for me to agree to whatever ridiculous thing you've gotten yourselves into." She stretched her arms across the back of the sofa.

"I thought you could accompany Hope to Medusa tonight." Shaun smiled, his hand squeezing my shoulder. I felt his strength in his touch.

"Okay, why exactly does she need an escort?" Her eyes narrowed on Shaun. "She looks more than capable taking care of herself."

"Maybe I just want to have a little fun." I glanced to Shaun and Reed. "These two are a bore. I need someone who's willing to play. I'm not even sure Reed knows how to dance."

"Mmm, I like her. Okay, let's have some fun." Gracefully, she stood up from the couch.

"The last girl I went with couldn't handle it. Are you sure you're up for my kind of fun?" I cocked my head to the side, studying her. I liked the way she was with these men. But I wanted her to know she wasn't going to railroad me the way she seemed to be able to do with them. Plus, I wanted to know more about blowing up the Mercedes.

"Oh honey, I can handle it." She hooked her arm around mine. "Don't wait up, boys." She strode out the door with me at her side.

When we got downstairs, a car was waiting for us. A tall man in a black suit opened the backdoor. "You have a driver?" I asked.

"Of course, don't you?" she asked, bemused.

"No, unless you count Reed."

She laughed. "You've got Reed driving you around. A girl after my own heart." She ran her hand across her chest. She dipped into the backseat, and I followed behind.

"So, tell me about the Mercedes." I wanted to hear what made her torch his car. Not that it wasn't something I wanted to do, but I wanted to know what her reason was.

"How about you tell me what we're really doing? I don't believe for a second that I'm here for you to have fun. I don't think you know how well I know the two men upstairs." Her eyes bore into mine. I could tell I wasn't going to be able to play this off. Alejandra was a smart woman.

"Oh? I would love to hear more about that." I folded my arms. I wasn't going to give details about a Raven case to just anyone. I had no idea who this woman was beyond Shaun and Reed knowing her.

She studied me. "You're not a Raven yet. You're too newly made. Do they have you doing their dirty work?" Her brow furrowed.

"No, I'm doing my own thing. Someone from the club kidnapped my friend last time I was there. I plan to pay that person a visit and show them just how much I don't like people fucking with my girlfriends. She's a Svanti so she wasn't able to defend herself against them." I crossed my legs and looked out of the window. We'd made it to downtown. Tall buildings stretched on either side of the car as we drove down Marquette.

"Now that's what I'm here for." She stared at me. "Don't lie to me. I know when someone is lying. I will absolutely help you get revenge for your friend. I don't like when men fuck with women. I am absolutely for making anyone who does, pay." There was a danger behind her words. She enjoyed that idea far too much.

Chapter 18

Alejandra briefly paused at the door before the bouncer lifted the rope to allow us in. We didn't even need to say anything. Was that because of her or me? Not like it really mattered. A tall man in a suit coat walked up to us. "You have a VIP suite reserved upstairs." He bowed. "If you'll follow me." He turned and escorted us to the balcony where I'd sat before but this time we were brought to the section alongside Vincent's section.

"Where's your boss tonight?" I asked, nodding toward his private section.

"I am to relay that he will be with you shortly. Until then, everything is on the house." He snapped his fingers and a waitress appeared. "Patricia will get you anything you'd like." He bowed his head again before leaving us.

"Anything?" Alejandra's brow rose.

"Can I start you ladies off with a few cocktails?" she asked, ignoring Alejandra's remark.

"I'm feeling a little frisky tonight. I'll have a Cosmo." I smiled at Patricia. I wondered if any of the workers knew about the disappearances. I thought I'd take a chance and ask. "Were you here three nights ago?" I asked. I should be able to remember, but I hadn't paid enough attention to the waitresses. She wasn't the one who helped us.

"Yeah, I'm here most nights." she nodded.

I pulled out my phone. "Did you see who she left with?" I asked.

The waitress studied the picture on my phone. "He was a tall blonde I think. Handsome, but he had one of those man-buns. I know a lot of guys think they're trendy, but I just think they're weird." She tucked her pencil into her tight twist. All the women who worked here had a uniform. Tight black V-necks and shorts. She had large silver hoops in each ear. I wondered if Vincent picked out every detail of what they wore. I noticed she had silver polish that matched the decor.

Alejandra smiled up at Patricia. "Is he here tonight?"

"I haven't seen him, but I know he's a regular. I can let you know if he shows up." I could hear the steady beat of her heart beneath her perky breasts. I wondered if Vincent would allow me to take anything I wanted from his staff. Was that why she was dedicated only to us?

"I'll take a Cosmo as well. Let us know as soon as he's here." Alejandra purred. I loved the way her voice sounded. Her green eyes reminded me of a black cat I'd had when I was young. I wondered if she could see as well as a cat.

"Will do. Anything else, ladies?"

Alejandra waved her hand dismissively, "No, dear, that will be all." She turned to face me. "So, you've made friends with the owner?" I could see the curiosity sparkling in her eyes.

"Yes, he's like me. He enjoys the finer things in life." I rested against the sofa.

Alejandra nodded. I had informed her about Vincent being a vampire before we entered the bar. I also let her know the name I had used when I was here last time. She'd agreed to help me find out who'd hurt my friend. "Well, a girl could get used to this." She leaned back.

"It's going to take a little more than this to impress me." I crossed one leg over the other. I had a part to play. Alejandra smirked at me. Patricia was back with our drinks in record time.

"Anything else?" she asked.

"What else did Vincent ask you to do for us?" I was curious. I couldn't help it.

"Whatever you asked," she answered immediately.

"Interesting," I smiled. "I think I'd like to dance. Would you like to come dance with us?"

Alejandra cocked her head. She didn't know what I'd done the last time I was here but Vincent did. If he didn't want me to drink from her, he'd be out here to stop me soon. I wanted to know what he was willing to give me. What would he do for me? I needed to know what my limits were with him, but also what he would allow. It would help me gauge if he'd let one of his employees get away with murdering his patrons.

She shrugged. "Sure."

I stood, holding my hand out to Alejandra. "Time to have some fun." Her eyes narrowed slightly. I wondered if she could scent what I was feeling.

We weaved between the crowd until we were in the center of the dance floor. I let the music move me. Alejandra's body moved gracefully as she towered over me in her heels. Patricia swayed with us. She seemed a little nervous but quickly let loose. I wondered if Vincent would be upset that I distracted his waitress.

My hands ran over her curves. "Your boss won't mind that you joined us? I certainly don't want to get you in any trouble." I moved closer to her.

"He said that I was to give you whatever you want." She breathed. I was using my charming ability. My hands ran down her neck.

"Turn around." She did as I asked and I swayed with her against me. I could hear her fierce heart beating beneath her chest. I wanted to taste her. I licked her neck, then sank my fangs into her delicate skin. Her blood tasted divine as I savored a few mouthfuls. I sealed the wound, not wanting to take too much. She may have to work late. "Thank you, Patricia. Will you go watch our table? You look like you need to relax."

She moved away from the crowd and back upstairs. I found another to dance with. I found it unnerving that Alejandra's eyes were on me, watching my every move. Was she going to accost me for indulging in my vampire nature. I licked my lips, wondering what she would taste like. I ran my hands over the chest of the man I was dancing with. He'd been similar to one of the guys I'd danced with the other night. Lost to the euphoria of the dance floor and the energy, I sank my fangs into his neck. I took a swallow and almost coughed. I sealed his wound and wondered what it was that made his blood so vile. My body instantly rejected it.

Alejandra was next to me in a second. "Okay, time to take a little break." She looped her arm in mine and guided me upstairs. My head spun but I managed to stay with her until she sat me down at the table.

I held my hand to my head. "Why do I feel so weird." My words came out slow, like I was drunk. I didn't like the way I sounded. My head felt like I was under water. The pressure was intense. "You didn't happen to do that same thing last time you were here, did you?" she asked.

"Yeah, so?" I mumbled. It wasn't a big deal. Vincent thought it was hot. I'd wanted him so bad after drinking my fill. I asked him to join me but he had to leave.

"So, did anyone else see you?" she asked. Her voice sounded muted. My head was pounding.

"What's going on, why does my head hurt?" I blinked. The light was so damn bright. They needed to make it darker in here.

"I need to get you out of here." She shook her head. "Patricia, can you ask my driver to bring the car around?" I closed my eyes and laid on my side.

"I'm just going to close my eyes for a minute."

"Girl, if you make me carry you out of this club," her words were cut-off.

"Who may I ask, are you?" A man asked. His voice sounded familiar.

"Alejandra, her bodyguard. Who the hell are you?" I could hear the confrontation.

"I'm the man she came here for, I believe I will be taking her with me now." There was a lilt to his voice, like he wasn't from here. I couldn't place it though. It was a mix of a few dialects. That was weird, why would someone have more than one.

"Over my dead body." I heard Alejandra say.

I moaned. "What's happening to me?"

"Nothing I can't fix. Now tell your friend you want to come with me now, Aurora or should I say, Hope." Shit, there was something very wrong here. My head was spinning. Why wasn't he supposed to know that name? Every muscle in my body felt like lead.

"What did you do to me?" I asked.

"I warned you to stop investigating me." His voice was far too close to me. Where was Alejandra? She wouldn't let him get to me, right? Not that I knew her all that well. Maybe this whole thing was a set-up. If I lived through this, Reed was going to kill me.

"So, it was you." I said before everything went black.

Chapter 19

My mouth tasted like metal, my heart pounded like a drumbeat behind my eyes. "Damn, can vampires even get hangovers?" I asked. My eyes refused to open as I pressed my hand to the side of my head, regretting all my life choices in that moment. Whatever I was laying on was soft at least. "Did you put me back in the fucking cage?" I cursed.

"Hmm, who put you in a cage, Hope?" I jolted. I knew that voice, and it wasn't the one I was expecting. I blinked my eyes open. I was in a four poster bed with red satin sheets. What the hell was this?

"No one, what am I doing here?" I asked.

"I couldn't have you investigating me for them." He moved closer to me. There was a glass in his hand with thick red liquid. "Here, this will help."

"Are you serious? You think I'm going to take anything from you." I pulled myself up and sat against the headboard. The room was lavishly decorated and dim. I liked the dimness. My head was pounding. There was a floor lamp in the corner providing the only light. Not that I needed it. Vampire vision was amazing. I could see even better in the dark.

"I am not your enemy." He sat on the bed next to me, pulling one leg up. He held out the glass. "It will help the headache." I glanced down at the glass and narrowed my eyes. I was not about to trust the man who drugged me.

"A headache caused by you. There's no way I'm drinking anything you give me." My eyes shifted down to the glass then back up to him. "Why should I believe anything you say?" I shook my head. There was something I was forgetting. I knew it, but trying to think through the pain was difficult. My thoughts kept scattering anytime I tried to focus by the thrumming pain.

"Because, I'm not the one using you. Who sent you to my club?" he asked.

"I'm not telling you anything." I pressed my lips together. I wasn't going to trust this guy. He drugged me. "How did you drug me anyway?"

"I knew you would go back out on the dance floor. You have a type." He set the glass on the nightstand and stood. He walked over to the window, pushing the black drapes to the side. "If you're not going to tell me, how about I tell you a little story? Maybe then, you'll drink the blood." He crossed his arms over his chest, leaning against the window frame. His lean muscular body took up almost the entire frame and I couldn't help but notice the muscles straining beneath his shirt.

"You can say whatever you want. I'm not going to trust you."

"I think you'll want to hear what I'm going to tell you. It would be nice to know what your sire told you, but considering the comment about the cage, I can understand why you may distrust others." He glanced over to me. I looked down. I was still in my pink dress from the club. I felt exposed in the thin low-cut fabric. The sheet had slipped to my knees and I pulled it up to my waist. I didn't like feeling exposed in front of him. Wait, the club, he took me from the club. Alejandra, where was she?

"Where's my friend?" I asked. I knew other supernaturals had disappeared from his club. She was with me. I remembered her telling him she wasn't going to let him take me. What happened to her?

"Don't worry, she's fine." He waved his hand dismissively, not bothering to look away from the window.

"Like I'm just going to take your word for it. Did she end up in an alley like all the others?"

"Others?" His brow rose as he turned towards me.

"Yeah, there were five people drained of blood after visiting your club. Tell me you don't know about that. You know everything that goes on at your club, right?" I cocked my head to the side as I paused. Waiting for him to deny it. When he didn't I continued.

"One of them turned up dead when you were called away from me on the dance floor. Too bad, I would have had a real good time with you. I was lost to the euphoria of the moment. I can't say you'll have a chance like that again." I looked away from him. He was in a pair of black cotton pants and t-shirt, which he managed to make sexy. He'd definitely dressed differently at the club. He looked more relaxed now.

He lowered his head. "Yeah, I am aware." He sounded bothered. I wasn't going to believe him. Men could just as easily lie with their tone as with their words. He pulled the chair from the corner next to the bed and sat down resting his ankle on his knee. "Have you heard of the Redcoats?" he asked.

"I'm not saying anything to you." I spat.

"Okay, well then allow me. They are an organization based out of Europe. We've been around as long as the Ravens have existed. We were created to manage those who are supposed to uphold the laws. The Redcoats are the ones who make sure those who uphold the law do not break it. We're a sort of checks and balances for the supernatural world. There's a council, just as the Ravens have but we're allowed to work outside of the law in some cases." He paused, looking over at me. Did that mean killing indiscriminately without consequence?

"Sure, so killing innocent people who come to your club is one example of you working outside of the law." I huffed. "What am I even doing here?" I pulled the blanket up to cover my chest. My dress was low-cut and suddenly I felt even more exposed around him. If he was one of the redcoats, he was probably going to kill me. Apparently, he could do that without any worry that it would backfire on him. Speaking of checks and balances, I wondered who watched over them.

"You are here because you were investigating me, when I am the one here investigating your partner along with a few of his acquaintances. I believe someone in the Raven organization is breaking our laws. They are supposed to be better, but I believe they are responsible for the murders of others leaving my club." I could hear the frustration behind his words. He didn't like that people were being killed after leaving his club. Did he feel somehow responsible? "You have been making my job incredibly difficult in that regard."

"Well, it was your mistake to assume I was easy." I glared at him.

He chuckled. "Apparently it was."

"Oh? Do you have anything on Reed to believe he is the one committing murders?" I suspected him too, but I wasn't going to let Vincent know that.

"Not yet, If I did I would have taken swift action. I thought you may have been involved, but I have been watching you. The detective in you wouldn't allow someone to go unpunished for murder. I believe you are just as interested as I am in finding out who the killer is." He paused, his eyes focusing on me. "I feel drawn to you. I have a deep need to protect you that I don't quite understand." his words sounded intense just as his gaze.

"Well, just so you know, for future reference, drugging me and taking me against my will is the opposite of what someone should do if they are trying to protect you. Where did you get your damsel in distress manual, Manson?" I threw up my arms. I was fine. "Can I go?" I asked.

"You need to know what I'm about to tell you. Then it is your choice to leave or to stay." He bowed. "I am a man of my word, Hope." He had me on the hook. I wanted to know if Reed was behind the killings. I only suspected, but couldn't actually say anything since there is a rule against that as his progeny. But if someone else accused him...

"Okay, so get on with it." I was tired of this same story. Reed explained the Redcoats were trying to kill me. Now he was telling me they were the ones who kept the Ravens in check. I understood the need, but who was keeping them in check if they were allowed to go around the laws. This was a backward system if I'd ever heard one.

"We think a Raven is behind the recent murders. I've been assigned to investigate the local chapter. The Ravens are charged with keeping the secret, we're charged with making sure they don't take advantage of their position. Our world needs to trust them. Not many know of our existence. But we were created when one vampire Raven went beyond what was acceptable behavior and used his position to do the unthinkable." He stopped, his eyes focusing on mine.

"Like impregnating a witch." I finished.

"So, you know?" His brows drew together. He looked young in that moment, almost innocent. I clutched the sheet tighter against my chest. Was this the part he told me he needed to kill me to right the balance or whatever?

"Yes, I know." I glared at him.

"We were created to make sure nothing like that happens again. Ravens have unlimited resources and connections. We have to keep them from using their power indiscriminately."

"Is that why I'm really here? What happened to keeping me safe?" I asked.

"What do you mean?" He looked honestly confused.

"You want to kill me to keep the secret. I'm not going to make killing me easy for you." I rested my hands at my sides, ready for anything. I certainly wasn't going down without a fight.

He chuckled. "Kill you? Heavens no, I am here to protect you. I believe that is why your sire changed you as well. You have been a heavily guarded secret, although there are others who have similar secrets." He paused. "If you become one of them, they no longer have to worry about the repercussions. That is until you use your power."

He clasped his hands together in his lap. He looked far too relaxed. I was so confused. Reed told me the redcoats were trying to kill me. Now, he was telling me I was recruited because I was a mistake the Ravens have been trying to cover up. Reed turned me into a vampire to ensure I wouldn't have children. One line would stop with me. Is that the real reason he changed me? My head was spinning. I didn't know who or what to believe.

"Have they recruited you to do a job yet?" he asked.

"You are my job, along with the people who had been found exsanguinated. Did you have something to do with that?" I asked. It was time he told me the truth. I wasn't sure I believed anything he'd told me. He was probably getting me on his good side so he could use me. I wasn't going to be used by anyone.

"No, the person killing is a Raven. They are the reason I'm here. I told you, we police the Ravens. We believe it's someone working outside the organization." He paused. There was one thing I didn't understand. Well, maybe more than one thing, but this one pertained to the case.

"If it's a Raven killing other supernaturals, how is he getting into your club? I thought you forbid vampires from coming in." I was told that others had tried, but no vampires, especially male vampires, hadn't been able to get into the club. So, how could it be a Raven if they weren't allowed. Unless that was their motive. They waited for them to leave the club, then took them. That would explain why Laura thought she was fine and then disappeared after leaving.

He turned, his eyes narrowing. "How do you know about my rule?"

"Because I am helping the Raven's investigate the case." I rolled my eyes. "Would you answer the question?"

"I don't know how he's getting the victims, but they are not getting into the club to do it." His voice was firm and I almost wondered if he was insulted. Served him right for taking me.

"What else do you know?" he asked, his eyes boring into me.

"Only that the phone used was pinged near the council, so I suspect it's a Raven." I crossed my arms. It couldn't hurt to confirm what he already knew. I just wanted to know what exactly I was doing here. "What is the point of telling me?" I asked.

"Do you think it's at all weird how you were recruited?" he asked.

"I thought it was because I was good at what I do." I glared at him. I wanted to hear him deny that. I was a damn good detective. My skills led me to him. Yet, I wondered about what he'd said. Reed could have turned me to stop the line with me. I certainly wouldn't be having children. But, he'd told me there were others. Was the Raven's plan to turn them all into vampires, thereby stopping the line?

"I don't doubt that." He tried to hold back his chuckle but failed. "Ravens don't recruit. They never have. They also don't put anyone in their league out on cases until they've finished at least a year of training after the trials. Yet, here you are, in my club, investigating. Nothing about that situation seems off to you?" he asked.

"I don't know. I haven't been a vampire long. I don't know enough to know what would be strange about that." I leaned back against the headboard. My head still hurt. This was a bit much to think about after being drugged and waking up in his bedroom. I wanted to go home, to my apartment and forget everything, especially every man who thought they were trying to protect me. At this point, they could all leave me the fuck alone. Maybe I was the exception since I was a detective and Reed knew how I worked. There was a first time for everything.

"How did that come about?" he asked.

"I'm not sure I'm ready to tell you anything more. You drugged me. I don't have a reason to trust you." I pulled my knees to my chest and wrapped my arms around them. I was covered with the sheets but I felt exposed. If what he was saying was true, Reed was back to being my number one suspect. Was everything he told me a lie?

I had to admit, kidnapping me from a crime scene and turning me into a vampire had been damn suspicious. I hadn't trusted him either. Especially after he locked me up for my protection. Maybe I needed to get the hell away from here.

"That's fair, what do you want to know? I am an open book." He held his hands out, resting them on his knees. He did look incredibly relaxed. I hadn't known too many people to open themselves up like that.

"Seriously?" I asked.

"Yeah, ask away. I don't actually want to hurt you. I only drugged you so I could get you back here without a fight. I needed to talk with you and this seemed the easiest way. If you drink the blood in that glass, you will feel a lot better. I promise. I am not here to hurt you." He seemed genuine. It was hard to trust someone who'd drugged you. He had to go to some serious lengths to get whatever was in that guys blood.

"You seem different." I took the glass, taking a hesitant sip. What's the worst that could happen? He already had me in his bedroom, or at least I guessed it was his bedroom.

"Yeah, I like to kick back more when I'm at home. I have a certain persona I must attend to in the club. I am playing a role just as you were." He smiled.

"Okay, so, why me and why did you take Laura?" I asked.

"I didn't take Laura. She left with the blonde guy shortly after you did. I didn't know she would be taken by another. That was my mistake." He lowered his head. "I am sorry that happened to your friend."

"Do you know who took her?" I asked.

"Hasn't she been located? I am so sorry. I thought she was found and that's why you were here. I didn't realize you were here to find her. I will send others to search for her now." He stood so swiftly that I blinked.

"No, she's been found. I was trying to figure out who took her. I thought you were involved since she was taken from your club." I took another drink. It was touching that he was ready to rush off and save my friend. It gave me a little comfort that Alejandra was probably okay. I figured she could take care of herself. I wondered what Reed and Shaun were doing. They were probably freaking out after we didn't return. I was surprised they weren't breaking down the door to get to me. Reed was so hell-bent on keeping me safe after all.

He sat back down in his chair. I stared at the strong angles of his jaw. He had the tell-tale flawless skin of a vampire. I wondered at how long he'd been a vampire. That wasn't something I should be wondering about my enemy. I should be figuring out how to get the hell out of here now that my brain seemed to be functioning again. He was right, whatever was in this blood helped. "Thank you for the blood." I looked down across the bed. I still held my knees, but I felt more relaxed than I had earlier.

"It's my fault you weren't feeling well. I won't take such a drastic action next time. After today, I trust you can make your own decisions about me." His voice was cool and confident. I hoped he was right about that. I was sick of being taken against my will.

"So, if it's not someone in the club targeting people, they must be waiting until they leave. If they are a vampire, they can't come in. Are you sure it's not one of your guys?" I asked. I saw the other men at his table the other night. Most of them were vampires. They must be the only ones he's let in.

"It's not one of my men." He said with such finality.

"How can you be certain?" I asked.

"I have known these men for centuries. I trust them. It is not one of them." He looked almost angry at my accusation.

"Okay, so if it's not them, that means it's someone who is watching your club. They have to be targeting you for a reason. Why else would they be killing people who leave here specifically?" I was trying to figure out the motive.

"I'm not sure." He sounded honestly baffled. The man who was so sure of himself a minute ago was questioning himself.

"So, considering it is a Raven, is there anyone who would want to get back at you for something? Was there anyone you accused who could be targeting you specifically?" I asked. These murders had to be connected to him. If they weren't done by someone in the club. "Someone is working awfully hard to connect the murders to your club specifically. Why?" I shifted to drop my legs over the side of the bed. I was feeling better and I had work to do.

"I hadn't actually thought about that." he admitted.

"Well, I'm going to need a list of names of anyone who would want to hurt you." I felt the cold air from the room hit my legs and shivered.

"Most of the vampires we go after are killed. They don't live to hold a grudge." He said that so matter-of-factly that I snapped my head up to look at him.

"Okay, so it's not someone you went after, but it could be their lover or a family member. It's not like you take out their entire family, right?" I scanned the floor for my shoes.

"What are you doing?" he asked.

"Looking for my shoes. I need to go." I stood and scanned the room.

"Wait, what? You can't leave yet." He stepped in front of me.

"You said I could leave after I listened. I did. Now I have to go." I stared up at him. "Are you not a man of your word?" I challenged.

"You are just going to go back with them? What if your sire is the murderer? You mentioned being put in a cage. If he finds out you suspect him, he could lock you away for good." The concern I heard in his words was touching.

"I openly accused him of murder since the day we met. That's not going to change because you told me the murderer is a Raven. News flash. I knew that already. You've given me a new group to investigate but that's about it." I slipped one heel on then the other. I felt like I was about to do the walk of shame even though I had nothing to be ashamed of.

"You what? You know you could die for that accusation?" His brows pinched together.

"I do." I turned, resting my hand on my hip. "Now, if you'll excuse me I have things to do today." I was done spending time with Vincent. I wanted to go back and talk to Reed and Shaun. I planned on coming back tonight and watching the club. I needed to figure out what all of the victims had in common and possibly why Vincent was a target.

"What about the Ravens? The murders? Does nothing I've told you change anything?" He looked perplexed.

"I plan on investigating who has issues with you. It would help if you gave me that list before I leave."

"Don't you think it would be a good idea to work together on the investigation?"

"Not if the murderer is targeting you. They'll be watching you. I'd prefer it if they thought I was another one of your groupies. The sooner I leave, the better shot I have of catching who may be watching you." He was connected to the killer. He must have angered someone over the years. Especially if he could kill indiscriminately. Someone was pissed off over one of his murders. That was the only explanation for why they would be targeting his club.

"Come back to the club tonight. I'll give you the list."

"Fine, but the longer you wait to get me the list, the more people you put in danger." I strode to the door. He used his speed to stop me. "The club is closed tonight. Meet me at the back door at seven." His eyes darkened. He ran his finger down my arm. "I would like to get to know you better."

"Maybe you should have thought of that before you drugged me." I cupped his face before giving it a light slap and striding out of the room.

CHAPTER 20

I walked into Reed's apartment. Both Shaun and Reed turned wide-eyed at my entrance. "Where were you?" Reed demanded. He'd gone from relieved to pissed in two seconds.

"I'm glad you're okay." Shaun closed the distance between us and wrapped his arms around me. I felt warm in his embrace. I looked over his shoulder and noticed Reed tense when our eyes met.

"Where's Alejandra?" I asked. Vincent said she was okay, but I didn't believe him.

"Her driver brought her home a little bit ago. He said she was brought out to the car, unconscious. He wasn't allowed to go into the club. His job was to protect her so he brought her back here hoping we could put the pieces together." Shaun explained.

"Good," I breathed a sigh of relief knowing she was okay.

"So, what happened to you."

"Oh, the usual, another guy swearing he's trying to protect me by drugging and holding me hostage." My eyes met Reed's, and I noticed him flinch before he schooled his features into its normal mask. "If you'll excuse me, I need a shower."

"What? You need to tell us what happened," Reed growled.

"I need to shower. You can wait." With that, I strode past the men and went to my bedroom. I needed to think about what Vincent had said without an audience. The Uber ride over had been short and I wasn't ready to start answering all their questions yet. I wasn't sure how much I was going to divulge considering the insight Vincent had given me into the Ravens. I didn't know who I could trust, if anyone. I wanted to go talk to Laura. She would be the person I'd confide in when I was having life issues.

I sighed. How sad was my life that my only real friend was my colleague. I'd lived my life for my job and in a few days, Reed had completely ruined that for me. He didn't know how much I'd put into my work, or he didn't care. It was probably the latter. I was growing more hateful of him every day. What if Vincent was right? What if Reed made me to stop the line? What if I was only being recruited because of whatever mysterious power I obtained from the witch line? I had no idea what to think about that.

I stepped out of the dress and under the hot shower. I needed to cleanse my thoughts and get to the bottom of everything. I needed to find out the truth, but I had no idea who to ask. I planned on questioning Reed but I had to be careful. Reed was volatile and I would not end up caged again. I would run before he even thought about it. Being an outlaw vampire couldn't be as bad as being a locked up one. I didn't even know the rules, but I'd bet it was death. All of their laws seemed to carry the sentence of death if broken.

I knew I'd spent too long in the shower when Shaun was waiting for me in my bedroom. "Can I help you with something?" I asked. I didn't mind his interruption last time. I especially liked the apology he'd made. But today I wasn't in the mood. I needed time to think alone.

"I just wanted to check on you. Make sure you were okay." He dipped his head submissively. I wondered if Reed sent him in here knowing I would be more open with him. I was starting to believe that every part of my life had been calculated by someone else.

I remembered how I was almost pushed into the academy. I was reluctant, but then one day, all I wanted was to be the best detective. Was that because I was charmed into it? Did Reed plan all of my life without my knowledge? I needed answers that I was sure he'd never give. I needed to find a way to get Reed to trust me enough to tell me everything.

"I'm fine. I will join both of you as soon as I am dressed." I turned away from him and toward my closet. A memory of the last time here filled my thoughts, but I pushed it away. I was not going to be distracted today.

"Okay, Hope, we're here for you." His voice was soft and reassuring. He may be telling the truth about himself, but I didn't believe the same applied to Reed. I was starting to think of him more as an enemy than an ally.

I slipped into a form-fitting black dress. This one had lace around the neckline and around the bottom. It was an off the shoulder dress. I put in simple diamond studs and a silver chain. I planned on going back to the club tonight, but I wanted the two men distracted enough to tell me what I wanted. After a little make-up I went down the hall to meet the boys. They were sitting on the sofa and loveseat, their heads bowed in quiet conversation. It ended abruptly when I strode into the room. "What were you two talking about?" I asked.

"You of course, come have a seat and fill us in on what must have been an eventful evening. You mentioned you were drugged?" There was a subtle anger behind Reed's words.

"Angry that it wasn't you who got to drug and hold me against my will this time?" I mocked. I was tired of him thinking he owned me or some such nonsense. I was done playing by their rules. At this point, I didn't give a fuck what they did to me. Apparently I was valuable alive so I planned to use that information. I had power that they wanted. Why else would I be the only person ever recruited. I'd read between the lines. Everyone seemed to want me for my power.

"No, you are my progeny. Anyone who wishes you harm will be dealt with by me." He threatened. "Was it Vincent?" he asked. I knew he was itching to get something on him to have reason to take him out. I figured that's what I was there for in the first place. I wondered if Reed knew Vincent was actually investigating him and the other Ravens. It put me in an interesting spot between the two.

"No, he didn't hurt me. He actually offered to help me find the person who'd hurt Laura. I assured him that matter had already been dealt with by you." I relaxed down on the couch next to Shaun, crossing my legs.

"He offered to help you?" There was surprise in Shaun's voice.

"Yes, he is here looking for the same people we are. I suspect that the person killing other supernaturals after they leave his club has a vendetta against him for something he'd done in his past. I won't divulge the details he entrusted with me, but I am meeting him tonight to collect a list of names of people who may be involved." I paused.

"You are not going there again. You said he drugged you and held you against your will. I will not have you harmed by another vampire. What if he is part of the Redcoats? It could be a trap to kill you once and for all." Reed's words were rushed. For a minute, I wondered if he actually cared about my well-being. He sure put on a good show.

"Vincent is no threat to me. I'm not going to let your petty jealousy stop me from solving these murders. You've already ruined my reputation at the office. I will find out who's behind these killings. I owe it to the families of the victims." I crossed my arms over my chest. I had to be careful. Reed still had that stupid box downstairs. I wasn't exactly free of his command just yet. I still needed to follow him in some respects. "I am the only one who can stop these murders. Vincent trusts me. He will help me find out who's behind this." I waited for the men to object.

"Are you sure he's not using you?" Reed asked. "You have a tendency to trust the wrong people." There was a spark in his eyes.

"Are you referring to yourself?" I narrowed my eyes at him. Reed was always such a conundrum. I thought he was joking, but I never could be sure.

"You have to admit. You have trusted more than one vampire you probably shouldn't have. Are you absolutely certain he is not using you for information or trying to get you away from the protection of the Ravens?" His mouth was pressed into a hard line as I processed the information.

"Am I under the protection of the Ravens? I am not one yet." I glanced over to Shaun, unsure of how much he'd known. I had done an excellent job at keeping the information about Cassandra hiring me to do this job away from everyone. Had he told Shaun?

"Normally no, but being my progeny comes with certain perks." He crossed his leg, resting his ankle on his knee. I could see that he'd put on another of his tailored suits today. Was he planning to go to Cassandra if I hadn't come back?

"Okay, let's pretend that's true. What exactly do you plan to do?" I asked. Considering he looked like he was ready to make a trip to the council, I thought he might actually be on his way to help me. That would be a first.

"I was going to alert the council about your disappearance. I planned to get a team together to raid the club." I knew he was just looking for a reason. He put me in danger to get the council to act. Was that the same with my change? Reed had given me reasons for why he wasn't the murderer we were looking for, but I still wasn't so sure. He didn't have an alibi for his whereabouts during any of the murders.

"Well, now you have me. I told you I would get Vincent to trust me. I am good at what I do." I squared my shoulders and gave Reed a self-satisfied smile. I liked rubbing in that I'd gotten what he wanted. "I am meeting him tonight. I will need a list of Ravens who would have been in the area when Laura's phone pinged. I know you said you got the guy who took her, but I believe there is more than one person involved." I glanced next to me. Shaun was waiting patiently. "Can you get me that list? I know how skilled you are at getting information off of your computer." I cupped his face and drew closer to him.

"Yeah, I can get the information." He nodded.

"I do appreciate it." My eyes flicked to Reed. His jaw was tense. I smirked before I leaned in to kiss Shaun. It was a slow and sultry kiss. I wanted to see the jealousy in Reed's eyes. I needed to see where we stood and how much I could manipulate him. I also liked the feel of Shaun's lips on mine.

He didn't hesitate. He wrapped his arms around my waist and pulled me closer. I stroked the hair at the nape of his neck before pulling away, my cheeks flushed. I bent my head low and blinked up at Reed. He glared at me. I only gave him a shy smile in return. Two could play at his manipulative tactics. I planned to win this round.

"What can you offer to help, Reed?" I asked. Shaun would get me the names to investigate. Vincent would help me narrow down the list to who may be targeting him. I was wondering what Reed's role was going to be in all of this.

"I'm going with you to meet Vincent," he growled.

"Vampires aren't allowed in the club." I hadn't expected that.

"As my progeny, it's customary to meet the men you are seeing. They must ask my permission before courting you. Vincent knows the rules. He will have to let me accompany you." He folded his arms over his chest. Another time he didn't give me all the information. I wanted to throttle him.

"You are going to ruin everything." I glared at him.

"No, I am simply your escort." His voice drawled.

"The club isn't even open tonight." I snapped.

"Well, then your new lover should have made his intentions known. I will confront him about it at our meeting tonight. What time did you say we're expected?" I wanted to punch that smile off his handsome face. He'd let the hairs around his mouth grow a little longer and he looked damn sexy with the dark hairs lining his bronzed face. He was sexy and I wanted to pummel him. Would our relationship ever be normal.

"Reed, you can't go with me. I will get more information if I am alone."

"But it would be unfit of me to let you go into another vampire's home alone. You do not understand our customs." The side of his mouth quirked up.

I glanced to Shaun. "Is he serious?" I asked.

"I'm afraid so. As long as he is your sire, until he grants you freedom, any men who are interested have to ask his permission." Shaun lowered his head.

"Did you?" I asked.

He nodded in confirmation. "I did."

My eyes widened. "So, you have both been using me this entire time." I flew up from the sofa. I'd made it to the door before Reed's body pressed against me. He held me firm against the door.

"Where do you think you're going?" He growled.

"Out, I need some fucking air." I spat back.

"You can't go anywhere. We need to plan our outing this evening." His lips brushed against my ear. The more time I spent in this world with him, the more I hated him. I vowed to get my freedom as soon as fucking possible. As soon as I thought of him as sexy, he destroyed it with his possessiveness.

"You know, most women don't like to be considered someone's possession. Maybe your vampire society needs to get with the times. Nobody owns me." I fired back, turning my head so I could see his eyes.

"It would be the same if you were a man. It is not about your gender." He released me.

"So, it's about possession. Great, my point is still valid." I pushed off from the wall and went into the kitchen. I needed coffee to deal with all this bullshit.

"You might want to rest up. It sounds like it's going to be a long night." Reed smirked.

"I could say the same to you. Too bad we don't have that luxury. I believe we have some planning to do. Shaun, would you be a dear and go get that list. I have some things I need to work out with my sire before tonight." My voice was like honey, but I hoped he heard the veiled threat beneath my words.

"I'm on it. I'll be back as soon as I can." He jumped up from the couch and went for the door. Obviously he understood what I needed. Shaun was good in that way. He understood me. That was more than I could say for Reed.

"No rush. I'm not meeting Vincent until seven." I took another sip of coffee. Reed and I were going to settle a few things before tonight. I could tell by the smirk on his face he knew exactly what I had in mind.

Chapter 21

I squared off with Reed. "Meet me in the training room in five minutes."

"Why not now?" He stood, a smirk on his face.

"You want me to kick your ass in a dress. Fine," I changed directions and went for the basement. I hadn't been down here since he'd locked me away. I hadn't planned on coming down here for a long time but I needed to clear some things with Reed. I'd learned the only real way to get anything across to him was through battle. I probably wouldn't win, but I would go down kicking, and that earned Reed's respect far more than anything else.

I stopped in the center of the training room and took a fighter's stance. He casually walked in, a swagger to his step. He was in his tailored suit, but slipped the jacket off and laid it on the bench near the door. "Is there something we need to discuss?" His voice piqued with interest. He loved a good fight, and I planned to give him one.

"Yes, I need to go alone tonight. What is it going to take for you to let me do that?" I squared my shoulders, holding my hands at the ready.

"You think we are going to settle this in the training room. Let me enlighten you. There is no way I am letting you go alone tonight. It would not be proper." He stepped onto the mat, stopping a few feet from me. He still hadn't looked like he was ready to fight me, but I knew he would counter anything in a second.

"Vincent is not going to talk openly with you there. He trusts me. I had to build that trust. I can't have it threatened by your damn male ego." I lunged forward, my fist connecting with air as I went for a jab to his side. He'd moved so quickly, I stumbled when I hit air.

"It's about time you become the aggressor. I see you have learned a few things from your last fight." His lip curved up but he still looked as relaxed as ever. I circled around him, yet he still didn't move. I balanced on the balls of my feet, attempting not to make a sound so he wouldn't hear my next attack. I dipped down, sweeping my feet out to kick him down. He simply leapt out of my reach and turned to face me. His shoulders were still relaxed. He was getting on my damn nerves. I grabbed down one of the swords we practiced with. If he was going to be an asshole, I was bringing weapons into our skirmish.

"I have learned many things from you. Many of them I shouldn't have learned." I jabbed the sword forward, aiming for his abdomen. He dodged, and grabbed down his own blade.

"So, you believe me to be an unfit sire? What exactly do you plan to do about it?" he mocked. I hated how his tone boiled my blood. He knew there was nothing I could do about it. Not until he granted me my freedom. At least with this case, I could earn my freedom through the Ravens. He'd given me that much. He said it was because he cared but everything he'd done caused more pain. I wasn't sure how he thought he was a good man. Maybe he didn't think that. Maybe that was my hope for him that he could be, if he cared enough to try.

"Do you even consider yourself a good man?" I asked. His eyebrow rose at my question. "You tell me that you blame yourself for my parents death, and you say you turned me to save me, but the only thing I have felt because of you was heartache and pain. What has been good about anything I've experienced since the day we met?"

I wanted to distract him. He honestly looked lost in thought. I lunged, using the distraction. I plunged my sword into his side and he gasped. I yanked the blade back. Triumph spread through me at the shocked look on his face. "Now you have some semblance at what I feel every time you do something for me." I glared.

He clutched his side for a second, then held his sword out again. "A man such as me could never be considered good, Hope. I am sure you are aware of the numbers of men I've killed. Good is not something I aspire to be."

He parried my next blow and metal clashed against metal. I knew he would not make another mistake with me. His guard was up and we continued in our dance, swords clashing until my forehead was slick with sweat. I felt triumphant no matter what happened. I wanted him to think about all the pain he'd put me through. He said he turned me to protect me, but he was the one I needed protecting from.

"I am going alone tonight." I ground out between clenched teeth as I held his blade back from my throat.

"No, I will be accompanying you." He fired back.

I threw his sword off me and went on a full attack, metal clanging against metal. I used my frantic movements to throw him off balance. I dropped and swung my legs around, dropping him to the mat on his back. I held my knife against his throat. His sword had fallen when he'd landed. I was surprised at how easily I'd taken him down. Unless he let me. "I am going alone." I dropped the sword next to his head and stalked out of the room. I was done arguing with him.

He flew at me. His entire body pushed me against the wall. He turned me around to face him, our bodies flush against each other. The trim of the door bit into my back. He grabbed my hands and held them above my head with one hand. "You are mine."

I narrowed my eyes on him. "No, I am mine. You may have changed me against my will, but I will not be owned by another. You know that to get information tonight I have to go alone. This bullshit claim you think you have over me needs to end. I am not a woman who will accept ownership. If you want me to listen, you should try asking." I held his gaze. I was tired of him thinking I was his property. I didn't know what era he was from, but I was my own woman. "Didn't your mother ever tell you that you get more flies with honey than vinegar. You should try being nice. It will get you much further with me. Now are we going to work as a team, or am I going to have to stab you again?"

I saw a flicker of respect and frustration in his eyes. He wasn't used to people pushing back on him. I wondered how many people listened to his bullshit. I was sure he'd manipulated a number of people in his lifetime. I wasn't going to be one of them. I deserved respect. He was going to give me that.

"Fine, I want an update as soon as you have anything new." He shook his head. Holy shit, I won. I smiled as a feeling of elation rushed through me. I didn't really think before my lips crashed into his. The minute our lips touched, a fire erupted inside of me and I clutched him closer. He kissed me with a hunger I hadn't felt with anyone else. It was like we needed the other to breathe.

My hands gripped his hair as he pressed his body against me and the wall. His hands gripped my hips and I wrapped my legs around him. I could feel his erection press against my core. My dress had ridden up, exposing me to the cool air. I ran my hands down his muscled arms as our tongues danced.

It took a few minutes before my mind caught up with what was happening. I felt like my body was on fire and he was the only thing that could quench the fire. But this was wrong. My rational brain knew that, but the animalistic part of me wanted him to take me against this door, right now. I dropped my legs to the ground and went stiff under his touch. He backed away, his eyes searching mine. "We can't." I breathed.

His eyebrows slanted down. "Why not?" He honestly looked confused at why I stopped.

"Because I don't trust you. I can't give myself to someone I don't trust." I pushed him away from me and he let me. He nodded and stepped further away.

"I will earn your trust again, Hope." He bowed his head and moved around me and up the stairs. I wasn't sure that was true, but at least he'd agreed to let me go alone. I needed to get my plan together before tonight. I also needed to speak to Laura. She was the only person I felt like I could confide in. But first, I needed to ask her forgiveness. Something I wasn't especially good at doing.

I knew Laura would be at home. She didn't have to go to work for a few more hours. I felt bad that I might be waking her, but I needed to talk to her. I knocked on the door and was surprised by how fast it opened. Laura jumped back as if startled to see me. "Hey, can we talk?"

"Ah, yeah, come on in." She held the door open and I walked through. I was a bit uneasy, but Laura and I both believed in the importance of burying the hatchet sooner rather than later. She would respect me more since I came to her.

"I wanted to apologize for leaving you the other night and everything that happened as a result." I bowed my head, staring at the white linoleum floor. "I wanted to come sooner, but Shaun said I should give you some time." I cocked my head to the side. "That and Reed decided to lock me in a box for a few days."

"Wait, what?" her eyes were round as she stared back at me.

"Yeah, it's kind of a long story. I came here as soon as I could. I am so sorry. I don't know the details of what happened to you, but I never should have left." I stopped, looking her in the eyes. "Can you ever forgive me?" I asked.

"Yeah, I can forgive you. I was the one who told you I'd be fine. It was stupid to go home with a guy I met at a club." She shook her head. "It would have been nice to know that you were there for other reasons though. I would have been a bit more guarded." She glared at me, resting her hand on her hip.

"Yeah, I deserve that. I thought you figured it out when I used a fake name." I bit my bottom lip.

"I knew you were up to something, but I didn't know we were in danger. You should'a gave a girl a heads up, ya know." She shook her head and made her way over to the red couch. Laura was an interesting individual.

"I know, I should have told you everything." I walked over and sat in her oversized gray chair, flinging my feet up on the matching ottoman. I loved relaxing at Laura's. It felt like forever since I'd been here.

I could hear the scratching of Laura's dog on the other side of her bedroom door. "I locked her up in case it was someone else. You know how yippee he can be." She rolled her eyes before opening the door to let out her Jack Russell terrier, poodle mix. He had curly black hair and dark eyes. She named him Cass after the angel in Supernatural. Laura had random artifacts around her house, including the famed Chevy Impala replica.

"He's just protecting you." Cass ran to me and I scratched behind both ears. I loved her dog. He was so chill. As soon as he got some lovin' he laid down at my feet. I thought he was adorable, but she had adopted him because she thought no one would. Most people went for cute labs or golden retrievers. Cass was a shaggy looking pup. I knew there was more to him.

"Yeah, I wish he'd stop protecting me from all the squirrels." She plopped back down on her couch, tucking her feet beneath her. "So, what are your plans for the day? I know you didn't just come over to apologize." She clasped her hands together, waiting.

"Well, I needed someone to talk to who I can trust. I've learned a whole lot of information and I need help sorting it all out. I need someone analytical like you." I bit my lip. Laura had always been my go-to when I had something to work out.

"Alright, what's going on?" she asked.

"Well, where do I even begin?" I looked down at Cass before dumping everything on her. The fact that Reed was supposed to protect my parents, what I'd learned about the Redcoats, not being sure which side is actually trying to eliminate me, including the story about my supposedly being descended from a vampire and a witch. I unloaded it all on her. I should have probably been concerned, but I trusted Laura implicitly. "So, needless to say, I have no idea what to do next." I sat back on the chair after I'd told her everything. I appreciated how Laura sat back, listening intently to everything I said to her.

"Okay, so you have to meet with Vincent tonight. Are you absolutely certain he's not behind the murders?" she asked.

"I guess not. I don't know why he would want to attract that kind of attention to his club." I pondered. "I had been out of it for who knows how long. He was gone every time a murder was committed. I could say the same for Reed. Not one of his supposed alibis has checked out. For now, it could be anyone." I huffed out a breath. "How am I going to find the killer?"

"You're going to do what you always do. You're going to devise an amazing plan to trap them. You know you're good at what you do. It's how you got in this mess in the first place." She sounded so sure of me. I wished I felt the same.

"I'm not so sure that was the reason, but I like it. Let's go with that." I rolled my eyes and she laughed.

"Have you thought about setting a trap? Let the guy who's watching Vincent know you are important to him. Get Vincent to go along with it. If it's true that whoever is killing these people are doing it to go after him, they'll jump at the chance to get to you." She folded her arms across her chest. I recognized her self-satisfied look.

"That could definitely work. How many other girls have gotten the special treatment I have at the club. Plus, we have a date tonight. As long as the person after Vincent is watching, it could be the perfect set-up." I flung myself next to Laura and kissed her cheek. "Have I told you how much I love you?" I kissed her again for good measure, Cass barking at my sudden excitement. I bent down to ruffle his fur.

"I have to call everyone. Shaun and Reed will need to be on the lookout for my date. I'll be the bait and they can look out for anyone suspicious." I clapped my hands together. I knew Laura would help me figure this all out.

"Don't forget me." She stood up from the couch.

I shook my head. "No way, you are not getting involved again. I don't know all the details about what happened last time, but I am not taking any chances. You are staying out of this."

"Hope, you don't know all of my gifts. I have the ability to heal other supernaturals. You may need me if you get hurt." She rested her hand on her hip. There was no way in Hell I was putting her in danger.

"That may work with another Supe, but I am self-healing. You are staying here, or working the cases from your lab. You are not coming with me tonight. I may need you to run some tests on the evidence. I do not need you putting yourself in harms way again." I shook my head.

I could see the stubbornness behind her eyes. "Hope, I could help."

"Laura, you already have." I rested my hands on her shoulders. "Now, get some rest. I may need you in the office tonight." I kissed her cheek before leaving. I loved Laura, but there was no way I was letting her get hurt again.

Chapter 22

Reed glared at me as I slipped on a new dress. He was supposed to be waiting for me outside, but he'd been arguing with me and chose to follow me back as I slipped on another dress. I wanted to look spectacular but I also wanted to be able to hide weapons under my dress. That meant I needed to wear something a little less form-fitting.

I'd already alerted Vincent of my plan for luring out the possible murderer. If it was either of these men, they would have put up a fight. Either that or they would go along easily knowing I wasn't in any danger. Both of them fought with me on it, but in the end I won. Well, I won with Vincent. I was still fighting with Reed.

"Listen, I already told you that you need to be with Shaun outside of the club. The plan is to lure the murderer to me, but I will need back-up, even with all your training sessions." I rolled my eyes as I adjusted the straps of my new dress. I'd chosen to wear a burgundy off the shoulder flair dress. I could strap any weapons to my thighs without anyone noticing. I slipped on my black strappy heels and grabbed my purse. I could hide my firearm in my purse. I had three weapons strapped to my person.

Reed watched as I armed myself. His muscular frame took up the doorway as he leaned against it. It didn't even bother him that he'd followed me to watch me dress. On the other hand, he watched me fuck his best friend so this wasn't a big deal. I still had on my black lace bra and panties. I hope he enjoyed the show.

"I don't like not being with you. If you're going to make yourself bait, I should be there." He folded his arms over his chest. The fire behind his eyes was more about his desire than his anger. I bent over, applying my lip-gloss. I glanced at Reed staring at my cleavage through the mirror. I thought back to what happened in the training room. I felt my cheeks flush. It was hard not to think about how he'd kissed me. How hungry we both were as we'd ravaged each other.

My brain told me I needed to block all of that out, but with him looking at me with heated eyes, it was hard. I got wet just thinking about his hands gripping my thighs, taking me. It was good I'd stopped it. I couldn't have sex with the man who insisted on controlling me. That wasn't who I was and he needed to understand that. I would not give myself to someone who thought of me as their possession.

"You will be there. You will be in the car watching my back. I need your keen observation skills to search out whoever might be watching Vincent. I won't be able to because I will be the one they are watching. My life depends on you figuring out who it is." I ran my hands through my hair before I turned to face him. I closed the distance between us and looked up at him through my lashes. "Please, don't fight me on this. I need you."

He sighed. "Fine, I will be watching. I won't let anything happen to you." His eyes closed and his head bowed. Was he being submissive to me?

"Thank you," It was nice to not have to fight about every little thing. He was actually letting me win. Maybe he'd seen the error of his ways. I doubted it. Maybe he was just realizing that my way was better.

I strode into the living room just as Shaun was coming in. He whistled. "You look amazing!" He lifted me and turned me in a circle before kissing my cheek and setting me down.

"Someone's in a playful mood." I laughed. I wasn't used to seeing Shaun this free and it lightened my spirits after having to fight with the other two men who were currently in my life. I actually had butterflies in my stomach for my date with Vincent. Somehow I got to spend my time with three very attractive men. I wasn't opposed to this turn of events.

"I got the list you asked for." He pulled out a folded up piece of paper and handed it to me. "Now you can compare it to Vincent's list to figure out our murderer. I always love a good mystery." He beamed.

"You are so weird. I guess that's why you got into criminalistics." I smiled.

"Yeah, I like the science part of investigations but it's fun to also be involved in solving the case beyond the evidence. Usually I just collect evidence and pass it off to the detectives. This is one of the first times I've been included." He sat down at the table after pouring himself a cup of coffee.

"I thought you've been doing this for a while. No one else asked you to work with them on a case? What about your work as a Raven?" I was surprised. On the other hand, I guess I didn't always ask the crime techs their opinions about the evidence. I just ran with whatever they gave me. Shaun seemed to be a first for me, too. It might be that he is also a vampire.

"I'm asked about cases that may link to the supernatural. I don't actually do any investigating for them. I am one of their inside men who helps make sure the supernatural world stays hidden from humans." He paused, scratching his chin. "Could you imagine what humans would do if they found out about us? We'd either become lab rats because they would want to know how to become immortal, or it would start a full-on war."

He shook his head. "There's a reason we need to keep the secret and why there are Ravens in every city. If word got out, we'd be fucked." He took a casual drink of his coffee. I hadn't actually thought about what would happen if others found out. I just knew I didn't want anyone to find out about me. Yet, most of the people I knew were also supernatural. With Carson as the exception. I wasn't entirely sure how he'd react.

"So, you ready for tonight?" I asked.

"We're the lookouts. I have images of all of the men on the list for Reed and I to scan through. We'll make sure no one gets to you tonight." He stopped, his eyes lifting to meet mine. "I actually think this is a brilliant plan."

"Thank you, I can't take all the credit. Laura helped." I sat across from him at the table, my hands wrapped around my own mug. There was something comforting about having a warm mug of coffee. Like all your troubles melted away with each blissful sip.

"Great, so you two made up then?" He waited.

"Yeah, Laura and I have been friends for a long time. I knew she would forgive me." I took another drink from my mug. I loved how the hot liquid felt going down my throat.

'Did you say she was coming with us tonight?" he asked.

"No, she tried to convince me that she could come along because of her healing ability, but I told her we needed her in the lab in case any more DBs came in. She reluctantly agreed." It wasn't an easy sell. Laura could be as stubborn as me.

"So, what time are we leaving?" he asked.

"As soon as Reed gets his ass out here." I stood. He should have joined us already. "I'll go get him. I'm supposed to meet Vincent at the club at seven. I'm already going to have to deal with traffic."

I hurried down the hall. Reed must have gone to his room after fighting with me. I opened the door and he was standing there with a towel wrapped around his waist. Water slid down his toned chest. I licked my lips at the sight of him. The thin towel barely latched around his waist. I followed the dark trail of hair that disappeared beneath the cotton. He was damn sexy. I knew I'd been gawking for too long when he smirked.

"Like what you see?" he mocked.

"I was wondering what was taking you so long. I have to meet him at seven." My voice came out weaker than I meant it to. I was too busy drinking in every bare inch of him. It was one thing to see his muscles in the workout room when we were sparring, it was quite another to see him in his bedroom. I really needed to pull it together. It's not like I was lacking in the sex department. I thought back to him stroking himself as he watched Shaun and I together. My cheeks flamed and I swallowed hard. The smile never left Reed's face.

"I needed to change." he turned back to his bed. His entire ensemble was laid out on the bed. He glanced up to me before dropping the towel. I wondered if he was waiting for my reaction. I took in every square inch of him. He seemed to be into watching me so it was fair play that I got to watch him. "Are you planning on staying?"

"I figure a little tit for tat is in order, so yeah. I think I'll watch you for a change." I folded my arms over my chest and leaned against the doorjamb just as he had done earlier while I changed. If it didn't bother him, I wasn't going to let it bother me.

He chuckled, and continued to get dressed. He didn't seem even the least bit bothered. Not that he had anything to be bothered by. He was perfect, well, perfectly fuckable anyway. When he slid his tie around his collar, I closed the distance between us. "Here, let me."

He gave me a playful smirk and dropped his hands. "Yes, ma'am."

I rolled my eyes and grabbed the two parts a little more forcefully than I needed to. A low rumble went through him. I knew he liked to push people around, but I wondered if he liked when someone else took control. The way his eyes hooded when I yanked him closer by his tie let me know he liked it. I tied his tie, pushing the knot up tight around his collar. I pressed down his collar with both hands and smiled at my work. He watched my eyes the entire time. "Are you sure I can't come with you?" he murmured.

"No, you get to watch. It's what you're good at." I patted his chest before turning and heading out of the room. I was feeling confident after bending Reed to my will. I thought about all the other ways I could push him. I had to admit, I was enjoying our little games.

Shaun was still at the table when I returned. "You ready?" I asked.

"I was waiting for his highness." He stood when Reed walked in. "You really went all out considering we're spending the night in a car." Shaun rolled his eyes.

"You will be spending all night in the car. I have a date." Shaun and I both gawked at him.

"What? I said you couldn't come with me. You need to be watching for the guy who may try to murder me." I couldn't believe him. He'd told me that he would be there for me. Now he was going out with someone else just when I needed him to be there for me.

"Don't worry. I made a reservation at the place Vincent is taking you. I will be watching you in the restaurant." He clasped his hands in front of him. I narrowed my eyes. Every time I thought I had Reed figured out he threw another curve ball.

"You said you would be there. I didn't mean for you to be in the restaurant. I don't even want to know how you found out where our reservations are." I threw up my hands and turned away. All the sexy daydreams I had about him while he was getting dressed fizzled away. He was so infuriating.

"I have my sources. Don't worry, Shaun will still be outside, scouting for suspects. He's the one who has all their pictures after all. I will be inside making sure you're safe. See, it all works out in the end." He loosened his tie a little. I smiled. I hoped it was strangling him. I sure would like to.

"You did this so you could watch us on our date." I fumed. "What? You going to follow us back to his place, sneak into the room and watch us fuck too?" I curled my hands into fists, my nails biting into my flesh and drawing blood. I was pissed.

"Wait, what?" Shaun asked.

"Don't tell me you didn't see him the other night." I glanced over at Shaun. His brows pinched together like he was trying to work out a difficult math problem. "Really? You didn't notice him come into the room?" I was surprised. He was a vampire after all.

"I was a little preoccupied." His gaze flew to Reed. "Seriously, you watched us?"

Reed shrugged. "You were in my house with my progeny." Like that explained everything. Shaun looked a little confused. He was probably trying to figure out how he hadn't noticed or why Reed would even do that.

I stepped closer to Shaun, taking his hand. "I thought you knew."

He dipped his head next to mine. "I didn't." He lifted his gaze to Reed and shook his head. "We have more important things to get to. Let's go." He didn't wait for us to move, he walked out the door and closed it behind him. I wasn't sure which one of us he was mad at. I thought he heard him come in. He couldn't be upset with me for letting it happen. It's not like I had any control over Reed's actions. I didn't want to admit how much I liked it at the time. It was hot to know how much I'd affected both of these men. They were mine.

CHAPTER 23

I pulled up to the back of Club Medusa and parked. Vincent had told me where he'd be waiting. We would have normally met at his place, but I was trying to lure out the murderer. I'd already made several appearances at the club. If the murderer was really after Vincent, I would be a clear target for him. Vincent was waiting for me. He was leaning against his Audi, his foot propped against the wheel. "Am I late?" I asked.

"No, you're right on time." His eyes drifted down my dress. "You look stunning." He held his hand out for me. He spun me around, making the bottom of the dress bell out. "Absolutely stunning." He admired me.

"You don't look so bad yourself." He was wearing a black suit with a metallic blue tie. I thought it was a nice touch. He looked sexy in all black. He opened the passenger door for me.

"So am I your secret? You asked to meet me at the back of the club?" I waited for him to answer, the car door between us.

"You could never be my secret. I plan on showing you the world tonight." He leaned forward, kissing my hand. "Now, if you don't mind. We have an eventful evening planned."

I smiled and ducked to slide into the car. The leather seats were heated and felt good against my skin. His car was decked out with the finest of everything. I even liked the tinted windows. No one would see anything that went on in this car. "So, where are we off to?" I asked. I hadn't asked Reed because I was so irritated that he basically admitted he was hijacking my date.

The corner of his mouth curved. "I wouldn't want to ruin the surprise." He pulled up in front of Manny's and a valet opened my door. He took my hand and helped me out of the car. Vincent met me on the sidewalk.

"Oh? Manny's is fabulous." He took my arm in his and escorted me into the lush bar.

"Hello sir, we have the hideaway ready for you." The man lead us to the back.

My eyebrows rose. "The hideaway?" I asked.

"Yes, I reserved one of the back rooms for the evening. I know you wanted me to show you off, but this is how I do things. I do not want anyone prying into our time together."

He wrapped one arm around my waist and continued to guide me through the restaurant. My stomach fluttered as he pulled my chair out for me. It looked as though the room had been decorated for us. Fresh cut roses filled the room in large vases. The scent was intoxicating as I took it all in. The lights were dim so it didn't hurt my eyes. There was a single table in the middle, two tall candles burning in the middle. It was elegant and cozy. This would be exactly what I desired in a perfect date. Did he know that somehow?

He smiled at me. "What are you thinking?" he asked. I wasn't used to having anyone ask that. "I've seen a myriad of emotions cross your face in seconds and I have no idea what any of them mean. Is this acceptable to you?"

"It's absolutely divine." I beamed.

"Good," he motioned to the waiter. "I ordered us the oysters to start." The man in the corner came with a platter of oysters which he sat between us. He also poured two glasses of wine. "Don't worry, I'll have them bring your martini later. This wine compliments the flavor of the oysters."

"How do you know me so well, already?" I asked.

"I'm a man who pays attention." His voice came out husky and it sent a thrill through me. "Now, please try the oysters. They are the best in town." He held his palm out toward the platter.

"You know, it's an interesting choice. Do oysters have the same effect on us?" I was curious as to Vincent's intentions. I wasn't sure if he was actually interested in me after drugging me at the club, but the way he'd gone all out for this date told me he was very interested.

"You will have to try them and find out. I am curious as well." He winked.

I blushed. "If I didn't know better, I would think you were trying to seduce me."

"Oh, Ms. Matthews, I am." His eyes blazed as he looked back at me. I felt my cheeks flush and the heat of his gaze swept through me. A girl could get used to this. He was certainly one to lavish a lady. I loved how he'd thought about every detail. I wished all the men in my life were this attentive. Maybe I wouldn't be so hesitant around Reed. I took a shell and let the oyster slide down my throat. It was an interesting feeling.

After we finished our entrees, I asked, "Did you reserve the room because you knew my sire was coming here too?" I needed to know if he was doing this all to thwart Reed, or if he even knew about him.

"Your sire? He was coming here?" he cocked his head to the side.

"Yeah, he told me he made a reservation at the same place. Shaun is outside watching for anyone who might be a little too interested in our plans." I lowered my voice in case anyone was listening.

"I knew of your plans, but I was unaware your sire would be here too. Should I make my intentions known?" he asked.

"Oh God, no." I reached my hand across the table to take his. He had smoothed down his jacket and looked like he was ready to go find Reed. I didn't want him to do that. I wasn't even sure why I was telling him all this. He'd made me feel special tonight. I was ruining it by bringing in my problems. I would take care of Reed. No one should have to ask his permission to date me. I'd only known him for a few months. He was not the owner of me. I intended to make that crystal clear.

"You know it is our custom as long as you are in the care of your sire to at the very least make one's intentions known. Any future coupling could be denied if I do not inform him of my intentions." He sounded so serious I couldn't help it. I belted out a laugh. Quickly raising my hand to cover my mouth.

"What century do you guys live in? That's ridiculous. I am a grown woman who can make my own decisions. How have you, a group of vampires, not changed with the times? This is borderline insane. I will not have anyone asking his permission to be with me. Everything about my life is my decision. I will be the one making it, we clear?"

I waited. I was not going to have anyone ask Reed for his permission to date me. I didn't even think men did that with girls' fathers anymore. It was archaic and it was time the vampires got up to speed. I was an independent, strong woman. I would not be belittled by some stupid vampire customs. I would make my own decisions.

"As you wish." He bowed his head. "Would you care for dessert?"

"I don't think there's anything on the menu that will curb my appetite. What do you say we take this back to your place?" I knew I was supposed to be out parading around the town but after the dinner, I wanted to show Vincent how much I appreciated all the small touches. He'd obviously put a lot of thought into dinner.

"Tsk, tsk, the night is young and I haven't even begun to show you a good time." He stood up from the table and held his hand out to me.

"Oh? What do you have in store." I asked.

"You'll see." He guided me out the exit. We turned down the street until we made it to Dakota, a Jazz bar.

"What are we doing here?" I asked.

"I believe I owe you a dance. It was rather rude of me to leave you on the dance floor the other night. I thought I could make it up to you." The smile he gave me was mischievous. Was he suggesting what I thought he was? I glanced around at the people in the bar. They weren't dancing close like they had in the club. How would we be able to drink from them without anyone noticing. I pinched my brows together as I took in the scene.

"I don't think that's such a good idea." I leaned in close. He took my hand and kissed my palm.

"Nonsense, I will show you how." He guided me through the door and instantly whisked me away to the dance floor. He pulled me flush against him, and we danced to the beautiful melody coming from the band. I particularly liked the saxophone. I'd lost track of how long we danced.

"Let's have a drink." Vincent led me to the bar. He ordered two martinis. He knew just what I liked. I smiled when the bartender set the glasses in front of us. "I hope you aren't too put out only dancing with me." He looked adorably shy for a moment. I could see his insecurity. It was not something I'd seen in him. He was always so confident at the club. I liked seeing this other side of him.

"I've had such a good time tonight." I smiled and sipped my drink.

"Are you assuming the night is coming to a close?" His eyebrow arched.

"I wouldn't assume anything with you." I smirked and took another drink. "If you'll excuse me a moment. I need to freshen up after all that dancing." I stood from my stool and went to the ladies room. I knew the plan was for Shaun and Reed to follow me, but I wanted an update. I'd totally forgotten why I was really doing this. It was too easy to get swept away with Vincent. He was so easy to be around.

I pulled out my phone in the privacy of the bathroom. I didn't want to alert any vampires who might be listening to what we were doing. I sent a text to Shaun. *Have you seen anyone following us?* I waited for an answer, staring at the three dots.

A woman. He responded after three agonizing minutes.

Are there only male Ravens? I asked.

No, he responded.

I waited to see if he would catch on. The person could be a woman. Why was it that men never suspected a woman of murder? It wasn't like it happened often, but it did happen. When he didn't say anything else I called. "Is she still following us?" I asked.

"What? Ah, I don't know." Shaun stuttered.

"Are you serious? You are supposed to have my back." I threw up my hand and paced the small space of the women's restroom. There were two stalls and a large sink area. The door opened and a red-head smiled before she bowed her head and went into one of the stalls.

"I'm sure she's harmless." Shaun shot back.

"Men, never mind, I guess I'm on my own." I hung up the phone and tucked it back into my purse. I touched up my lip-gloss and admired myself in the mirror. The woman in the stall came out and smiled at me. There was something familiar about her. She had rich auburn hair and wore a short, black A-line cocktail dress. "I love your dress." It fit her so well.

"Oh, thank you, I saw you dancing out there. It looked like a lot of fun." Her voice was more sing-songy than I expected.

"It was," I smiled. I turned away to leave.

"Who's the guy you're with? He looks familiar," she asked.

"Oh, he owns the Medusa club. That's probably where you saw him." I pushed the door open wondering about her questions. It seemed innocuous, but also a bit weird. Vincent held his finger up to let me know he'd moved from the bar to a booth along the wall. I made my way around tables and people to take a seat next to him.

"So, what women have you scorned?" I asked. If it was a woman following him, maybe it was an ex-lover he'd angered. He stared at the band playing across the room. He looked faraway.

"Why do you ask?" he said after a moment. I knew that he'd made someone mad enough to do this. There was something in his eyes.

"Do you want to tell me about it?" I asked.

"Not here," his eyes scanned the room and stopped, his mouth dropping for a second. "We should go. We can talk back at my place." His words were hushed. If the woman he was reacting to was a vampire, as I suspected, she heard him.

"Trying to get me back to your place already? I don't know if I should. You might be trying to take advantage of me." I leaned back in my chair, sipping my martini. I scanned the room, trying to discern who here was a vampire. I assumed she was beautiful.

He chuckled. "You were already in my bed."

"Oh, so you just expect that I'll be there again. I see how it is." I scanned the room. It was hard to see the entire room because of the angle of our booth. The bar was behind us, the stage was across from us. I loved how the lights dimmed and purple and blue lights replaced the bright overhead lights when the band played.

"So, what made you want to be a detective?" he asked.

My gaze slanted down towards him. "What made you ask that?" Was he trying to distract me from asking about the woman who may be after him or me?

"I'm curious about you. Is it a crime to want to get to know you?" He took a drink from his glass, eyes scanning the room again. I wondered who he was looking for in the crowd. I really wanted to know more about the woman who was after him, but I guess keeping up small talk couldn't hurt.

"My parents were murdered when I was young. There was this officer who was assigned to the case. I didn't actually know they had been murdered, but the officer kept tabs on me. He checked on me to make sure I was doing okay. I saw the caring side of the law in him." I stared off into space remembering him. He was as stable a part of my childhood as anyone. "He reminded me that there were good guys fighting evil, and I always wanted to be a part of that."

"So, you've always wanted to help people." He was watching me.

"Not in a traditional sense. I see people on the worst day of their life. I just want to make it a little better for them. I want them to know that someone is looking out for their loved one. It means something, more than I could ever really explain." I took a drink. This wasn't exactly a first date conversation, but this wasn't your typical first date. I was doing what I always did, hunting another bad guy. It didn't really matter that this time the bad guy wasn't human. At least, I assumed they weren't human. "So, you ready to tell me about the one who got away?"

He chuckled. "You don't give up easily, do you?"

"No, it's why I'm so good at what I do." I observed an elderly couple dancing to the slow jazz beat. There was something about good Jazz music that settled in your bones. It seemed to resonate within some deep part of you and latched on. I couldn't help but sway to the sound. It was mesmerizing.

"What's your favorite sin?" Vincent suddenly asked.

"What?" I turned to face him. There was a playful smile spread across his lips.

"Haven't you ever been asked what's your favorite sin? I think it's a marvelous way to get to know someone." He tapped his finger against the rim of the glass studying me. I had no idea where this conversation was going. It reminded me of a line from Firefly, was he a fan?

"I guess it depends on the day. Sunday has always been good for sloth and gluttony. I've been partial to lust on the weekends, and wrath, well wrath is my day job." I tucked a lock of my hair behind my ears.

"Damn, you're sexy." His gaze smoldered as he looked at me. "There are very few so young, who are wise beyond their years. I am curious to see who you become after a few thousand years." He continued to stare. I averted my gaze and went back to watching the couple. They seemed so carefree among everyone else in here. Maybe that was the secret to old age. The older you got, the less you cared about the inconsequential things.

"I'm not sure if I would consider my beliefs about sin, wise. I just like to have fun." I looked down to my empty glass. "I think I'm going to mingle and get another drink." I slid over.

"What? No, I can get a waitress over." He waved over to someone helping another table. She nodded but continued talking to those at the table where she stood.

"It's fine. I want to stretch my legs. I also want to see who is more interested in you than me. Shaun mentioned there was a female following us. I would like to see who that might be." I slid to the end of our booth. He grabbed my wrist.

I looked down to where he held my arm. "Please, you can't put yourself in danger. You don't know who you are dealing with."

"So, tell me." I stared into his dark eyes, waiting.

He lowered his gaze. "I can't tell you here. There are things that no one can know. If anyone in here were listening..." he trailed off. I knew there were others listening. Reed was probably here somewhere, or at least I assumed he was. He told me he planned to follow me tonight to make sure I was safe. I wasn't sure how true to his word he would be. Although, knowing him, he wouldn't be able to stop himself from creeping on my date.

"Don't worry about me. I bite back." I winked. He squeezed my arm before reluctantly letting go. I pulled out my phone and sent a text letting Reed know that I suspected the murderer was a woman. I went to the bar to get another drink.

"Can I get a Cosmo?" I asked the bartender as soon as he made his way to me. I wanted the woman to see me away from Vincent. I planned to go outside like I was going to have a cigarette. I didn't smoke but it would give me a chance to lure out whoever may be after Vincent. I set my drink on the table. "I'm just going to step outside. I'll be back."

I swerved around people and tables, scanning the crowd as I went. I thought I saw Alejandra as I made my way outside. I didn't see anyone who was paying me particular attention, but whomever had committed the murders was good at being invisible. I wondered if Shaun was actually paying attention. I couldn't believe he would dismiss someone because they were female. I was more than capable of killing. I walked around the roped off area where groups sat outside. I wasn't sure why you wouldn't want to be inside enjoying the jazz music.

The woman from the bathroom came out, she was tapping a pack to get out a cigarette. "Hey, you need one?" she held her pack out to me.

"Oh yes, thank you." I took the cigarette and pressed it between my lips. I dug through my purse. I didn't have a light, but I needed to keep up the ruse. She held a lighter in front of my face. I leaned toward the flame. I inhaled a deep drag of the unusually sweet cigarette. I realized she was intently watching me. "Thank you," I smiled.

"You're very beautiful." She pulled out her own cigarette. "I can see why he likes you."

"Who?" I asked. "Oh, I saw you in the bathroom. Do you know Vincent?" I asked.

"You could say that." The way she was watching me sent a chill down my spine.

"How do you know each other?" I knew I should be getting one of the guy's attention, but I was curious why she was doing this. Why did she kill all of those people?

"We were lovers once." She kept a keen eye on me as she spoke.

"Oh? What happened?" My hand flew up to my mouth. "I'm sorry, that was rude. You don't have to tell me." I tried to play innocent, but I wasn't very good at it. My head spun when I took another drag of the cigarette. I hadn't had a cigarette in so long I'd forgotten the effects.

"Why don't we take a little walk. I will tell you everything you want to know." She smiled. I don't know why she wanted to go for a walk, but she seemed nice enough.

"Oh, you asked me to text your friends. Here, if you'll give me your purse, I can do it. I will let them know you've had a little too much to drink." She continued to guide me to a car parked down the street. It was weird because cars weren't supposed to be parked here. Something was wrong, but I couldn't seem to get my brain and body to cooperate with me. What was in that cigarette? I hadn't even thought about the action when I handed over my purse. My rational side was screaming in my head that I needed to get back to the club. To tell someone who she was. Shaun had laughed when he thought it was a woman. Vincent knew who it was. I didn't feel like I had control of my own actions. I was a prisoner in my own body. What the hell was she going to do to me?

The woman opened the door and guided me in. I didn't understand how I wasn't able to control myself. I did whatever she wanted. Was this some new form of charming me? I noticed Shaun come running up to the car. She whirled and hit him in the head hard enough that he dropped to the ground. *Shit, who was this woman?*

I watched as she loaded Shaun into the backseat and got into the driver's side. "Wha..."

"You are probably wondering what is going on. Well, I slipped a little something into that cigarette. It helps you be a bit more suggestive to my power." She turned the corner away from the city. "You won't be able to do anything I don't approve of. I can read your thoughts so I will know if you try anything."

I tried to empty my mind of all thoughts. I didn't want her to know what we had been planning. "What is your plan?" I asked.

"I am taking everything Vincent cares about. Eventually they will connect everything to him. They will take his club and end his life." She got onto the freeway. She weaved between cars like a mad person.

"I was only on a date. Why would I matter to him?" I asked. Suddenly I couldn't move again.

"Just a date?" she threw her head back and laughed. "He hasn't put in an effort in centuries. You may believe you are just a date, but I know him. You are special to him. He will come after you. I'm hoping he comes after you."

"How are you able to do this, to control me?" I asked. It was something that she seemed to be able to change. I could speak when she let me. It was irritating.

"You don't know much about our world, do you?" she glanced over at me as she dipped into the right lane and exited onto another highway. We were headed south.

"No, I've only been a vampire for six months and my sire is an asshole."

She laughed again. "Aren't they all. This is nothing personal."

"Just like the others you killed. How many have there been?" I asked. I suspected that she had been doing this for a while, long before coming to my city.

"You are right to think that I have been doing this a while. I was hoping the you would get the information I desired against Vincent. It's why I chose you to lure him. I knew you would be exactly his type. But you seem to be slow on the investigation. It's probably because you're using newbies instead of a seasoned Raven." She shook her head. "It's sad. What is coming of the organization. I never intended to give you what you wanted. I just needed you to bait him for me. I want him to lose someone he cares about."

I gaped at her. She didn't look like Cassandra, yet here she was, telling me what only she would know. "How?" I was so dumbfounded.

She waved her hand in front of herself and she shimmered and changed. The woman next to me was Cassandra. "I am a Satori, like you I have magic as a vampire. The drug I gave you helps make you more amenable to my mental suggestions. I was also one of the descendants. It's why I chose you. Vincent will know your importance, but I needed him to care about you first. I plan on killing all of your kind." She pulled into a long driveway. We weren't in the city anymore. I didn't know how anyone was going to find us. Shaun had been the one who traced phones. He was our tech guy. He was unconscious in the backseat. To say we were fucked was an understatement. I glanced back to see that his eyes were open. He had been listening, but she hadn't noticed. I tried hard to clear my thoughts. I didn't know if she could read my thoughts all the time.

"So, are you going to tell me more about Vincent? I'd love to know what turned you into a scorned lover." I also wanted to know more about the magic she mentioned, but she seemed to be more focused on Vincent. Keeping my head forward, I planned on keeping her distracted so she wouldn't notice Shaun. I wondered if Vincent was her sire.

"Yes, he was." She answered my thoughts. *Oh shit.*

"Is that why you have been trying to get the Ravens to take him out? It's against the law to kill your sire." I ran my hands down my dress, paying close attention to how much I could move under her power. I might need to be able to surprise her. "Why didn't you just pay someone to kill him? I mean, how long have you been trying. There had to be an easier way."

"I couldn't. If they traced any of that back to me, I would be killed. I have worked too hard to get ot where I am to lose everything." She stopped in front of an older looking white farmhouse. The paint was chipping away on the wood siding. There was a half-fallen gray barn on the other side of the house. A sidewalk led up to the cement steps, but it looked like the grass had taken over most of the sidewalk.

There wasn't another house around for miles. The road was a good mile away from the house and a line of trees blocked the view to the road. There was another line of pines on the left behind the barn. I wondered if anyone had even lived here. "Nice place you got here."

"No one lives here. I needed something outside of the city to set up shop." She got out of the car. I still wasn't able to move. How long did her drug last?

"Do you have a plan?" I whispered to Shaun.

"Yeah, don't say anything. Don't even think about me," he whispered back.

"I'll try but you better come up with something quick. I don't know how long I can keep up not think about you."

"Do math problems or think about fashion or something."

"Seriously, I have a better idea. How about I think of how much fun we had the other night? Then maybe she will realize I am nothing to her sire." I ran through the images of Shaun buried inside me. She stopped after opening the door to the house. I couldn't believe she was just leaving me in the car. I could run at any time. I rested my hand on the door handle and found myself frozen again.

"Dammit, who the fuck is this woman?" I growled. I'd met her with Reed. I thought they were involved. It was probably another ploy to get what she wanted. I was starting to wonder if Reed was involved in the murders. He gave me a bullshit alibi every time I asked. Maybe he's been helping her the whole time.

"You don't want to fuck with them. She must have been a Satori before she was turned. They have the ability to read and manipulate minds. She can plant suggestions in your head. The fact she's also a vampire makes her dangerous. Somehow she can charm a vampire. It shouldn't be possible, yet here we are." Shaun was speaking low.

She went all the way in the house, leaving us here. "You want to make some kind of escape while she's in the house?"

"I planned on surprising her when she opened my door."

"What? So we can both be under her control. No, go get fucking reinforcements. You at least have a phone. Go behind the barn or something, quick before she comes back." I couldn't believe he was just going to play dead and surprise someone who could manipulate others minds. She could make him kill me. Then we'd be fucked.

"Fine," he opened the door furthest from the house and slid out as quietly as possible. I watched as he looked over the hood of the car before taking off for the tree line. How in the Hell were we going to beat a mind-controlling vampire?

Chapter 24

Cassandra strode out of the house, another man at her side. He looked familiar. Was he at that stupid bar where Reed and I met the Loup Garou? She pointed to the backseat, and he hurried down the steps toward the car. She followed at a more leisurely pace. At what point would this wear off, and I would be able to resist her? I continued to think about the sex Shaun and I had the other night to distract myself. I didn't dare think of the other men. I wasn't interested in an immediate death.

When the guy opened the back door, he looked so dumbfounded, it was comical. "Lose something?" I asked. He turned to the woman. She glanced between us.

"There's no one here," he called back.

She flung open my door. "Where is he?"

I pushed against her power. I had to be able to fight her. It was my only chance. "Gone," I said between gritted teeth.

"What do you mean gone?" she asked.

I pressed my lips together. I didn't want to tell her anything. "Just gone."

She turned to the man next to her. "You're a tracker. Find him." She grabbed my arm and yanked me out of the car. "You're coming with me." I tried to pull against her. The more I resisted the more pain I felt. It was like a sharp pain jutting across my head. I didn't care. I didn't want to be manipulated. The pain was a sign that at least something was changing. You would think I would know better than to take anything from anyone by now. How many times did I need to learn that lesson? "I need to send a message to Vincent."

"Is my dead body the message? Cause I can think of a few more ways you could get your point across. Have you tried flowers with a card? Maybe a robot. Everyone loves robots." I tried to pull against her arm. I didn't want to go willingly to my death.

"Are you delirious? I don't love him." She yanked even harder when I tried to pull away. I needed to get my damn mind back.

"You could've fooled me. No one goes to all this trouble unless they loved the person once. I'm sure you two could work it out." What was I saying? I hated my sire. If Vincent had done anything like Reed had, I wouldn't be accepting my ideas either.

"I loved him once. True hate can only be born from love. It festers like an open wound until it consumes you. I plan on spending my life taking everything he cares about until his life is over." She said the words with such malice I blinked. "I'm surprised you of all people are so forgiving. I was there the day you were turned."

She had me there. "What did he do to you?" I asked, slack jawed. I couldn't imagine having that much hate for someone. I could, but I hadn't even felt that toward Reed. There was still a part of me that pulled toward him. I could tell that any love she felt was long gone.

"He broke my heart, of course." She threw me into the house, yanking the door closed behind her. Hauling me to my feet, she flung me into a metal chair in the kitchen. There wasn't much in the abandoned farmhouse. A few chairs, a couch that looked like someone left it in the seventies, a broken picture on the wall of a family who may have lived here. There was even a broken plastic truck on the floor in front of the couch. It made me wonder how long ago this house was abandoned.

"I think there's more to it than that. I can help you take him down. Us women should stick together. Maybe there's a deal we can strike here that can be mutually beneficial. See, I'm not a fan of my sire either. He changed me against my will, as you well know. I would love nothing more than to see him dead. I've gotten close to Vincent. Closer than anyone else. I believe we can help each other." I knew I was rambling a bit, but I hoped she could see the wisdom behind using me instead of killing me. "If you kill me, he'll just keep going on as he's always done. The Ravens don't even think it's him doing the killing. But you know this, you're one of them." I stared at her, waiting for confirmation.

"You think you're so smart don't you?" She crossed her arms over her chest. "You think if I agree to this, I'll let you go? You'll go running back to the sire you claim to hate. I've been watching you, Hope. I don't think you hate your sire as much as you claim."

She wasn't wrong. "Did I mention the part about him taking my life against my will? I hate him. He ended my life. He was also responsible for killing my parents. I may not act like I hate him, but trust me, I am plotting his demise just as you have been plotting Vincent's. You have to see we can help each other here." All I could think about was getting myself out of here.

I rested back in the chair, crossing my legs. I knew I had made her think. She was staring at me, probably wondering if I was telling the truth. She knew about me being turned, but I doubt she knew it was against my will or about my parents. Reed knew where the Loup Garou's' lived. He would come looking for us. I was sure of it. "Did your maker kill everyone you've ever loved, including ending your own life? I probably have more justification than you. Did he leave you for another woman? Never told you he loved you? Come now, you can't have more reason than me to want him dead." I noticed she didn't have me pinned to the chair. I swept my hair behind my shoulder and waited. She would let down her guard and give me an opportunity. I just had to wait until she trusted me.

"I have reason enough to want him dead. Let's leave it at that." She glared at me. Most women who'd been wronged, loved sharing what it was their lover had done. I wondered if it was really so bad or if it was so horrible she never wanted to speak of it again.

"Okay, so are we killing the bastards or what?" I asked.

"I told you the reason I never had him killed was because it could traced back to me. I am not making a deal with you that will get us both killed. Do you not know enough to know the Ravens will kill us both, even if we aren't the ones to do the official killing?" She shook her head like she was speaking to a child. I hated my naivety. It wasn't my fault Reed had left out so much of the information I needed to know. "Has Reed really taught you so little?"

"It's not my fault my sire is an asshole only doling out information when he feels like it." I pressed my lips together. "Another control tactic. You wouldn't know anything about that, though would you?" I wondered if Vincent had been one controlling bastard and that was why she hated him. I wanted to chip away at her. Find out what it was that he'd done.

"I know a little something about control." Suddenly I couldn't move. "I'm sick of all your blabbering." She went to the door and strode out. I knew I had been starting to break her hold. If I could get to a phone, I could let the others know where we were. I wanted to check outside to see if Shaun had gotten away, but didn't dare. It took a few more minutes before I could break her hold. I don't know if that was because the drug was wearing off or because she'd gone far enough away.

She returned and threw my purse on the table. She took out my phone. In her other hand, she had a rope which she used to tie me to the chair. "I thought you could control me, what's with the rope?" I asked.

Her eyes narrowed on me. "I suspect the drugs are beginning to wear off." She tightened the rope. Then pulled out a knife. "Let's get to that message."

"What are you going to do?" I asked.

"Don't worry, it might heal if you find a witch. Let's see how much you actually mean to Vincent." There were etchings on the knife she held. As she pressed it across my neck, I felt the cold steel burn. Hot blood ran down to my chest. So much for my dress. Blood wasn't going to come out. She used my phone to snap pictures. I wondered if I would live through the blood loss as a vampire. Could I die of exsanguination? Is that how she was able to kill? Some magical knife?

My instincts kicked in, I needed to stop the bleeding. "Pressure, I have to put pressure on the wound." Too bad my hands were bound behind me.

She smiled. "Come now, you don't actually think that's going to work?" It was then that I realized I had said that last part aloud.

"We could have been great together. Now you're going to be caught, if not killed. Go ahead, send those pics." I felt the blood continue to move down my chest, soaking into my dress. She'd cut the artery. It wouldn't be long until my body pumped out the blood.

"I'm not going to be caught." She smirked.

"I'm going to hunt you and kill you for this." I glared at Cassandra. I didn't care who she was. I was going to kill her.

She laughed. "You'll bleed out soon. Even vampires can't survive blood loss. It'll be slow and painful. You'll be thirsty, it will eat you up from the inside." The smile on her face made me sick. She was enjoying my pain. "I think I'll be leaving now. Thanks for the cash." She held up the wad from my purse. "I won't be seeing you around. But of course I will be there to console Reed. He will be devastated by your loss."

I watched as she walked outside. I heard the car start. Did she leave her tracker or did she have another place nearby? I yanked against the restraints, but this wasn't a typical rope. I didn't know what it was reinforced with, but even with my vampire strength, I couldn't get my hands free.

The fucking bitch left me for dead. She was on my hit list now. I wasn't kidding about how we could have helped each other. Now I was going to make sure she died. Hopefully in as painful a way as possible. First I needed to figure out how to get out of this damn chair. Where the hell was Shaun?

CHAPTER 25

My head felt dizzy. All I wanted to do was close my eyes and sleep. I didn't know how long it had been, but I was close to losing consciousness. I could feel my blood soaked into my dress. It was becoming sticky against my skin. I'd lost a lot of blood. I wondered if Vincent got the photos and if anyone was coming. I didn't want to die in this damn house. My perfect party dress was destroyed, and I probably looked like Hell. This was not how I was going to die.

The door slammed open. Reed stood there with Laura at his side. "Holy shit," he ran to me and pulled at the rope.

My eyes fluttered. "It's some special rope. I can't get free."

Laura bent down, wrapping something around my throat. "It's spelled. I can break it, but it will take a minute." She took something out of her pocket and bent at my side.

"How?" I whispered. I'd lost a lot of blood and it was hard to speak.

"Laura traced your phone." Reed bit into his wrist and held it to my mouth. "Drink."

I narrowed my eyes and jerked my head away. "You're stubborn. Do you really want to die because you're unwilling to drink my blood?" He pushed his wrist into my mouth. I swallowed a few mouthfuls and pulled away.

"Why am I not healing?" I croaked.

"Who took you?" Reed asked.

"Cassandra, she's a Satori or something. How could she also be a vampire?" I asked. I didn't know enough about this world. "What did she do to me?" I asked.

"What did she cut you with?" Laura asked.

"A knife, it had some kind of etchings on it. Why?" I drank Reed's blood, but it didn't feel like I was healing. Reed was staring at me, his mouth agape. He hadn't said anything since I revealed who'd taken me. I didn't know what his relationship was with her, but they'd seemed close. I guess there wouldn't be any consoling.

"It was probably spelled like the rope. We need to find a witch to undo it." Laura had freed me from the rope and stood. "We need to go."

"Where's Shaun? He was with me in the car. He tried to save me and got knocked out. He ran when we got here." I tried to stand and fell back into the chair. Reed lifted me into his arms. "Since when are you a gentleman?" I mumbled.

"I'm not, but I'm not going to let you die today." He held me against him as he carried me to the car. He slid into the backseat with me in his arms.

"What about Shaun?" I asked.

I heard a moan coming from the tree line. "Laura, get Shaun." I begged.

She looked over to where the moan came from. Reed held me close and Laura drove closer to the trees. She jumped out of the car. Shaun stood up with her help. He leaned on her as she helped him into the car. "What the Hell happened to you? You were supposed to get help." I scolded.

"I'm fine by the way." He was holding his side. "I called Laura before I was blindsided by that fucking werewolf. He got in a few good blows before I was able to take him out. I saw the bitch leave. I'm surprised she left you alive in there." Shaun turned but moaned at the movement.

"Yeah, alive but dying." There was a scarf wrapped around my neck, but I could still feel the blood oozing from my neck. I didn't know how long I had before I died. Cassandra told me I could die from blood loss. "You wouldn't happen to know any witches, would you?" I chuckled. I knew I shouldn't be laughing, but it was how I coped.

"Don't worry, I know one." Laura was speeding down the highway.

"Oh good, I'm not sure I trust either of these two to save me. They were supposed to protect me from this happening. Look where that got me." I leaned against Reed's chest. I hoped I was bleeding all over him.

"Hey, I tried to save you." Shaun protested.

"Yeah, and you got taken with me. So, I hope you weren't hoping to win any points for being the savior." I glanced up at Reed. "And where were you?"

"I was at the bar." He pulled tighter on the scarf at my throat. I felt even more light-headed. He bit into his wrist again and held it out to me.

"You made such a big deal of going everywhere I went with Vincent. Where the hell were you? I trusted that you would be there for me." He tried to push his wrist into my mouth, but I turned away.

"You need to keep taking blood. The more you lose the more you will need." He held his wrist to my mouth. I grasped his hand and drank his blood. I deserved it. He was supposed to have my back.

"So much for trusting my partner," I mumbled as I pushed his wrist away. My eyelids were heavy. I just wanted to take a little nap. Reed shook me as soon as I closed my eyes.

"Hope, Hope, you can't go to sleep. You need to drink regularly until we can get back to the city and reverse whatever that bitch did to you." Reed tapped my cheek. It felt a little too close to a slap, and I turned to glare at him.

"Laura you need to step on it." Reed shook me again.

"What the Hell? I'm just closing my eyes for a second." I tried again, and he shook me.

"Shaun, give her some of your blood," Reed demanded.

"Yeah, his is probably better." I reached out. Shaun twisted and held his wrist out to me.

Reed helped me reach Shaun's wrist. I drank down a few mouthfuls and leaned back against Reed. I wouldn't shut my eyes again. I didn't like being shook every time I closed them. Laura pulled in front of an older brick house in the South side of Minneapolis. The houses on 50th street were some of the nicer ones on this side of town.

"Reed, can you try to hide the blood while you bring her up. I'll go ahead and make sure it's okay. Wait, until I wave, then follow me up." Laura didn't wait for them to agree. She ran up to the house and knocked. A boisterous woman opened the door. She had a scarf wrapped around her dark curls. She wore a long blue dress that flowed when she moved. Laura waved for us to join her. Shaun opened the door and Reed lifted me out of the car.

Laura held the door open. "This is Melanie, she is one of the most powerful witches in the city." Reed carried me into the house. Shaun was behind us.

"Bring her in here." Melanie called from what I guessed was the kitchen. Reed held me close. She pointed to one of the chairs. "You can set her in one of the chairs." Reed sat with me in his lap. He hadn't let go of me since we left the house. You would think he actually cared about me. If you didn't know him, you would. I knew him. He didn't care about anyone but himself.

Melanie rolled her eyes when she looked at him. "Take the scarf off. I need to make a salve and put it on the wound before I speak the incantation. When I'm done, she's going to need blood."

Laura glanced at Shaun. "We're on it, right Shaun?"

"Yeah, we can do that." Shaun was still gripping his side. At least he would heal at some point. I didn't know what this damn woman did to me, but I hated that I wasn't healing. I didn't think vampires could feel pain. Since I'd been turned and trained with Reed, I knew that part of the myth had been a lie. I could feel all kinds of pain. I was getting tired again. I tried to hold my eyes open. Getting slapped again for falling asleep didn't sound fun. Finally, after a few minutes, I couldn't do it. My eyelids slid closed. I felt something cold around my neck. I blinked my eyes open.

"That feels weird," I mumbled.

"It will heal you, dear," her voice was deep.

"Sounds good," I murmured. My body felt heavy, and I couldn't open my eyes. I heard the woman say something, but I was too far gone. Her voice sounded so far away. Distantly I knew I should try to stay awake, but I couldn't resist the pull of darkness anymore.

The first thing I noticed was that my mouth tasted like metal. "What the hell?" I croaked.

"She's awake," Shaun called. "Hey, Hope, how are you feeling?" he sounded way too cheerful. I blinked open my eyes.

"I feel like Hell. What's going on?" I asked.

"Melanie healed you. It was pretty bad. We had to do a blood transfusion to get blood back into you since you were unconscious." Shaun took my hand and squeezed.

I tried to sit up. My head spun. "Why do I still feel like shit?" I asked.

"It's going to take a bit until you're back at it. The loss of blood will affect you for a few days." He held my hand.

"I don't have a few days. We have to find Cassandra. I'm going to kill that bitch." I sat up but my head spun. I held my hand against my forehead.

"We are going to kill her. You just can't do it yet." I glanced up at the door. Reed was leaning against the door jamb. His body took up the entire door. He was wearing a white tank and his muscles bulged when he crossed his arms over his chest.

"No, she's the one we've been looking for. We have to go after her. She's trying to frame Vincent. Eventually she will do it, and the Ravens will kill him. But it's her. We have to tell the council so she can be stopped." I didn't like the way that they were looking at me. I felt like a child under their gaze. "What?" I asked.

"Hope, we can't go after her." Shaun shook his head. He still gave me a look like he was appeasing a child. I glared at him.

"Care to explain why not?" I asked. I was going to kill that bitch for trying to kill me.

"She has the power to manipulate vampires. You'll have to excuse us for not wanting to go after someone who can do that to any one of us. The only reason you're alive is because she wanted Vincent to watch you die. She had your phone set up to send live video to his feed. We can't exactly go accusing a council member of murder. She'll make sure we die before anyone finds out." Shaun explained.

I glanced to Reed. "You're just going to let her go? What's the point of being a Raven if we can't stop killers?" I asked. I was dumbfounded. One of the council members was a murderer. "Does she know I survived?" I directed my question at Reed.

"You won your early trial. Cassandra granted it a few hours ago. You should be pleased, you got what you wanted." Reed held an unreadable expression. I couldn't believe he was just going to let her get away with it. Did he know?

I threw my hands up and dropped them back onto the bed. My bed. It took me a minute to realize I was in my bed. "So, what? I'm just supposed to stay in bed while she goes off killing more people. She almost killed me. What's going to happen at the trial? I know too much already." I spat. These two were worried about what would happen if they said anything to the council. She just moved me up on the list to be in the Raven trials. Reed had already told me how difficult they would be. He said people spent years training for them. How long was she going to give me? She knew how little I knew.

"I think if anyone has reason to go after her and kill her, it's Vincent." Reed frowned.

"What? Is he going to go after her? I want to know what his plan is. How is he going to kill a council member? I want to be a part of it." I was stubborn. But looking between the two unflinching, I knew I wasn't going to get anywhere.

"You can't be a part of catching her. You have to focus on not dying in the trials. It's no coincidence that the moment she found out you lived, she listed you for the next round." Shaun explained. I hated how still Reed was against the door. He was like a fucking statue.

"I'm not going to win this argument am I?"

"No," Reed growled. "You got what you wanted, princess." He was right. I did all of this to be able to get into the Ravens. I was one step closer to having my freedom, technically, if I didn't die in the process. There was no way that bitch was going to let me win. She would find a way to kill me if I didn't kill her first. Looking at Reed, I suspected he knew the real reason I wanted to become a Raven. I wanted my freedom. Hunting bad guys was a perk of the job. I would get to hunt the baddest of all. Starting with that bitch Cassandra.

"You're right. I should be happy." I pressed my lips together. I would do whatever I needed to become a Raven. It looked like I was going to get my wish.

"Now, we just have to get you ready. Most people took years to train. We've only got six weeks." Reed glared at me.

"Six weeks?" I asked. "I thought Cassandra was only getting me in a year earlier."

"Well, it looks like you motivated her to move up the timeline. We have six weeks to get you ready. It's good you don't have to be the detective anymore. We're going to need every minute of every day to get you ready."

"What happens if I'm not ready by then?" I asked. "If I lose the trials?" I knew the answer, but I wanted to hear it from them.

"You lose your life. The trials are life and death. That's why I wanted you to wait. You have to be prepared. If not, you don't get a second chance." Reed sounded grave.

"You waited to tell me that until now?" I gaped.

"You're the one who wouldn't listen to me. You wanted to get in as soon as possible."

"Yeah, but maybe I would have thought twice if I knew it was life or death." I rolled my eyes. Again Reed was leaving important information out. How in the hell was I going to be ready for whatever the trials entailed in six weeks?

"Yeah, well maybe you should listen to me sometimes." I had to smile. Reed was mocking me. At least I'd lived through my first case even if the bitch who'd assigned it was the killer. Now I just had to live through the damn trials. I knew Reed would help me. He wouldn't want his progeny to fail. He was too damn proud for that. I had to admit, I kinda liked that about him. It was something we had in common.

If you enjoyed this, make sure to sign up for my newsletter to get exclusive excerpts, new releases, and more. Sign-up here.

Stay tuned for Book 2: Scarlet Corrupted Coming Soon!

Printed in Great Britain
by Amazon

81302320R20120